"Now, eat it!"

"There is a place," he said. His voice was very different now. He'd dropped his role, his cover; this was the man himself, a human being stripped of pretense and disguise, risking everything he'd carefully and painfully assembled through the years, his tenure, for this one mere high school kid, a person who meant nothing to him.

"Here," he whispered. He took a fountain pen and a mini-pad from out of a secret drawer and scribbled an address in purple ink on a tiny slip of paper. "Memorize it." Herbie did. "Now, eat it!"

Also by Julian F. Thompson

Goofbang Value Daze
The Taking of Mariasburg
Simon Pure
A Band of Angels
Discontinued
A Question of Survival
Facing It
The Grounding of Group 6

HERB SEASONING

Julian F. Thompson

SCHOLASTIC INC.
New York Toronto London Auckland Sydney

ISBN 0-590-43024-6

12 11 10 9 8 7 6 5 4 3 2   2 3 4 5 6/9

Printed in the U.S.A.   01

Whatever it turns out to be,
this book's for Polly, lovingly.

1
BACKGROUND
INFORMATION

From *The New York Times*, Tuesday, December 29, 1987:

> As it happens, 1988 will arrive a little late this year — one second late, to be exact — and thereupon hangs a tale.
>
> By international agreement, the world's time-keepers, in order to keep their official atomic clocks in step with the earth's irregular but gradually slowing rotation, have decreed that a "Leap Second" be inserted between 1987 and 1988.
>
> So at precisely 11:59:60 P.M. on New Year's Eve, there will be a one-second void before the onset of 12:00:00 A.M. New Year's Day . . .
>
> For various reasons — the sloshing molten core, the rolling of the oceans, the melting of

> *polar ice and the effects of solar and lunar grav-*
> *ity — the planet rotates on its axis at irregular*
> *rates, and on average has been slowing down by*
> *about one-thousandth of a second per day.*
>
> *Thus, every few years a full extra second is*
> *accumulated on the clocks. So periodically, to*
> *get the clocks back in step with earthly rotation,*
> *a leap second has been inserted to remove the*
> *extra second from the clocks. Without much fan-*
> *fare, it has happened 14 times since 1972 . . .*

Here's what Dr. Dennis McCarthy, an astrono-
mer at the Naval Observatory, had to say about the
meaning of a second, according to the same *Times*
article:

> *"A second is a relatively long amount of time.*
> *If you're flying a plane by instruments, and*
> *you're off by one second, you're going to miss the*
> *runway by nearly one-fifth of a mile."*

Unbeknownst to him, or anybody else, Herbie
Hertzman was born during a "leap second," the one
that happened more than sixteen years ago.

So, you *could* say that he wasn't born *at any time*.
You *could* say that he missed the runway, that he
wasn't *ever* born.

2
AUTHOR'S DISCLAIMER

I'm not saying any of those things. You're going to have to make up your own mind about this character, and about the larger question of whether people can occur — can be allowed — with no time on the clock. Or whether they should be like baskets in a game of basketball, which only count if they have left the shooter's hand with time still showing. But otherwise are disallowed. I leave that up to you.

I don't know. A lot of Herbie Hertzman's story sounds incredible to me, but yet I still believe it. It's possible that that's because I'm just about as gullible as . . . well, old Herbie is, or was, or might have been. You, I wouldn't know about.

3
T.K.

To the extent that it's possible for anyone to learn anything in high school, Herbie Hertzman probably learned that Tyche was the Greek goddess of luck in Miz Potemkin's History of Western Civilization class, required of all sophomores.

And, if boys like Herbie remember anything important for more than fifteen minutes, which his putative mother almost surely doubted, he still retained that information twenty-four months later.

The memory would be, and was, a little flawed, however. Western Civ is hard to get down pat. It's full of words that almost everyone misspells, like "peasants" and "cavalry," and others that are tricky to pronounce, for instance, "Arkameedeez" and "Cardnal Rishloo." Not to mention those you don't remember what they mean, like "putative."

Fall of sophomore year, Herbie wrote down

Tyche in his notebook just the way that Miz Potemkin mizpronounced it: "T.K." Ever after, he imagined T.K. as a youthful, perky, fun-type goddess in an extra-short, white, silky tunic.

"T.K.," Herbie wrote, that time. And then he wrote, "Good luck."

4
TWO YEARS LATER

By the time he was a senior, Herb was seventeen and six feet two, with a fine, round head of shiny coal-black hair cut close to it in ringlets, like you see on ancient statues of Apollo. In general, he had a mildly puzzled look in his surprisingly blue eyes.

Most days he wore a collared long-sleeved shirt to school, with blue jeans and a dark brown leather vest, and he always had his big, wide, buckled belt on upside down. Can you imagine that? When he was little and his mother dressed him, she would slide his belt in from the wrong direction, upside down. She wasn't being mean or careless; some people *don't* know any better. So, of course, the buckle wasn't ever on the proper side, and he, both young and ignorant, always kept it that way. And naturally he drew a lot of stares at school, whether he was there or not.

He also, more than ever, *hungered* for good luck. He believed that with good luck a person might attain the two things that, it seemed to him, were key to being happy:

1. Love (he always put that #1, so's not to seem a grubber, or insensitive), and
2. Money

He also knew there were some other means that lead to one or both of those same ends, supposedly. The ones you hear the most about are:

a. Natural Ability, and
b. Hard Work

And of course you also hear people say that the surest way to find Love is to have:

1. Money

And the only way to be sure of having Money is to have:

1. Rich Parents

Well, Herbie knew he didn't have Money or Rich Parents. And when it came to Natural Ability, it seemed as if the evidence was mostly on the side of . . . undecided. As a rule, he "got" things right away, but he didn't always seem to *keep* them. Or, put it this way, he'd retain a lot of stuff he didn't even need (like where both Holden Caulfield and that Frank Viola went to school, and who the hylozoistic monists and Bailey Quarters were), and then forget how to extract the square root of 237. It seemed to him the things he learned just on his own had a way of hogging all the airy, light, high-ceilinged rooms up in the front part of his brain, and of forcing certain school "material" to stay in narrow closets with the bulbs burned out.

Herb couldn't figure out if he was "college

bound," or not. He didn't like the *term* at all. It made him think of "snowbound," which he knew was *trapped*. But at least it was okay, an accepted thing to do. He hadn't ruled it out. What he needed was some reason he could use to rule it *in*.

Older people more or less encouraged him, but not that much. "You've got a real good head on your shoulders" is something that a lot of parents tell their kids, some of them named Herbie. They almost have to, though. Face it, he is *theirs*, a mixture of their genes, and if he doesn't, how do they explain it, short of saying they're a pair of dullards, too?

"You are perfectly capable of being a B+ student in this course" is more what *teachers* feel compelled to say, because they know that if they're doing even a quarter-way decent job, a bowl of bread dough could make C, by simply being plopped down in the room, most days.

I think the truth of the matter is that Herbie was or is or might have been acutely smart, but like you and me and the lamppost, he didn't really know exactly what that meant, so he couldn't get a lot of satisfaction out of it. He couldn't count on it to bring him Love or Money.

Not the love of Tyree Toledano. Not its equivalent in money, say, the contents of the U.S. Mint.

So, he told himself, he'd probably be smart to put his faith in T.K.

"But what about Hard Work?" someone in the room will always say. And not *just* to prove he was paying attention a while back. There's a certain type of person who will *always* drag that concept in. *Hard Work*. Even people with so much natural ability

you'd like to *kill* them try to act as if it's really ol'
Hard Work that got them to whatever pinnacle, or
pedestal, they're up on. Also, once you get to be a
certain age, it seems as if you've got to shove your
way into the world of youth and put up lots of verbal
temples to this boring, sweaty god.

Herbie wasn't sure that he was ready for it,
though, this Hard Work deal. He *wished* he was, or
would be. He wasn't afraid of the stuff, he didn't
think; it was more a question of . . . well, if he *could*,
or not. So far, there'd always been resistance, coming from a yawn mine deep inside his system. He
hadn't managed to produce Hard Work on anything
for more than maybe forty minutes, tops.

No, T.K. seemed more likely than Hard Work
to get him what he wanted, needed, *had to have*, if
he was ever going to be a happy fella. You remember: Love and Money.

Not that Herbie Hertzman was, like, notably *un*-
happy, either; please do not misunderstand. He was,
like many of the rest of us, more in-between, like,
there. If, years and years from now, he lives or dies
peculiarly, or marries in a way that calls for national
attention, and members of the media go digging up
his past, I bet they get a lot of "Herbie Hertzman?
Sure. He was in my bio class, I think. He seemed
to be a sort of easygoing guy, I guess. What's that?
No, nothing special, really. . . ."

But meanwhile, at the age of seventeen, he had
his ordinary daily life to lead. And that included
dealing with the question everybody seemed to ask
about his future:

"WHAT *ARE* YOU GOING TO *DO*, LIKE,
WITH YOURSELF?"

9

5
GETTING GUIDANCE

The best place to head for in any high school, if you're trying to figure out what you're going to do with yourself, is *not* the boiler room, not anymore. It's generally locked, for one thing, and even if it isn't and the custodian is there, the chances are he may not be as wise and caring as the old *janitors* used to be — the "After all, they're only kids . . ." guys. Vocations are way down, and lots of modern ones are in it for the benefits, from what I hear.

Because he knew that, Herb decided he would try the Guidance Office, first. He was pretty desperate. He set up an appointment with his counselor, as he had done at other times, in other years, for other reasons. The very first time he'd done so, he'd expected to meet someone who'd be pretty much like his *camp* counselor, whose name was Quint, and who was on the JV tennis team at Yale. In fact,

Herbie'd almost expected that the guidance counselor's office would have a bunch of bunks in it, and he would lay around on one, and his counselor on another, and they'd sort of shoot the bull about the pennant races or the difference between being intense and a bad sport, before they got around to what he'd scored in first-year algebra.

It hadn't been like that at all, of course. Not then or any other time. And it wasn't just the lack of bunks. The way that Herbie finally figured it, "camp" and "guidance" were completely different kinds of counselors, the way that "baseball" (say) and "window" are two different kinds of fans.

"Hey! Herbivorous!" said Mr. Alexander Rex, his guidance guy, that day. Mr. Rex — when you said the name, it *had* to come out "Mister X" — had wraparound dark glasses on, and high-top silver sneakers covered with tiny mirrors, and a great big knitted purple sweater with a huge, white, knitted question mark right in the middle of the front of it. Everybody knew he was the shortest, smartest, blackest member of the guidance staff. He did his hair the way that Ziggy Marley does, and he was five feet four.

"COME-Come-come," he said to Herb and took him to a half-partitioned cubicle. He went behind the small, plain desk and sat. Herb took the chair that faced it. On the floor, beside the counselor, there was a topless wooden box — or file drawer, possibly — that seemed to hold a lot of folders, maybe student records.

Mr. Rex then cocked his head a little — up, as if in thought. Because of the very dark glasses, Herbie couldn't tell where he was looking. But suddenly the shaded eyes came down to level, and Mr. Alexanderex commenced to give out guidance, à la Socrates.

"What you be goíng to do with you, young blood?" he asked. His head jerked back and forth, and he spoke fast and with a boppin' beat. "What's shakin' in between Ol' Lady Want and Mister Should?" The students didn't know it, but he talked like that to keep from getting bored.

"Well, as a matter of fact," said Herbie, shaking his own head and allowing himself a small, self-deprecating smile, "that's kind of what I want to talk to *you* about. I know I'm expected to *make* something of myself, but I don't know exactly what that is. Everybody's asking me what I'm going to *do* with myself" — Herbie pulled his handsome, longish nose and shook his head again — "and I'm not sure at all. Maybe that's because I don't know what I want to *make*, yet. Of myself, I mean. Other than, well, something different than whatever I am now." Another sigh, this one ending in a totally self-conscious chuckle. "But I'm sure I'm not too clear on all the possibilities. What I might be *suited* for, or anything like that."

During the last part of that speech, the guidance guy leaned over to his right, twisting his body and reaching for the hanging files and folders in the open box. This was a real familiar sight to Herb. In fact, it happened every time he went for guidance. And always with the same result.

As Mister X's fingers did their walkin', he began to rap, again.

"I be tryin' to find you' RECORDS-Records-

records, man," he said. "You' grades which whisper what you' *done*, you' test scores screamin' what you *can*."

Finally, however, he sat up again, and empty-handed; no telling what was in his eyes. His head shook back and forth.

"Somebody musta *borrowed* them," he said, no longer upbeat. "Somebody *always* borrowin' my records. Make me sick, I tell you, bro'. Can't sing without my music on, y'know."

Herbie swallowed hard. The situation seemed acutely serious. High school wasn't everlasting; it would soon be over. You didn't have to *do* stuff with yourself in high school; stuff was done *to* you, by *it* — or sometimes *them*. But sooner than he liked to think, all that would change. If he didn't do some *something* with himself, he wouldn't be a player in the game of life. He'd be a nobody, a man without a number.

"Well," he said. He'd try to be a good sport, anyway; Quint had counseled him on that. "I guess there isn't anything that anyone can do. . . ." He started to get up.

"No, wait," said Alexander Rex. He said it in a hoarse, but somehow friendly, whisper. He slid out of his chair and, crouching, put his ear to the partition on his left. Then, very slowly, he stood up; when he was up on tiptoe, he could just see over it. He nodded, then crouched down again and did the same thing on the right partition. When he was seated in his chair again, he flicked a switch atop the little speaker on his desk. Cheerful background music issued forth, the kind that gives you something to despise when you are put "on hold," sometimes.

Then he leaned way forward, elbows on the desktop.

"There is a place," he said. His voice was very different now. He'd dropped his role, his cover; this was undiluted Alexander Rex, a human being stripped of pretense and disguise. He'd decided to risk everything he'd carefully assembled through the years, his pension, for the sake of this mere high school kid, a person of no consequence whatever.

"Here," he whispered. He took a fountain pen and a mini-pad from out of a secret drawer and scribbled an address in purple ink on a tiny slip of paper. "Memorize it." Herbie did. "Now, eat it!" Herbie hesitated. "Hey, don't worry," Mr. Rex assured him. "It's all completely pure and natural. The ink is Concord grape juice, no preservatives." Herb did as he'd been told. It really wasn't bad. The paper had a vaguely nutty taste to it; it turned (returned?) to pulp inside his mouth quite quickly.

"The person that you'll see is, like, a consummate professional," continued Rex. "You'll be presented with a range of options to consider. You won't be pushed or pressured into anything."

Herbie raised a finger, had a question, but the counselor had read his mind.

"Your parents needn't ever know," he said. "It's up to you to tell them, if you choose to. Myself, I think it's better if you can, and do. But as I said, it's up to you."

Herb cleared his throat in some embarrassment. "Money," he croaked out. "Is there a fee? I haven't got but maybe three-four dol — "

"No," said Mr. Rex. "The services are free to those who can't afford them. Their funding comes from God knows where." He sighed. "We'd do what they do, here in school, except that you-know-who put in those regulations saying that you can't *do* certain things with public money." The guidance person and the newly guided boy both shook their heads, together.

Then Rex pulled down his shades enough so Herb could see him raise his eyebrows. "Is that it?" they clearly said. Herb nodded. Rex flipped off the music and stood up.

"So, keep your nose clean, just say no, my man," he boomed, "an' instead of 'It's too hard,' tell homework, 'Hey, I can!' "

Herb found his own way out. As usual, he hoped he might run into Tyree Toledano.

6
TYREE TOLEDANO

The trouble was: Tyree was not that sort of person, the kind you always happen to run into. She was made of airier, more insubstantial stuff, the stuff that dreams are made of.

That's why she never did attract attention at the places Herbie saw her, even if she was more beautiful than any girl he'd ever seen.

She came into a class of his one time, and he'd just sat there staring at her for the entire period, although nobody else seemed to notice her at all. She had intensely dark, thick eyebrows, and huge dark eyes, and a mouth that seemed, to Herbie, wide enough to slide a half a bagel into — halfway, anyway. Her dark brown hair was soft and wavy, and it settled on her shoulders, either side. That day she had a buttoned woolen sweater on, but not a shirt — a smooth, light tan one made of cashmere, Herb was pretty sure. She hadn't done the top two buttons, though, and on a fine gold chain around her lovely neck she wore a curious black amulet, shaped like . . . well, a cough lozenge. Mr. Roland didn't call on her all period, and she never came back to that class again. Herbie didn't blame her.

Another time, he saw her doing cartwheels in the hall in school, barefoot in a minimal blue leotard, her straight blonde hair pulled back and knotted in a dancer's bun, her lower lip between her teeth, and her blue eyes focused on some distant, but important, goal. Herb watched her then until she reached the Girls' Room door, through which she disappeared.

One other day, she came toward him on the street, with a small smile playing on her frosted lips, and her flaming hair tied loosely just behind her neck by what he took to be a multicolored silk bandana. She wore a pale green shirt that afternoon, and very tight, white, narrow-legged pants and bright red patent leather pumps with spiky heels. After she'd gone by him, and he'd turned to watch her slender gracefulness some more, he was surprised to find she'd disappeared. It was as if the ground had opened up and swallowed her, or she'd been magically transformed into a bus stop sign, two women pushing strollers, or that leggy Irish setter, there.

Not seeing Tyree anywhere inside, or just outside, the school that day, Herb decided that he might as well head home. It was, perhaps, a little late to go to the address that Mr. Rex had given him. And anyway, before too awfully long, it would be suppertime.

7
A YOUNG PHILOSOPHER WALKS HOME

Herb always liked his journeys home. He didn't have a car and didn't like to ride his bike. He walked. And thought about . . . well, things. Sometimes — after he had passed the window of Belinda's Lingerie, for instance — his thoughts were fairly junky. But at other times they were extremely philosophical, he thought. For example (from some thoughts he'd had while walking home two weeks before):

A person's life is somewhat like the wardrobe in his closet (Herbie thought). Most of it is everyday: not too great, but not real bad. And the extremes, they balance one another out. For every real sharp jacket (the equivalent of hearing that you've made somebody very, very proud or happy), there is also a disgusting pair of stupid checkered pants with a spaghetti stain on them (which are like finding out you totally destroyed the social studies final).

What that means is that a wise man *must* remember that his life and wardrobe never stay the same for long. Things go back and forth from good to bad and back again. And as they do, it is important (he decided) to *appreciate* the goods, and not just curse and moan about the bads, the way so many people seem to do.

And so he'd made a resolution that he'd try to do exactly that, and more. Every time he had good fortune, he'd not only take the time to notice and enjoy it, he would also thank the source of it: T.K. (or her present-day equivalent; Herb didn't think names mattered much). He could and did imagine perky little T.K. smiling when she saw him being grateful. And maybe even taking notes about him on a pad of old papyrus that she had right by her hot tub. High up on the slopes of Mount Olympus.

So anyway, on that day Herbie strolled along quite happily, just Doing Nothing With Himself but stepping over cracks, admiring some passing cars, and thinking, oddly, of the first line of *The Handmaid's Tale*: "We slept in what had once been the gymnasium."

But then he couldn't help but notice some excitement, up ahead. There were some twenty, maybe even fifty, people gathered on the sidewalk just outside a church, with others partway up its steps.

"Frank Pizarro," Herb said merrily, out loud, invoking (as he did) the memory of that *other* great discoverer/explorer. "What's all this about?"

Apparently "all this" was all about the stuff that happens after lots of weddings. As Herb got closer, he could see the bride and groom were posing on the church's upper steps, while people took their picture. Beside the curb there was a long, white limousine.

When he was *very* close, Herb realized that hardly anyone was speaking, but that many people in the crowd were saying things in *sign language*. ("Hey, Vic! Hey, Vera! Smile!" presumably.) The newly married couple were a prematurely balding fellow with a short black beard and a pleasant-looking girl who wore blue sequined glasses. Because they, too, were signing ("Cheese!"?), Herb figured that they also didn't hear too well, the same as many of their friends.

Herb mingled with the people on the church's steps. One thing about him was, he really *did* like almost everyone, all different kinds of people. In hardly any time at all, he felt a part of this occasion and was happy for this happy-looking couple. Vic and Vera both looked very nice to him. If Vic became completely bald in another three-four years, so what? Herb was sure that Vera'd go on loving him.

Just then he noticed that the fellow he was standing next to on the steps was talking and laughing with the person on his other side, *while also signing at the couple up above*. Herb thought that *that* was pretty special. This guy, with just one brain, could carry on two different conversations at one time!

"Excuse me," Herbie said to him, interrupting both of them, "but could you show me how to sign something?" He thought a moment. "Like, 'I hope you have a really happy life'?"

The fellow, confident enough to have on cowboy

boots, said, "Sure," then smiling in a very friendly way, he made about a half a dozen movements with his hands, which Herbie duplicated perfectly, the first time that he tried them.

"Boy, you got it," cowboy boots informed him. "Perfect." And he clapped Herb on the shoulder, communicating further friendliness.

"Great," said Herbie, "thanks." And he did the movements with his hands a second time. He felt as if he'd learned another language, which'd be his third, if you included Spanish, which he'd had in school three years. He wondered if the hand gyrations that this guy had taught him meant the same in Spanish.

"Here, show my friend." Cowboy boots was tapping Herbie on the shoulder, the same one that he'd clapped, before. "Hey, Vinnie, look what I just taught this dude to say to Vic and Vera. Go on," he said to Herbie, who then did his sentence still another time: "I hope you have a really happy life," or as Herbie told it to himself this time, as he was doing it: "*Espero que ustedes tengan una vida muy contenta.*"

But Vinnie didn't nod and smile and clap Herb on the shoulder. Instead, he grabbed the two of Herbie's hands in his own pair, while glaring, at the same time, at the guy in cowboy boots.

"What's the matter with you, Elmer, anyway?" he snarled, and clearly he was not amused, no way. He switched his eyes, now back to Herbie. "Look, you just forget that, kid, okay? My buddy here's a wise guy — see? — a real *jerkisimo.*"

"Well, what?" said Herbie, puzzled, looking at

his captive hands. The Vinnie guy still had him muzzled. "I asked him how to say 'I hope you have a really happy life.' "

Vinnie looked from side to side, then bent his mouth toward Herbie's ear.

"What you were going to say," he said, "was, 'Hey, I think you both look like a pair of jerks.' " Except, instead of "jerks," he said a vulgar word you seldom hear at weddings — even if it may be thought by former boy- or girlfriends of the bride or groom.

"*What?*" said Herb. He turned back to the cowboy-booted man. "That's really rotten of you, Elmer." Now he wanted to get out of there. He tried to think of something else to say, an exit line.

"Your mother ought to wash your hands with good strong soap," he sneered.

Halfway home, he thought he'd better stop and get some offerings for T.K. Luckily for him, he hadn't left the real America; there was a fast-food place a half a block away.

8
OFFERINGS

Magdalena Orgalescu, Herbie's mother, had married Big Ben Hertzman eighteen years before. Ben wasn't all that big; although he did stand six feet three, he was and is quite slender. It was more that "Big" and "Ben" are words that go together in a lot of people's minds, just like "Ho" and "Jo" and "Squirmin' " (I am told) and "Herman."

Lena (short for Magdalena), *she* was big, however. For a while, that is, when she was younger. She'd come over from Romania at the age of twelve, and in the first ten years she was here, she more than doubled what she weighed.

You couldn't really blame her, though. Romanian immigrants are apt to eat most everything in sight, when they are able to. Although it's one fantastic country, and the homeland of a lot of dandy human beings, some of whom are gypsies, Romania hasn't done real well, in certain ways, since World War II. There have been a lot of shortages, for instance. Of almost everything, some say, but especially of food that's fun to eat. Butter, milk and bread are rationed to this day; salad at a restaurant is often just four pickles on a plate. The Fudge Banana Brownie is endangered, possibly extinct, in Bucharest.

But once she was completely Americanized, and had started to make something of herself, Lena got into serious dieting. She cut her weight in half and met Ben Hertzman. Then she married him and sometime later Herb was either born, or not. There isn't any question that she *could* have given birth the day and month and year that Herbie called his birthday. Even that "leap second." Nowadays, Ben Hertzman sometimes says that Lena has a "perfect" figure; other times he'll say that she is "skin and bones." It all depends on whether he's kidding around or not — which is almost impossible to tell. Even Lena says she doesn't know, herself; that's rare for a Romanian.

"Hey, Mom! Hey, Dad! Anybody home?" called Herbie, coming in the door.

"Hi, honey," Lena Orgalescu Hertzman answered. "In the kitchen. With good news."

"Hey, Mom," said Herb again, arriving in the kitchen. He bent and kissed her cheek.

"You're late," she said, but not complainingly. She was wearing an embroidered robe and sitting at the kitchen table. In front of her there was an almost empty teacup and a deck of cards. She'd been relaxing after work. By day, she was a stockbroker.

"I was at the windup of a wedding," Herbie said.

"And I made a pit stop, after, at Phast Phil's. Tell me some good news."

"Two things," she said. "The first one is, your Uncle Babbo wrote. He's coming for the weekend, and he wants to talk to you. He's got some thoughts about your future, possibly a proposition, I believe." She smiled. "The second is" — she looked down at her teacup — "an idea that came to me a little while ago. It's another line of work you might look into, if you don't get into college." She held out a clipping to him. "Take a look at this."

It was from a magazine. He looked at it. It was an ad that also had a picture in it. The picture was of twelve young men, all dressed the same. They were wearing light blue leather boots, the soft and floppy kind, and light blue trousers, sort of pirate's pants, with white scarves looped around their necks and little blue boleros. They were members of a dance group called "The Wedgwoods" who, the ad explained, "performed on stages coast-to-coast, as well as for the heads of state of many foreign governments, abroad."

"What?" said Herbie, grinning in surprise. "My mother wants that I should be an *entertainer*?" He shook his head. "That's crazy, Mom. I'm not a fun-type guy. And I'm a *lousy* dancer. Just ask . . . anyone."

"It's just a thought," his mother said, and shrugged. "You've got a lot of dancing in your blood, your *genes*. And you've got the looks, like all the Orgalescus. Did you know your Uncle Babbo was a model, once? But just the very top part of his head, and pictured from above. He was the 'after' in a hair restorer ad."

But Herbie only shook his head again. His mother's brother, Babbo Orgalescu, was extremely dark and hairy. Sometime after his arrival in America, he'd come upon the motto that he'd lived by, ever since: "Use it or lose it." The last that Herbie heard, he was involved with something by the name of "Your Mane Man: The One Complete Hairstyling System."

"I don't know, Mom," Herbie said. "I guess I'll have to sleep on this one. I'm not sure I'm right for it. I see myself as more the sedentary type. More of a thinker, a philosopher." He grinned. "A guy who's into finding out the answers to Big Questions. Like, 'Why *can't* I put my dirty dishes in the sink?' " He tried to laugh it off.

His mother picked up the deck of cards and began to deal them out in four rows on the table. Herb knew that might be solitaire, but maybe not. He also knew he probably would hear some more about "The Wedgwoods."

"Pan Am was up five-eighths today," she said. "Does that say 'journey' to you, maybe? Or, even like a *tour* — from 'coast to coast'? And possibly 'abroad,' to where the heads of foreign governments are found?" She took a glance up at his face. "I know, I know — to you that sounds like superstition. 'How could the New York Stock Exchange have anything to do with *me*, my future line of work?' you ask. *But*" — she smiled at him and closed one eye — "I tell you dis: Stranger t'ings haff happened."

"Right," said Herbie, thinking of the food he'd bought while coming home. "I'll think about it, Mom. Upstairs." When his mother put the accent on, he knew that it was time to split.

* * *

When Herbie got up to his room, he lost no time in setting up the offering to T.K. It meant more if he did it at a time when he was really hungry, like right then.

The ruling principle, the one that animated quite a few of Herbie's dealings with the goddess, was simplicity itself. He believed the letters T and K had magic properties, at times, at least for him. When they were found in certain words, and in that order, those words become the names of lucky *things* (he had decided). And so, for instance, TiddlywinKs would be a pastime favored by the goddess and would be a lucky game for him to play, compared to baseball, say. BasKeTball, which had "the letters" in it, but *reversed*, was almost certainly a no-no — as were KilTs and sKirTs (at least for him). In order to be realistic (also fair and open-minded), the boy permitted some *exceptions* to the rules, as in the case of KiTchen. *It* could be a *very* lucky room, as on the nights his mother cooked roasT chicKen.

But he only made these offerings to T.K. on *extremely* rare occasions, special times when he had special needs for great good luck. And he always made them properly, with ceremony, the way he did right then. First, he'd TaKe a shower, to get clean and worthy. Then, he'd put fresh sweaTsocKs on, and nothing more — hence, nothing hidden from the goddess, up his sleeve or anywhere. After that, he TooK Ten nicKels, and he put them in a circle just a foot across. (In Brazil, they make the magic circle out of candles, and you can see where *that* has gotten *them*.) Inside it, went the offering

27

itself, always just two items: a TurKey sandwich and a real ThicK chocolaTe shaKe.

With all that finally done, Herb sighed contentedly and smiled, and lay down on his bed. For luck next day, he decided that he'd wear his deersTalKer, and TaKe his TomahawK.

He checked the magic circle and the food inside it. A quarter of an hour had gone by. He thought that T.K. *probably* was done with it by then, although mere mortals like himself could not (of course) be sure. The sandwich and the shake contained a lot of different nutrients, as everybody knew: protein, carbohydrates, vitamins and minerals. And also "nectar" and "ambrosia" (less well known), which were what a goddess drank and ate. Herb believed that T.K. would extract those parts of what he offered, and then leave the rest behind. The food would *look* the same, of course — just as it will do if you take all the vitamins away (the way the human processors still do, sometimes). So he could only go by time, to tell when she was done, and it was time.

His job was (then) to properly dispose of all the "scraps" (as he called them in his mind). He couldn't let them sit there on the floor. Mice would be attracted by them, surely, mice *and* roaches.

And so, Herb dressed and then sat down and ate the "scraps" himself, praising T.K. as he did so. After which he hurried down to dinner.

9
ON THE WAY TO CASTLES IN THE AIR

The address that Herbie'd memorized the day before was seven-dash-eleven Sunset Strip, and when he left his house to head for it, at 10 A.M. next morning, he realized he didn't know where he was going, where Sunset Strip might *be*. Not even more or less.

"Is this the story of my life, or what?" he said out loud.

He stood there for a minute, puzzling. The only thing that he could think to do was . . . well, *eliminate* the parts of town he was familiar with, and go to all the others, one by one, until he hit the right one. The thing that made *that* hard, confusing, was that he thought he'd been all over town, before.

The name of the — what would you call it? — *service* he was seeking was, according to what Mr. Rex had scribbled down, "Castles in the Air." That's all the counselor had written on that tiny slip of paper: "Castles in the Air, 7-11 Sunset Strip." That *sounded* fairly classy, Herbie thought, but he also knew that names could be deceptive. "The Church of the Supreme Transmogrified Redemptor" was a rather shabby storefront, and "Nathaniel's One-Step Quickie and Immaculate Dry Cleaning and De-Staining Empire" was not a place to go (he'd heard his mother tell a friend) with any dress you planned to wear again. Herb could only hope that "Castles in the Air" would be more solid and substantial than its name implied. He started out, as usual, with hope (but not prejudgment) in his heart.

A few miles later, he was finding unfamiliar streets, all right, and they were lovely; one of them was Sunset Strip. As Herbie walked its gently curving way, however, he seldom saw a house. *Driveways*, he could see; driveways made of gravel and of blacktop and of white crushed stone were nicely spaced, but plentiful. *Gateposts*, he could see, and also sometimes gates and even once a gate*house*, he could see. *Signs* with names of people or of properties were also common: B.D. SWIGOTT or THE LARCHES. He saw some other signs, as well, with messages such as NO ZEALOTS and PLEASE DON'T FEED THE GRYPHON.

Human beings seemed as rare as houses. In fact, the only person Herbie saw close up in all the miles he walked on Sunset Strip was this one fellow who was standing by a driveway with a large sign reading PRIVATE ROAD beside it. Herb thought he was a few years older than himself, and he was wearing a short haircut and a leisure suit that still had the price tag, as well as other labels, hanging from one sleeve.

"Who are you and what's your business, here?" he said to Herb, quite sharply.

"Herbie Hertzman," our young man replied. "I'm not in business, yet. I'm looking for a place called 'Castles in the Air.' Who wants to know, just out of curiosity?" He let the fellow see his tomahawk, ran a finger right along its business edge.

The stranger jerked a thumb toward the sign. "I'm Private Road," he said. "Private Buford 'Buddy' Road. I just came home on furlough for a week, to check on my estate, here. 'Castles' is a ways up there, someplace. Keep going, you can't miss it. And if you take my best advice, you won't ask anybody else you meet for any more directions. We've got some all-world goofballs living in this neighborhood, and two of the rock-bottom worst, I'm sad to say, are in my line of work: Corporal Punishment and General Nuisance. They're making it real hard for me to be all that *I* can be, I'll tell you that much. I'm pretty sure that I could find my future in the army, if they'd stop ordering me around. And they're apt to do the same to you, if you should cross their paths."

He looked Herb over, top to toe to top again. "And how do you keep hand and mouth together, Sherlock?"

Herbie thought that instead of "hand and mouth," he'd probably meant either "body and soul," or "realistic expectations and utopian dreams," or "old paperback books," or "families that don't play," but he decided not to take his chances with eccentric, snappish, Buford "Buddy" Road.

"Oh, fork *or* chopsticks," he said quickly, with an

easygoing smile. "It all depends what sort of mood I'm in, I guess. I can bring the bacon home with either one, heh-heh. But have a nice day, won't you?"

And with that he headed off, politely but with tomahawk still swinging in his hand.

A few miles farther on, Herbie finally reached a driveway with an *extremely* welcome sign right at the foot of it: CASTLES IN THE AIR. He paused again to check out his surroundings.

For the most part, they looked good; they even *sounded* good. The drive was white and crunchy — also smooth, devoid of potholes, pits or puddles. There were two sturdy fieldstone gateposts, columns really, flanking it — but no gate to block his way. Outside the posts, however, was a tall, black iron fence, made of slender eight-foot pieces up and down, and set about a half a foot apart. They were also curved a little on their upper ends, and sharply pointed, there.

Tied onto this aristocratic fence with bright red twine were half a dozen crudely lettered signs, bearing rather hostile messages, considering the neighborhood. IMPRACTICAL IDEAS ARE PRACTICALLY REPULSIVE, STUPID, said one. Another read HONK IF YOU'RE NOT DAYDREAMING. Two others were: CASTLES IN THE AIR IS FULL OF GOONY BIRDS, and KEEP KNOWLEDGE OF THE WORLD WHERE IT BELONGS, IN SCHOOL. Behind the fence, however, gentle rhododendrons grew, in some profusion.

Peering up the drive, Herb could see a slate roof in the distance, with a tower sprouting from one corner of it. He felt sure that he was seeing Castles in the Air itself, a building firmly grounded in a better part of town.

"Well, I guess it's not a storefront," Herbie said out loud, as he began to walk up toward the place.

Before he'd gone three steps, he was startled by two voices coming from his left, just past the gatepost on that side.

"Ahem," said one of them. "Ahem. Kaff-kaff-kaff-kaff."

"Chivvy-chivvy-chivvy-chivvy-chivvy," said the other one, and very sharply, too.

"What?" said Herb. He couldn't see the speakers — anyone, in fact. The voices seemed to come from somewhere in the rhododendrons. "Who's there? You want to speak to me?"

" *'What? Who's there? You want to speak to me?'* " That second voice was, clearly, making fun of his. "Yes, we-want-to-speak-to-you, you idiot. Who else would we be speaking to? You think we're out here for our health, or something?"

"To be honest with you," Herbie said, "I wouldn't know. It seems to me that this would be a pretty good environment — in terms of health, I mean. Actually, I barely know what *I'm* here for, myself. But — could I ask? — are you from Castles in the Air? You wouldn't be, like, *yeomen* of some sort — or would you?"

" *'Like-yeomen-of-some-sort-or-would-you?'* " It was that same sarcastic voice, mocking him again. "No, we're *not* like-yeomen-of-some-sort. Or yes-men-of-some-sort, or even *no*-men-of-some-sort. You don't have eyes, or something? Don't you know *pickets* when you see them? I suppose you're going to say you didn't see our signs."

"Perhaps you thought," another voice chimed in, "that you could just come waltzing in as if this was a disco, or a *dance* hall. As if it was some stupid *mall*. Or Constitution *Hall*."

"Look," said Herbie, "there's been some mistake, I think. What I'm doing here is completely consistent with the whole idea of a pluralistic, democratic society (with a well-established and accepted labor movement) in which every person regardless of race, color, creed, or rational origin can totally self-make himself in almost any way he chooses. Provided he can figure out what choice he wants to make, out of all the choices there might *be*, as well as counter work. Like, well, to give you one extreme example I can think of — and I'm not saying this is necessarily the choice that I'm about to go for, *but* — well, like, hey, I *could* be President, someday."

"The hell you *could*," said one of the first voices, the most vicious and sarcastic one. "There's laws to keep absurdities like that from happening, thank God. And what there also are is *ruts* for kids like you to settle down in and shut up, you follow me? You think you're better than your parents? They did what they were told, or else, I'll bet. And you, you'd better do the same."

"Oh, yeah?" said Herbie, getting just a little miffed. "Well, I've got news for *you*. This is a *real* free country we've got going here, and it's up to me to make my own decisions . . . er, once I find out what the choices are, that is. In fact, that is *exactly* what I'm going up to Cas — "

"Son," a voice said, interrupting him. It was a new and deep and southern kind of one. "We're not askin' you all this, we're *tellin'* you. We're just about to give you your instructions, boy. Lak judges do with juries, we got, lak, a *charge* to lay on you, a *pickets' charge*. So you just listen up and mind. You ready, boys?" he said. " . . . two, three, four. . . ."

And then the charge came rolling out from deep inside the rhododendrons, line after line after line:

> "We will tell you what to think,
> we will tell you what to do.
> Don't you dare to make a stink,
> or things will go real bad for you.
> And, above all, you little jerk,
> don't expect to like your work."

It wasn't any fun for Herb to stand there, in the open, hearing that — *exposed* to it — a threat, an existential horror of that magnitude. He didn't know if there was anything that he, a teenaged kid, could do to check it, counteract it.

But something told him that he'd better fire back a salvo of his own, and hope that it connected. And so he faced the rhododendrons squarely, with his shoulders back.

"Your threats won't work," he managed to blurt out. "I'm not that dense. I don't take orders from a fence."

With that, he turned his back on them and marched straight up the driveway. He hoped the pickets couldn't tell, from looking at his back, how all that talk of "ruts" and not expecting to enjoy what he was going to do had scared him.

Behind him, there was only silence. Except, of course, for groans.

10
BLAST OFF

For the most part, Herb wasn't into preconceptions. He took both things and people as they came, instead of working out beforehand how they might or ought to be, and having expectations of them. Some people call that "being philosophical"; others say it's more like bland, or dumb, or lazy. If asked what *he* thought, Herbie would have put it this way: "Pretty much, I trust to luck, I guess."

And so, he didn't think much of the fact that when he topped a final little rise of ground, he saw his destination was this enormous gray stone building with only slits, high up, for windows, connected to a big round tower with a battlement on top. Or that it had a nice wide moat around it, and a drawbridge that was open — down — with a sign on it which read not only CASTLES IN THE AIR, but also BED AND BREAKFAST — HOMEMADE FRENCH TOAST. Or that there was a woman in a wide straw hat kneeling by the flower garden running 'round the moat, and pulling weeds from it. Which weeds and other garden debris she was tossing into a two-wheeled cart beside her. He just accepted all of that, convinced that this was going to be his lucky day.

It seemed the woman must have heard Herb crunching up the driveway. When he was still about four bowling alley lengths from where she worked, she turned and waved at him and then, with sweeping motions of one arm (the one that ended in a trowel) she urged him to approach, to come across the close-cropped lawn and join her. Even at that distance he could see that she was laughing to herself, quite merrily. Herb, himself, had never found that doing garden work was that much fun.

When he got close, and doffed his double-visored cap, the way he always did when he was wearing hats and meeting ladies, she turned her head around again and peered at him.

"Great Hebe's junior jeebies!" she exclaimed. "You must be Herbie Hertzman!" And while he nodded "yes," she picked one knee up off the ground and, using it to push on with both hands, she made it to her feet.

"Sandy said you might be coming by," she said to Herb. "I'm Sesame deBarque." She pulled a muddy glove off her right hand and offered it to him, laughing much as if she'd just exposed a rabbit, or a squid.

Herb shook the hand enthusiastically. Sesame deBarque was older than his mother, also shorter, rounder, fair instead of dark. Wisps of blondish hair escaped from underneath her picture hat, and her full, strong-featured face was ruddy. She wore — indeed, she was enveloped by — a shapeless tentlike sundress cut from some material that would have made a cheerful cover for a couch, patterned as it was with large green leaves and ample yellow flowers that looked much like cabbages. This garment ended just above her knees on which were strapped two rubber kneeling pads; below them, her pink, sturdy calves were bare, as were her ankles and her feet. Her toenails gleamed bright emerald.

"Sandy?" Herbie said.

"Alexander Rex," she answered. "Cunning little devil, isn't he?" And then she laughed again, and slipping one hand under Herbie's arm and grabbing her cart's handle with the other, she began to walk both cart and boy toward the open drawbridge.

Unsure of how to answer that, or even if he should, Herb pointed at the sign tacked to the drawbridge.

"You know, it isn't really either bed *or* breakfast that I'm looking for," he said. "I thought I'd made that clear to Mr. Rex, although sometimes it's quite easy not to understand another person. But anyway, it's actually more something to *do* I'm hoping to find out about. With myself, you know? Although, to be completely honest, I've worked up quite an appetite from all the walking that I've done today." He paused and thought it over. "And I really like French toast a *lot*," he said, quite truthfully.

Sesame deBarque threw back her head and laughed again.

"And Russian dressing, too, I'll bet," she said. "But Herb, I know *exactly* why you're here. That sign is just to throw them off. The tourists and the busybodies — all the unbelievers. And, as far as cooking is concerned, it's all that I can do to toast *myself*, before an open fire. That's why I always have the other sign on, too. The little one above the archway, there." She pointed.

Herbie looked where she was pointing and sure enough, above the large main entrance to the castle was a small pink neon sign. NO VACANCY, it blinked, in Gothic script. It fit in very nicely with the architecture, Herbie thought.

"But," she added, "we can have a snack before we settle down to work. Just let me toss this junk out, first."

With that, she let go of his arm and pushed the cart up to the water's edge and dumped its contents into the moat. Herb was surprised at that. The driveway and the grounds were so well manicured, it seemed peculiar, out of place, to see this garden refuse floating on the moat's clear water.

His hostess must have seen the look on Herbie's face.

"Don't worry. Watch," she said. They'd crossed the drawbridge to the castle side, and there she seized the handle on a chain that hung down just outside the door and gave the thing a yank.

At once, the water in the moat began to move, from right to left as Herbie turned to look at it, and faster all the time until it was as speedy as rapids or a whirlpool. The water level kept on lowering, as well, until the last few inches swept from view and disappeared some place beneath the castle with this most enormous "Glug!" — after which fresh water gushed into the moat again. Herb stood there, staring, stupefied.

Sesame deBarque, however, clapped her hands delightedly.

"Isn't that a ring-tailed doozie, now?" she raved. "A scientific and hygienic miracle? This is the first one ever made, by the Arab prince, Walid Caliph, in 1323 A.D., and installed around his castle in North Africa. Do his initials ring a bell with you, by any chance? You bet they do." She nodded. "Then what happened was some movie mogul saw it over there in 1951, still working perfectly, and fell in love with it. He bought the whole shebang the way they do — castle, moat, the works — and moved it stone by stone to this location. But some years after that there was an awful . . . incident. Someone pulled the chain during a party — accidentally or on purpose, who's to say? — and a half a dozen starlets and a man named Sid were never seen again. The mogul sold the place to me and moved to St. Tropez with someone by the name of Bijou." And she shook her head. "Some say he got away with murder, that he'd had it in for that guy Sid for years. They say he planned it all, even to the choice of weapon. According to that theory, the starlets were . . . unlucky, you could say. In the wrong place at the very worst of times."

"Gee," said Herbie. "That's some story, Ms. deBarque."

"Please," she said. "I'd rather that you called me Sesame, or Ses. Or SDB, if you prefer initials." She winked and clapped him on the back. "So. How about we get ourselves a snack and go to work? Okay?"

"Terrific," Herbie said. She flung the portal wide and went on in ahead of him to turn the lights on.

40

* * *

"Sandy Rex and I did Outward Bound together, years ago," Ses deBarque was saying as she and Herb went down another vaulted corridor, one peanut butter sandwich later. "He was a great kid to have in your group, a real team player, but he had a terrible sense of direction. Put him in the woods without a compass and he'd just go 'round and 'round. That's probably why he went into Guidance. He'd have, like, perfect empathy, you know? I mean, he'd know the questions from the inside out. Like, 'Where am I?' and 'How do I get out of here?' "

"Yes, or 'What am I going to do with myself?' " said Herbie. "Which is my main question and the reason Mr. Rex suggested I come up here. What he didn't tell me, though, is how you possibly could help me."

"That's not surprising," she replied. "You see, he doesn't know. Nobody does, except for me and all the clients that I've served. And with them I have, like, an agreement."

They came to a door at the end of the corridor. She opened it and motioned Herbie in ahead of her.

He gasped. It was a gorgeous room. The words that came to Herbie's mind were "huge baronial hall." That is to say, the place was barnlike in dimensions, with those slits of windows high up in the walls on either side, and lots of banners, pennants, ensigns, streamers, flags, gonfalons and the like hanging from the noble rafters or jutting from the walls on staffs. Herb recognized the logos on a lot of them, and saw that many of them were from very major corporations and professions including, to his mixed emotions, all of these: Toyota, and McDonald's; IBM, the Minnesota Twins.

A huge refectory table, flanked by maybe forty high-backed chairs, ran down the middle of the room. At the far end of it was a handsome walnut desk, with swivel chair behind it and a client's chair in front. And against the farthest wall there was a huge, and most amazing, wheel!

The thing was twenty-five-feet high, at least, and flat, its surface sectioned off in pie-shaped pieces, eight of them, all in different bright, exciting colors. And each of those eight sections had some words in it. Here is what it looked like, provided you imagine all the different colors on the thing:

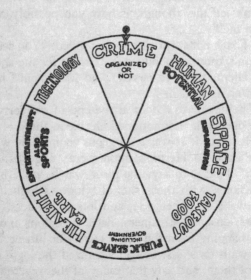

At the top, there was an arrow that would point to something if the wheel were spun and then allowed to stop.

"Let's get the paperwork all taken care of, first," Herb's hostess said. She led him past the big long table to the desk and took her place behind it in the swivel chair. He sat across from her and crossed his legs. It seemed to him that that would be the sort of thing a person taking care of "paperwork" would do.

"This is our basic 'dinner plate' agreement," Ses explained. She'd pulled out a loose-leaf notebook more or less three inches thick.

"Dinner plate?" said Herb.

"Yes, isn't that absurd?" she said. "It's something that we *say*, these days; don't ask me why, for heavens' sakes. Unless it's because it can hold four hundred and thirty-seven helpings of 'the parties of the first and second part,' and eighty-six side orders of 'whereas.' But anyway. We also have the short form, if you want to save some time."

She handed him a single sheet of paper that read: "I agree that I can't have it all.*" Below that was a line for him to sign on; it was dotted.

At the bottom of the page, beside another asterisk, it said: "Just thank your lucky stars for anything you get, and swear you'll never mention any part of this to anyone, so help you Hannah."

"So," said Herb. He signed the thing and sat back in his chair. So. He had agreed. To what, though? Really?

"I guess I'm set," he said. "But still. The one thing I don't understand is . . . is what it is you're going to do for me."

Sesame deBarque just stared at him a second, blinking. But then she wrinkled up her nose and shook her head, and started making sounds of comic self-disgust, while laying open-handed swats on top of her straw hat.

"Absentminded Minnie Thaw," she seemed to say. "I haven't told you . . . *anything* — now, have I? Well . . . " She reached across the desk and patted Herbie's hand.

"Here's the way it works," she said. She rose and went to stand beside the wheel. "First, you step up to our Winner's Circle, here, and give the thing a spin. What the little arrow ends up pointing to is *it*, the field you're going to sample. Seeing as you haven't got the foggiest idea of what you *want* to do, or what's involved in any of them — right? — it shouldn't matter in the slightest where the arrow lands. Correct?"

And Herbie nodded. That was true. For sure. He could sample any kind of work, he guessed. Why not? Of course he'd never thought of Crime, a life of crime (organized or not) as being one of his alternatives. He'd always had a tendency to blush, or giggle, if his mother asked who put the ice tray back with just one cube in it. But he knew there was a lot of major money to be made in shady deals, "white-collar crime," and other kids from real good families were doing it without their mothers asking them about it. He decided he would keep an open mind on Crime. Chances were, he'd never have to deal with it, other than as a victim. There were seven other "choices," after all.

"*Then*," she said, "we take you to the tower, where you step into our vehicle and get transported, almost magically, into the time and place where your job identity awaits you. There and then you try it out, and after you have done so, you return for your debriefing." Herbie blinked. "If the two of us agree that wasn't *it*, for you, we make a new appointment and you try again."

She sat back in her chair and smiled at him some more. "Any further questions?" she inquired.

"What kind of *vehicle* is that?" said Herb. "I'm not sure I've ever heard of — "

"No, probably you haven't," she said, interrupting. "It's called an Upwardlimobile. You'll see. And better still, *experience*. It's really on the cutting edge of space-slash-time vocational technology."

"I'll bet," said Herb enthusiastically. And then he had another thought. "But maybe, if you have a phone, I ought to call my mom. I told her I'd be back by suppertime."

"No sweat," said Ses deBarque. "You will be. A week in any of the places you might go lasts only fifty-seven seconds, here. We use a time compressor; it's a handy little thing. I wish that there was something half as good for hips and thighs."

Herb nodded and stood up. "Well, in that case I believe I *am* all set," he said. He went and spun the wheel.

Around and 'round it went. And when it stopped, it stopped, of course, on Crime — Organized or not.

"Zoo-eee," said Ses, excitedly, "you sure don't kid around! Gonna be real ba-ad right off the bat." She sobered up a little. "That's our very widest, *wildest* category, as I'm sure you've figured out already. You *could* end up on Wall Street, or in the halls of government — or in a long pink Cadillac with half a dozen rental properties named Misty. Only the Dispatcher knows, and it's not telling yet. But soon. . . ."

She started pushing buttons on a console on her desk. It reminded Herb of the automatic teller machine down at the bank.

"Come on, come on . . ." she said. She drummed her fingertips, impatiently. " 'Somewhere, over the rainbow . . .' " she sang, softly.

"Ah, here we are," she said at last, as a small plastic rectangle, no bigger than a credit card, appeared from out of the console's side. She glanced at it, and nodded and stood up.

"Let's go," she (simply) said.

She led him through three doors and down two halls, and so into the tower. To Herb's considerable surprise, the Upwardlimobile looked like a Ford or Chevy van, perhaps an '86, in tan. He'd been expecting something more along the lines of *Challenger*, *Apollo*, one of those. He was, in fact, relieved.

There was a slot between the windshield and the driver's door, and Ses inserted the small plastic card in that, before she slid the side door open.

Inside, it was exactly like a van, with breakfast nook and sofa bed and compact kitchenette. There was a calendar that had a color photo of Old Faithful on it. Behind the two big bucket seats up front, there was a heavy suede-look curtain, which Herb's hostess now pulled closed.

"So — I guess it's time for you to buckle up," she told the boy. "And we'll begin the countdown." She gestured toward the couch inside the van.

Herb clambered in, and sat.

"I guess they'll be expecting me, and all," he said.

"You bet they will," she said. "You'll see. All set, now, Mr. Argonaut?"

Herb had gotten his seat belt on and buckled tight. He smiled at her misspeaking "astronaut," like that. He was nervous, but not scared, he thought. It seemed to him he'd flown before, one time, when he was just a baby. He was pretty sure that he remembered landing. They had missed the runway, gone beyond it. But they'd landed safely, anyway.

"Roger, wilco," he told Ses deBarque, and flashed the thumbs-up sign.

"Five, four, three, two, one," she said, and slammed the door tight shut.

11
THE ISLE OF
WINCE 'N' WAILS

Herb was pretty impressed with the Upwardlimobile's ride. "Smooth" was like an understatement; there wasn't any sense of motion whatsoever, and it didn't make a sound. Nor was there any pressure on his ears, or anywhere, while taking off or landing. And because there weren't any windows back where he was, Herbie couldn't see what he was going through, or over. Also, the time compressor made it hard for him to even guess how long the trip was lasting, and he never saw a driver, either.

If he hadn't gotten there, it might have seemed to Herb as if he hadn't gone at all.

The door slid open suddenly, and there he was. Because he wasn't into preconceptions, he wasn't that surprised at where. The Upwardlimobile had landed on a hillside, it appeared, and from his couch the boy was looking down upon a — what? — a *settlement* (he supposed you'd say) that someone had established on a rocky, treeless island mostly covered up by ice and snow. At least Herb *thought* it was an island; it had a sort of shipwrecked look about it.

The settlement consisted of some twenty Quonset huts and other different kinds of structures (that included one big gray affair that looked to be inflated), most of them connected to another one or two by covered passageways. Wind had piled the snow in whale-sized drifts in places; elsewhere it had swept the ground as bare as blubber, revealing quite a grand array of trash: metal drums, black plastic bags stuffed full and broken crates of many shapes and sizes, some with weathered lettering on them. Herb saw one that read: Designer Leather Telephones. Taken as a whole, this didn't look like all that great a place to practice criminal activities — except, of course, for littering.

A moment later, he had company. It was a fellow wearing pac boots and a parka with that wolf's fur trimming on the hood.

"Don't anybody *tell* me!" he cried out. He had a cultured and enthusiastic voice. "*You* are — You *must* be — Herbie Hertzman. With the pizza that we ordered, am I right?" He laughed and stomped across the van with hand outstretched. He didn't look much more than thirty — *forty*, anyway — and was about the most clean-shaven guy that Herb had ever seen.

"Uh — I'm Herbie," said the boy. "Without the pizza, though. Nobody told me anythi — "

"I'm not surprised," the man went on. "We *are* a *tad* beyond the outer limits of deliverance, up here."

He winked. "But, *grand* to see you, anyway." He sounded almost English, but not quite. "*Welcome* to the Isle of Wince 'n' Wails! I'm Greenfield Hill, proprietor, in charge of the igloonatics who call this godforsaken outpost home!"

Herb let the fellow wring his hand. Greenfield Hill used both of his to do so, holding onto Herb's and kind of cupping it between the two of his. Hill's hands were very warm and smooth; Herb thought his grip felt honest and sincere. He welcomed both the warmth *and* honesty. An icy, arctic wind had blown in through the open door and almost set his teeth to chattering. And feeling that you're being dealt with honestly by someone who you know to be a crook is warming in its own way, too.

"Chop-chop, let's hand up Herbie's mitts and parka, Trev. Good *man*." Hill spoke to someone still outside the door. "Just slip these on, my beamish boy. There you go. How's that? A perfect fit, *I'd* say. I bet I was a haberdasher, in some other incarnation. Now, how about we scat-tail out of here and rush to sample Wince 'n' Wails's brand of northern hospitality? A warming cup of cocoa, or some Gray old Earl will hit the spot, I'll bet."

"The Isle of Wince 'n' Wails?" said Herb. The windproof parka'd made a difference right away. Now that he was pretty sure he wasn't going to freeze to death, he thought he'd better get a few things straight. Was he where he belonged? For sure? He'd heard of people flying from Seattle to New York (for instance), who'd had their baggage go to, say, Karachi, Pakistan. Maybe, in this instance, *he* was like lost luggage.

"Well," said Greenfield Hill, "its *real* name isn't

that, of course. According to the gang at Rand McNally, this *most* unprepossessing piece of real estate is Prince of Wales Island, and a part of Canada, District of Franklin in the Northwest Territories, *well* above the Arctic Circle and *not* far from the North Magnetic Pole. By most of us, however, it's thought of as *the* jumping-off place in the world entire — and hence the Isle of Wince 'n' Wails. But at the same time it's just *perfect* for our purposes because it *is* — except for inside, where we do our work — so *totally* unbearable! Now what say you to a jump right on that noisy little Arctic feline there, and letting our young Trevor whisk us to a place of warmth?"

Herb hesitated, still. Although what Greenfield Hill had said suggested that this place was, like, a hideout of some sort, he still had doubts about the guy himself. Vic, of Vic and Vera, his own dad and Dr. Bismuthson, his high school principal, all looked more like criminals than Greenfield Hill.

"One thing," Herb started, rather haltingly, "perhaps a stupid question, but, well — to save some time, just don't get mad, all right? — the stuff that's going on down there," he nodded toward the settlement, "it *is* illegal, isn't it?"

"Oh, you can bet your . . . Abenaki knicky-knacky there, it is," said Greenfield Hill, pointing at Herb's tomahawk. "Could you imagine any *homo sapiens* who hadn't been *lobotomized* living in a place like this for *funzies?*"

With which he laughed, delightedly, and helped Herb out the door, with an aren't-we-all-buds-together arm around his shoulders.

* * *

"The Mounties think we're just a bunch of silly science types — geologists and weather-weirds," Greenfield Hill was saying over dinner, hours later.

When they'd gotten to the settlement, they'd had a cup of cocoa in a room with a door that had Lounge on it. There were some other men and women there, but none of them was dressed in a chalk-striped suit with extra shoulder pads, or pointed, narrow shoes. But seeing how they greeted Greenfield Hill, Herb became convinced he was the *capo*, Boss, whatever — never mind his good-guy preppy look. After cocoa, Herb was shown his room and given lots of time to get "cleaned up" for dinner. No word had yet been said about what anyone was doing there.

"In fact," G. Hill was saying now, after sipping from the glass of light white wine that Herb had said "no, thank you" to, "there's only one RCMP, a Mountie corporal — I think his name is Truscott or McKenzie, a sweet young *Scottish* sort of person — for this *immensity* of space, about the size of our Alaska." He shook his head and laughed. "He told us he'd swing by again in fourteen-fifteen years, he didn't know for sure. That's about how long it takes him to go once around his beat, traveling by *kayak* and on *snowshoes*. Thrice around and they retire him, I guess. With a citation from Her Majesty and a clock set in a walrus tusk."

The three of them were sitting at the table in the living-dining area of Hill's apartment: Herb and Hill himself and Trevor Rhinelander the 4th, the "Trev" who'd handed in the parka and the mittens, and who'd been the driver of that snowmobile, an Arctic Cat. He seemed, to Herb, to be another pleasant person, lean and dark, but with a friendly, flashing smile, much closer to his age than Hill's. It had been Trev, in fact, who'd cooked the dinner; Herbie'd found that out from Hill, who seemed extremely proud of him for having done so. Hill had whispered to the boy when Trev was in the kitchen, saying it was very "now" of Trev to pick up gourmet cooking, to really get to know his sauces.

While he was eating, Herb tried to think of questions that his father might come up with in this situation, the sorts of questions he would ask another man about his business, when he didn't have a clue *about* that business, even what it was.

"So," he said, at last, filling an infrequent silence, "it sounds like this'd be a great location for your kind of . . . operation." The other two both nodded, vaguely, but they kept on eating, didn't speak. Herb tried another tack. "So, how long have you-all been . . . operating, here?"

"I wondered that myself, when *I* first came," said Trevor. "And I was quite surprised to learn they started up right after World War II. Which means — let's see" — he looked at Hill — "forty-five full years?" Hill nodded. "With but a single change in management, and that was just two years ago."

"True, true," said Greenfield Hill. "Our founder's heir, who was the president by then, he got a sudden urge one springlike Friday morning. To get into something else, I guess. An hour later, he was gone." He snapped his fingers. "Poof! Like that!"

"That was my second year up here," said Trev. "And thanks to him" — he bobbed his head at Hill — "we never missed a beat."

"*Well*," said Hill, "we had our programs going, and a product to . . . produce. Nature — as you know, Herb — just *abhors* a vacuum. I stepped in, picked up the reins, and here we all are now. Happy as a flock of larks." He smiled, and so did Trevor.

"Exaltation," Trevor said.

"What?" said Hill.

"Exaltation," Trevor said, again. "An *exaltation* of larks. That's another way of saying lots of larks. If not preferred, at least accepted."

"*Is* it, now?" Greenfield Hill seemed thrilled to get that news. "That's just *delightful*, Trev! And good for you for *knowing* that. I'm proud of you, I really am."

Trevor dropped his eyes in modest pleasure. Herb wondered what the story was with Hill and Trevor. He didn't care what larks were called. He decided he would have to switch to very pointed questions.

"You know," he said, "I'm really in the dark about . . . well, what you're *doing* here. What the 'programs' are, and what the 'product' is — all that. And what a guy like *me* could do, what *role* I'd play in . . . everything."

Herb hadn't planned on saying "role," but when he did, he was extremely glad he had. He definitely preferred to think he'd just be *playing* "criminal" on Wince 'n' Wails, walking through a *part*, like in a play. Greenfield Hill and Trevor Whatshisname were nice enough, but he just didn't see himself as one of them, their type. "Robert Cohn was once middleweight boxing champion of Princeton," went flashing through his mind. Those were the first words in *The Sun Also Rises*, he knew, a book by Ernest Hemingway.

Hill stood up, but not to answer Herb, to go for seconds. The food was on the sideboards. It consisted of what Herbie would have said were fish chunks and long onions in a thick white sauce that tasted slightly licorice-y, along with rice that had some kinds of nuts in it, and a salad that was only funny-looking lettuce leaves, no cukes or peppers or tomatoes. Herb gathered that this food was like what people ate in France; Hill and Trevor had French names for all of it. He'd seen a movie that was all in French, one time, and the girl in it was shown completely naked in one scene. Going by the way she looked, Herb guessed French food was good for people.

"Basically," said Hill, returning to his seat, "the thing we want for you to do is be yourself, over-qualified as you might be for that . . . responsibility. As for our little operation here. . . ." He took a bite of food, and chewed, and swallowed.

"What we're *up to* is what certain nasty tongues would probably describe as *smuggling*," Hill said, and sighed. "We don't, because it ain't — exactly. We see the work we're doing as a *service*. To our *products*, on the one hand, and our *country*, on the other."

Greenfield Hill then wiped both corners of his mouth. "Show Herbie how we manage, Trev, all right?" he said. "I can barely wait to see that look of utter aghastonishment, as it, like, spreads across his pure but honest countenance."

"Check," said Trevor, springing to his feet. "Just let me bring the world to him." And he strode into the living room and grabbed the big round globe from off the walnut desk. He put it on the table in between his place and Herb's.

"Everything begins down here," he said, "in Acapulco, *May-he-co*." He got his finger on the spot, on the Pacific coast of Mexico.

"We take our raw material from there and set off 'round the world on Route One Hundred," Trevor said, and he started to run his finger south, straight down the globe, down to Antarctica and (after picking up the globe and turning it) then up the other side.

"A.k.a. the one hundredth meridian of longitude," confided Greenfield Hill. "We just like to *call* it Route One Hundred." And he gave a cozy little chuckle.

"We *pause* in Bangkok, Thailand, here, a while," said Trev, "and then resume our journey up, right through Siberia, above the Northern Pole, and down the other side to end up here on Wince 'n' Wails, still smackeroo on Route One Hundred." His finger'd settled on a tiny island, well above the Arctic Circle.

"Where we unload," said Greenfield Hill, "and *process* for a while. In time, our products end up in the States, of course."

"The land of opportunity," and Trevor smiled, "for us."

"I *see*," said Herb, and so he did, but all too well, alas. What he saw was plain disaster, thanks to Alexander Rex and Sesame deBarque, drug lord and lady.

Beyond a doubt, he thought, the product was cocaine, the lady that became a tiger, Doctor White. Like everyone his age, Herb had an attitude concerning drugs, already. It was the same one that he'd had toward bullies, back in grade school: He both feared and hated them. Like bullies, drugs might kill him, he believed, even if they didn't mean to.

That's not to say Herb wasn't *curious*; indeed he was. He wondered how drugs made you feel — exactly how, the different ones. He knew the words and phrases for the feelings. People talked of them, sometimes, compared to how sex felt, or how they made sex feel. Herb had had some limited experience with sex, with what you might call "starter sex." He loved the way *that* felt. But the thing with sex was this: it was built in to everyone, and harmless, even maybe good for you, and with you all the time. You had to have, were *meant* to have, sex feelings. Drugs, however, were made up of chemicals you had to *get* and *take*, knowing they could hurt your precious body, and your mind. It seemed to Herb that people who took drugs were trusting, like, to *luck* — hoping they would not be hurt too bad. He absolutely wasn't going to do that; he would just stay curious. It wasn't fair to T.K., to ask her to protect him from himself. So it was quite unthinkable that he'd be part of getting drugs to other people, helping them to do what he believed they shouldn't. What he wouldn't do himself.

Even if he had a minor, temporary "role," that wasn't any good. There was a principle involved. The boy stood up. It was right to stand on principle. Then, if you had to run for it, you wouldn't have to take the time to get up, first.

"I'm sorry," Herbie said. "But I won't have anything to do with drugs."

He knew exactly where the door was, and that Hill's parka hung there on a rack beside it. Getting to the van might be a problem, and starting it and driving it.

"Drugs?" said Greenfield Hill, brows drawn together.

"Drugs?" said Trevor Rhinelander the 4th, eyebrows up, as in amazement.

"Yes," said Herbie Hertzman. "Drugs. Cocaine. That's the 'product,' isn't it? The 'raw material'?"

The other two cracked up. They looked at one another and they both said *"Drugs?"* again, but in entirely different tones. And then they started to guffaw. They laughed and laughed and pounded on the tabletop, and laughed some more, and said the magic word again, which made them laugh, if anything, much harder.

And when they'd finally finished laughing and had wiped their eyes and hiccuped, Greenfield Hill looked up at Herb and spoke.

"No, dear heart," he said, "the 'product' isn't drugs, far from it. Although we've *had* a dope or two come through, from time to time." He looked at Trev, and for a moment there, Herbie was afraid they might crack up again. But this time they controlled themselves, and Greenfield Hill continued.

"Our standards are at least as high as yours, concerning drugs," he said to Herb, "and possibly a good deal higher. Drugs are not our 'product.' But to give you an example of what is. . . ."

Hill started smiling once again, and then he pointed at the person sitting next to him, at Trevor Rhinelander the 4th.

"Well," said Greenfield Hill, "*he* is."

12
THE ERSTWHILE
JOSÉ BLOW

"What?" said Herb. He sat back down — collapsed, more like it.

"Mm-hmm," said Greenfield Hill. "Four years ago, our Trevor was some little José Blow, or might as well have been. A barefoot, brown-eyed *bumpkinito*, feeding chickens near Chihuahua. *But*" — he held a finger up — "he was our type: *intelligente*, ambishoso, not afraid of work. And thus, darn close to four years later, he's a man transformed, a product of the *most* intensive education ever offered anywhere, to anyone, at anytime. He is, as far as any eye can see, a perfect . . . need I say it? Rhymes with common word for baby dog? And next spring he'll have kennel space at Shearson Lehman Hutton."

He beamed at Trevor who beamed back at him and nodded, modestly.

"Each and every spring thereafter," Hill continued, "a quarter of his gross shall fly on home to roost with us. In a year or two that won't be chicken feed, my friend, but he will go on paying, gladly, for good reason. Paying his tuition in installments, you could say, and buying some insurance, and delighted to be doing so. Am I correct, young Trev?"

"*Por supuesto*," said the erstwhile José Blow, now grinning broadly at his mentor. Herb knew that meant "of course," of course.

13
STUDENT TEACHING

Two days later (time-compressed) Herb was standing in his "classroom," waiting for his "students" to arrive. He was extremely nervous, naturally enough, although the room that he was in was nothing like the ones that he'd inhabited before, in "school." There was a sofa and a love seat and a wooden bench; there were some poofy cushions on the floor and three upholstered chairs; there were assorted tables, end and side and coffee, one of them with leather on it, one with a brass tray on top. An oval mirror and three paintings graced the walls: one super-realistic still life of a hot dog and an orange drink, so detailed you could see the wiener and the tulip glass both sweat — also a beachscape showing bathers, in Brazil, perhaps, going by their brief and cheeky outfits, and another that was just a vase of quite familiar yellow flowers.

"This classroom looks more like a classy living room," Herb said out loud, just making sure his nerves had not deprived him of his voice.

He walked across the room and looked at his reflection in the oval mirror.

"The teacher of this class resembles some dumb ditzy dweeb," he told himself. "I *hate* him."

He went and peered out one of the wide windows, which was triple-glazed, at least.

"Nine A.M. up here could pass for nine at night," he said.

Herb sat down on the bench and ran his palms along his thighs again. He told himself it was *all right* that he was nervous in this role: The Teacher. He decided he felt more like an impala. All your life you've feared and hated lions, and all at once you're meant to *be* a lion. You go and get a drink and look down at the water hole, at your reflection. What you see is an impala.

Could he possibly be popular (he asked himself), convince his students he was "one of them"? The trouble was, he wasn't one of them, not even close. They were going to be a bunch of Mexicans, ten people from another culture altogether who, he understood, would range in age from under seventeen to twenty-seven.

And probably the ones his age would all have mustaches.

Greenfield Hill had told him that there wouldn't be a language gap. Like all the other students there on Wince 'n' Wails, these (he said) would speak American, "and maybe even *English*." And *without* an accent you could put your finger on.

"Incredibly enough, they all *arrive* in that condition, thanks to our dear founder's great discovery," he said. "And their four months in Bangkok, speaking only Thai — or, as I prefer to call it, Siamese."

"What?" said Herb. "You teach them Siamese *before* you teach them English?"

"Yes, exactly," Hill explained. "You see, the Siamese sets off a 'gross linguistical reaction' (as the founder said). When you put Siamese on top of Spanish, you completely 'cleanse the palate' (as that dear man would also say). The learner's slate is left as clean, phonetically, as any newborn babe's. Of course there *is* one *caveat*: too much Siamese and they get stuck in sing-song city. Four months of it is pretty nearly perfect. And at that point we can start to sock the English to 'em."

"Wait," said Herb. "Just so I'm sure I understand. . . . You're telling me that Siamese and Spanish are such different languages they more or less, like, *cancel one another out*?"

"Precisely," Hill agreed. "It reminds one of the process where you add some *chlorine*, which of course is poisonous, to *sewerage*, another poison. And you end up with a harmless glass of water."

"Yes," said Herb, "but doesn't — "

"The water may not taste that great," said Hill, "because it isn't truly natural. The same with these folks' English, in a way. It's kind of . . . *blah*, sometimes. Perhaps a little *yucky*, even. That's something you'll be working on."

"You mean," said Herb, still trying to get this straight, "that once they reach this state of 'speaking-readiness' that you've described, they *then* can pick up *English* on the trip between, like, Bangkok and the island, here?"

"Absolootle," Greenfield Hill replied. "We've found a journey through Siberia is just a *fabulous* accelerant to learning."

"How so?" asked Herb, the innocent impala.

"Well, just imagine," Hill confided. "Suppose that *you* were one of them, and someone said to you — your *teacher* said to you: 'Now, look here, kids. Everybody who *correctly* reads, out loud, the first ten paragraphs of the article "Why You Can't Laugh At Cher Anymore" in the Feb 88 issue of *Premiere* magazine (we use a lot of cultural material) will *certainly* be on a dogsled when we start from this location on Steppe One, tomorrow afternoon. The rest, the ones who make *mistakes*, will just stay here and do the best they can without, like, tents or food.' I mean, would *you* get words like 'Meryl Streep' — and even 'Chastity Bono' — down pat, or what?"

"I see," said Herbie, nodding thoughtfully. "Whoever wants a plate of musk ox stew say 'triskaidekaphobia.' Pronouncing it correctly, please." That was, of course, a very lucky word, for him.

"Say *what*?" said Greenfield Hill.

"Triskaidekaphobia," said Herb. "Fear of the number thirteen." He decided not to mention T.K.

"Oooh," cried Hill. "I *love* it! That's *fantastic*, Herb!" For a moment, there, the boy felt positively Mexican.

Herb's class came tromping in the room at 9:08 A.M., exactly. They were accompanied by Trev, who said he'd come along to "do the honors," introduce the group to its new teacher.

Herb was amazed. They didn't look like cartoon Mexicans at all, any more than Trevor did. None of them had on sombreros or huaraches, none of them flopped down against a wall and promptly fell asleep. Four of them wore sunglasses, but two of those had shoved them up onto the tops of their heads, and all of them had colorful elastic neck straps on the things. They all were dressed informally, but with a certain flair, the kind that spoke of uniformly carefree affluence. In other words, they looked as if they'd *shopped* in a Banana Republic, but not as if they'd *lived* in one.

One girl, in addition to her stylish, narrow cotton canvas pants and leather ranch boots, had on a dark green Dartmouth (in white letters) sweatshirt. Herb rocked back on his heels. Unless he missed his guess — was very much mistaken — *that* girl's name was — *might have been* — well, Tyree Toledano.

Trevor Rhinelander the 4th was doing the honors by then. He explained that Herbie Hertzman, seventeen, was now a high school senior, and that he'd spent his entire life being "a typical American kid." At that, a murmur of respectful awe swept through the room. One slightly older male was already evolved enough to say "fantastic." The fellow had on broken-in blue jeans by St. Laurent, a bright red Loft Wool sweater (L. L. Bean), and a bright blue baseball cap from Eddie Bauer. There was something funny written on the front of it; it said, *Mikey likes it*.

Herbie Hertzman, Trevor said, was going to tell them all about himself: his family, his school, his bedtimes, his taste in food and drink and television shows, the games and sports he'd played while growing up, the things boys did with other U.S. boys (and then with U.S. girls), the contents of his room, his pockets, his desk drawers, his bathroom cabinet, his *dreams*.

"He's going to give you folks the works," said Trev. "From soup to nuts, from ticktacktoe to tofu. Is that the pure unvarnished, double-H?" he turned and said to Herb.

Herb nodded. He noticed Trevor's easygoing, totally informal, casually idiomatic way of speaking had set off still more sounds of adulation. Clearly, all the members of this younger class could look at Trev and see the sort of person that they planned to also be. And, too, potentially as someone who, at some still unknown point in future time, they might just do a deal with. Trev was now, and always would be, an "*hermano*" — part of what they knew to be a network of "designer Mexicans" (as Hill referred to them behind their backs, from time to time) scattered all across the states, dug into power slots of one sort or another.

"You'd be surprised, I'll bet — I'm talking *real* surprised," Greenfield Hill had said to Herbie, day before, "at the number of . . . let's just say 'prominent Americans' who are, in fact, our products. Who are 'drybacks,' as I sometimes call them." Chuckling.

"What?" said Herb. "You mean that there are people that I've *heard of*, people who . . . well, people like my father just assume are real Americans, who aren't?"

66

"Ooh, yes indeedy," said Hill, with a mischievous expression on his smooth, pink face. That day he had a yacht club necktie on, and he was looking droll as any davit, sharper than a marlinspike.

"Of the thirteen major presidential hopefuls, back in early '88," he said, "seven Democrats and six Republicans in all, no less than four were once on Wince 'n' Wails. Of the CEOs of the Fortune 500 companies, some forty-six, just under ten percent, are ours. Real estate developers? We've got a dozen of the biggest in the country! Major auto dealers? More than you can shake an old transmission at. A third of the network news anchors. Nobelists: just one, and that was just a fluke; there isn't that much dough in prizes. Two of our people *did* win the Publishers Clearing House biggie, but that's because that fellow — what's his name? he's always on TV — he's one of us."

"Good grief," said Herbie. "And I suppose you're going to tell me half the guys who make a million bucks or more a year from playing baseball are *also* products of this program."

"Oh, heavens, *no*," said Hill. "*Baseball* is a game of *skill*. You have to *play* it, pitch the ball, or hit it. Baseball calls for some specific *talents*. Fernando is a Mexican, of course — Fernando Valenzuela, *you* know — but, hell, the guy was great. He *earned* the money that he made. That's like a different ball game altogether. *Terribly* old-fashioned." And he laughed.

"I see," said Herbie, thinking what Hill said made lots of sense. There was skill and talent, on the one hand. You either had them, or you worked real hard to get them. You *needed* them for certain kinds of jobs. Or you had to know a lot to do those jobs.

But, it seemed, there also were a bunch of other jobs, which almost anyone could do, and even be successful at, provided that they had a lot of nerve, looked good and had connections, and were lucky.

Herb thought about the fields a person could be real successful in and also be a . . . well, *dumb jerk*. Politics, it seemed, was surely one. And all those businesses in which a person's job was pretty much to "put together deals," and make (Herb had to gulp) a lot of money.

But was that necessarily so bad, he asked himself? Take what was going on at Wince 'n' Wails. Was this so terrible, the act of helping Mexicans to be productive citizens? Rich instead of poor? After all, the boundary separating us and them is artificial, arbitrary, really. It could be anywhere, or nowhere. People cross it all the time, and most of them end up in sweatshops, or the lettuce fields. Isn't this a far, far better thing?

When looked at in a certain light, Greenfield Hill was nothing more or less than a *developer*. Of course, this scheme of his had an Orwellian dimension in that he, Big Brother, made these people all the same. But he also, at the same time, was creating jobs and giving talent and hard work a chance to show what they could do.

Of course (and to be sure) Hill also took a heaping handful of the fruits that they had labored for. In that respect, the deal on Wince 'n' Wails was borderline *Fal*wellian, Herb thought.

"Your class was *fabulous*," said Tyree Toledano. Except that during introductions at the start of it, she'd said her name, her U.S. name, was Hepzibah

Medallion, and for "nickname" on her college application she'd put "Zippy."

She'd lingered after class, after all the rest of them had gone.

"I thought that that was really interesting," she said, "the stuff you said about how guys your age, *our* age, all want to . . . 'make a touchdown,' is it? With their girlfriends?"

"That's 'score,' " said Herbie, trying not to blush. "The word I used was 'score.' Making a touchdown just applies to football — that's our kind of football — and to space landings, I guess. 'Score,' or 'making points,' can either be, like, in a game or with a girl."

"That's cool," said Zippy, and she wrinkled up her nose and grinned at him.

Herbie'd never seen a girl at such close range to match her. Zippy Medallion. He decided that she had a "pixie-panther" sort of face, and beautiful. She had a thick and shiny mop of jet-black hair, parted in the middle, dropping down in waves until it hit her shoulders; and then there were those fancy-flashing coal-brown onyx eyes. Her lips made Herbie think of cherry bombs; her teeth were straight and white as ice cream wagons. She also had the smoothest golden tan, the best complexion, that our boy had ever seen. And when she'd slouched back on a poofy cushion lying on the floor, and her Dartmouth deep green sweatshirt had, like, ridden up a ways and bared five inches of her belly, Herbie also saw that it was equally as golden-smooth and tan.

"But what I *still* don't get," she said, "is whether girls like me would want to 'score' ourselves — or even, like, 'get scored on.' Or is it that a person who is 'scored on' is a 'loser'?"

"It's kind of complicated," Herbie said, and that was true. The more so in that he really didn't know the answers to her questions. What *would* a girl like Zippy *really* want? From boys, in general. From him, specifically, Rob Lowe, or football captains, anywhere. All he really knew was what guys *said*, what he had heard. But he surely knew the answer to another question, one she hadn't asked, and it was, "Yes, guys lie."

"In my own case," Herbie said, improvising as he went along, but also trying very hard to tell the truth, "I'm the kind of guy who . . . well, let me put it this way: if *I* scored on a girl, I'd never *call* it that, or tell another guy I had, 'cause if I did — I mean, like *when* I do, of course — I'd have done it, *did* it, with a person that I really liked a *lot*, which means I'd think about her in a different way than if I'd just set out to try and *score* on someone — anyone." He was almost out of breath when he had finished saying that.

"But when I get to *Dartmouth* . . ." Zippy said, softly but with great concern, "you know I'm going to *Dartmouth*, right? When I get *there*, I'm just afraid I won't know how to tell the guys like you from all the other ones."

"Well, up there at *Dartmouth*, the first thing that you've got to do," said Herb with great conviction, "is probably not believe a word of what they tell you. The guys up there will all be really smart — like thirteen hundred on the SATs and up. And a lot of them are big fans of . . . well, of guys like Oliver North and Elliott Abrams, if you've ever heard of them. That means they'll *say* — they'll tell you — that they'd never do it with a girl unless they really liked her. And they'll *say* they care about a woman's reputation and her feelings. Unlike all the *other* guys, they'll say, in 'this fraternity' — or club, or class, or dorm, whatever. But the chances are that they'll be what they call 'misstating,' half the time."

"Mmm," said Zippy, thoughtfully. "But let's suppose I meet a guy I *want* to score on . . ." And she looked at Herb and took a step, and then a glide, in his direction, smiling with her coal-brown eyes. ". . . someone tall, and with beautiful blue eyes, I bet."

She was standing right in front of him, by then.

"In fact," she said, "let's say that this is *not* a Dartmouth College situation, even. . . ."

And with that she took her sweatshirt by its bottom hem and pulled it up and over her head and arms, and tossed it on the floor.

Then, smiling up at Herb, she shook her mop of wavy hair, to settle it. When she did that, other parts of her shook slightly, too.

"Great goddess," Herbie said, and meant it from the bottom of his heart as he, responding quite reflexively, and following the program in his genes (and jeans), reached out for her. He hadn't for a moment thought — expected — this would happen, especially on this remote and frozen wasteland. He'd come to check out Crime — Organized or not, as a career. Now this other option had . . . arisen. And it seemed like something he would like to *do*.

"OH, NO! OH, NO! OH, NO! OH, NO!" said Greenfield Hill, as he came striding into the room.

He sounded and he looked extremely cross. He scooped up Zippy's sweatshirt, when he got to it, and handed it to her.

"You put this on at once," he scolded. "You're meant to be in C-15, and doing Nautilus this hour. Though on the *face* of things" — he smirked, clean-shavenly — "you have *some* muscle groups that don't need much along the lines of . . . more development." He shook his head, perhaps in awe and admiration, Herbie thought.

"But you have a lot of things to learn, young woman," he went on, "about . . . oh, making *proper* use of assets, just for instance. Luckily you've got some time to learn them in, before you get to college."

Zippy'd slipped her sweatshirt on while he was saying that, and with a guilty look, a half-apologetic smile for Herb, she sidled out the door.

"In your case, though," Hill said to Herb, when she was gone, and in a fury, Herb could tell, "there isn't *any* time left on the clock. You are through, *kaput*, and *finis*, boy; you're history. So get off my geography, before I totally forget myself."

"But," said Herb, "I didn't know . . . I didn't do, like, anything except . . . you see, she was — "

But then he broke it off, bit down on all the self-absolving sentences that jumped into his mind. He *wasn't* going to put the blame on her, and say that she'd come on to him. Even though he didn't know her — never would, it looked like, now — he wouldn't do that to her, make her out to be what other guys referred to as "some pig" or "that old slut." What he'd felt she was was, basically, a simple country girl, direct and truthful, warm and friendly.

Probably intelligent. Discriminating. Sensitive.

Hill was pacing all around the room by then, extremely agitated still, still shaking his blond, perfect haircut back and forth, and wringing his clean hands.

"We simply can't permit a member of the staff to be not only *stupid*, but a bad example, also," he was saying. "Even temporary staff. Overt behavior, like yours, can cancel out a month of drill, of classroom work, of memorizing theory. It's just *disgusting*. All the rest of us are trying to act a certain way, preach one solid set of standards, *practice* what we preach — and then I run spang into this . . . this *outrage*." Hill stopped and glared at Herb.

"Isn't it a *fact*," he asked him, "that if this whole curriculum were summed up in a single word, that word would be *Deceive*?"

Herb nodded, not exactly getting it, but keeping silent, anyway. He *had* seen, sure enough, that all the Mexicans were being taught deception, everywhere. Even on the tennis courts, inside the gray inflated bubble, they learned to say 'Just out,' and shake their heads, as if they were sincerely sorry. When opponents' shots were on the line, of course.

"We're not a bunch of straightlaced puritans up here," insisted Hill. "You won't hear me or any of my full-time staff suggest there's anything that's wrong with *screwing* people. In fact, day-in, day-out, techniques for doing just exactly that are what we teach. But if you do it right out in the open, where anybody in the whole wide world might come along and see exactly what you're doing . . . why, then you're screwing *up*! You've got to *sneak*, *pretend*, *be devious*, *lock doors*, *look innocent*, goddamn it! We

want our people to succeed in life, you stupid little
. . . *Hertzman*, you!"

With that, he started to make shooing motions,
flicking out the shiny, pink-nailed, *clean*-nailed fingers of both hands.

"Go on. Go on with you," he said. "You just get
out of here. I'll be in touch with Ses deBarque on
this. I'm *very* disappointed. You can leave the clothes
you borrowed in your room, and Trev will take you
to your . . . *van*." His voice was drippy with disgust.

"And don't forget your tomahawk," he yelled at
Herb's retreating back.

14
TEMPTATION

Herb's return trip — *dep* Wince 'n' Wails some time or other, *arr* Castles in the Air whenever — was every bit as quick and quiet as the one that got him to the Arctic to begin with. It maybe even seemed a little quicker, given how time tends to drag when you are going somewhere new, and feeling nervous, having peanut butterflies.

Sesame de Barque was in the tower, still, to greet him. That wasn't too surprising. If a week was time-compressed into a space of fifty-seven seconds, he had run through an entire criminal career in something under twenty-five, he thought.

"Well, here I am again," said Herb, managing a laugh, "ha-ha," as the van's door slid open. Ses had used the time that she had had alone to take one knee pad off, and as Herbie's Reeboks hit the floor, her other one did, too.

"That sure was *interesting*," he said. He knew that he was feeling awkward, having trouble picking out a tone to take. He really hadn't had sufficient time to cop a final attitude toward Crime — Organized or not.

His first reaction to the "work" of Greenfield Hill and Co. was homonymic (he believed), combining as it did both *awe*: amazement at the scope and ingenuity embodied in the scheme, and *"Aw"* ("they aren't doing anybody any harm"). No question that the field *did* seem to offer opportunities for someone like himself (without experience, or skills, or any special training) to both make a lot of money and succeed in one of the . . . professions: teaching.

Yes, he thought, he'd done a pretty darn good job of teaching that one class. They'd taken notes; he'd gotten laughs. No one had gone to sleep, or thrown wet garbage at a fellow student, or said out loud that "this class sucks." Maybe doing what he'd done was *technically* a crime — conspiracy or something — but still he had to think he'd scored real well, *professionally*.

However, on the other hand, he'd found it hard, apparently, to meet a certain set of standards, as defined, or anyway implied, by Greenfield Hill. The way he'd dealt with Zippy had been . . . unacceptable. He hadn't lied to her, or tried to sneak a furtive fondle well before she had invited one; he hadn't (just for instance) made a date to meet her underneath the stage at midnight, which would have been a major violation of the rules. And when he'd had the chance to put the blame on her for what had happened (and so save his own sequoia), he had held his tongue.

76

What that little . . . episode with Zippy caused was, like, a switch. Before, he'd been a young man trying out a job in Crime — Organized or not, a teaching job, as it turned out. After, though — and on the basis of that one so-called mistake — he was a has-been: judged, convicted and expelled. *His* crime had been *not* being sleazy, being chivalrous, in fact.

So, how (he wondered) was he meant to feel about this "failure"?

Meanwhile, Ses deBarque was looking at him. Analytically, he thought. Or, possibly, askance.

Was it possible, he had to ask himself, that she, somehow, knew everything about his trip, already? Knew all the details of that final incident? Knew who'd said what, *done* what, to (with/for) whom, to what effect? Blush City, if she did. He decided that he'd better tell her most of it himself, and right away. Sort of get his version on the books.

"I guess I'm not too, too surprised," she said, when he had finished. "As types, you and Mr. Greenfield Hill are not exactly rolls and butter." And she laughed.

Herb rubbed his nose and smiled at that one. "Well, I thought he seemed to have a real nice personality," he said. "But he didn't seem too tolerant of different life-styles. Different from his own, I mean."

"Well, *that's* a fact," said Ses. "He didn't used to be that way, but every year it seems as if he's gotten worse. More greedy. *And* unprincipled. As poor old Mason Furbish, Junior, probably found out."

"Mason Furbish, Junior?" Herbie asked.

"Yes," she said, "poor, rotund little dude. He

could make the finest garlic salad dressing in the world, I think. His father was the phoni-linguistical genius who discovered how the sounds of Siamese react with those of Spanish. That's the honest truth. You'll hear some people say it was a total accident that happened due to overcrowding in a Bangkok jail, one time, but I know otherwise. And then what happened was that Mason, Senior, realized that his discovery was meaningless, unless there was a use for it. So it was he who came up with the scam — who made the very first designer Mexicans up there on Prince of Wales. He ran the operation there for years and years."

"Huh," said Herb. "And Mason, Junior . . . ?"

"As you'd suppose, inherited," she said. "And ran it quite successfully, himself. Right up until the iceberg race, that is."

"The *iceberg* race?" asked Herb. "You don't mean *iceberg* race."

"Yup," she said, "sure do. It's something that the Eskimos and Inuits and them have done up there for centuries, in summer, when the ice breaks up. Two guys each choose an iceberg, big huge ones with peaks and ridges, you know what I mean. Each guy has a paddle and a push-pole, and a lot of freeze-dried food or blubber, I suppose. It's hard to get the 'bergs to go real fast, and they don't turn too easily, but once you're under way, those babies sometimes give you quite a ride. The idea of the race is just to see how far you get before you run aground, or melt, or winter comes."

"Mmm," said Herb. "That doesn't sound particularly exciting."

"Ordinarily it's not," she said. "But this one had

its moment, in a way. You see, the 'berg that Mason, Junior, got had other passengers aboard. A family of polar bears. How they got there is uncertain, but some think that Greenfield might have chummed them onto it the day before, using lemon sole and brook trout amandine, if I know him."

"Wo!" said Herbie, pretty shocked already.

"Right," said Ses, "and, well, the race got started on a Thursday night, I think it was — remember, it's as bright as day at night up there, in summertime — and either then or early Friday morning Mason, Junior, left the firm, real suddenly. I doubt he ever knew what hit him." She shook her head and smiled a crooked smile.

"He probably went bustling around a crag, or scarp, or cube of ice," she said, "going 'round to paddle on the other side, and bingo! Down the hatch he went. I'm sure those bears just loved the guy, poor little tenderloin." She changed her voice to speak the way she thought a bear would sound. " 'Fine full-bodied fellow, that — robust, and with a pleasant garlic aftertaste.' " She laughed, but bitterly. "The rule of fang and claw, I guess you call it."

"And Greenfield Hill took over," Herbie finished for her. He was remembering how Hill had said the founder's heir, who was the president by then, had gotten into "something else" — how on one specific day it just was "poof!" and he was gone.

"Brrr." Herb made the shiver sound. Gotten into "something else" indeed — the belly of a bear! "I'm just as glad I didn't . . . well, *work out*, up there."

By that time they were strolling down the corridor that led back to the castle proper.

"What's your pleasure now?" she asked. "Care to take another spin? It's early, yet."

"No, I don't believe I will," said Herb. "I'd sort of like to head on home and just space out a while before my Uncle Babbo gets there. He's got some thoughts about my future that my mom thinks might be pretty tempting. You just never know."

"That's true," she said, and bobbed her broad-brimmed hat, emphatically.

"Uh," Herb found his feet had sort of stopped, right there in the corridor. "Could I, like, ask you something? It's on account of what you just now told me."

"Sure," said Sesame deBarque. She stopped, too, and faced him, friendly-looking as the dickens. "Anything. At any time."

"Well," he watched his right-foot Reebok step right on the other's toe, for no good reason, "how come you'd even *send* a person — such as me — up to a place like Wince 'n' Wails? To work for someone who's a murderer."

"Because it's there?" she said, and then, "Of course that's not the answer; it isn't only there, it's everywhere. I guess the first part of the answer is: It wasn't my idea. That category's there 'cause people want it, though sometimes they'd rather call it by another name. 'Marketplacing,' or 'Intelligent Manipulation of the Status Quo.' The road to hell is paved with small deceptions, Herb. And Green-field Hill? A lot of folks would say . . . he's only human, after all. Ambitious. And he *does* fill needs. Everybody makes mistakes. Possibly the bear-thing was a little joke gone tragically awry." She didn't look at him when she was saying that, the last part. "Or just damn bad luck."

"I guess I didn't have to go," said Herb.

She didn't answer him. Instead, she put a hand out, held him by the arm a moment.

"All I hope is that you *do* come back, and try again," she said. "And that you don't regret the process."

They started walking down the corridor again. He thought that over, nodded to himself. Every nowhere that you got to was, in one sense, somewhere that you hadn't been before, somewhere that you maybe learned you didn't want to go to again. Getting lost is also finding out that's not the way to go. Maybe he'd get into fortune cookies.

"I guess I might be back," he said.

And she said, "Okey-doke. Like, anytime." And going on her tiptoes, she then kissed him. Herb felt approved of, close to her, and wondered why.

15
UNCLE BABBO

"Let's take a little drive," his uncle, Babbo Orgalescu, said to Herb when they had finished dinner, Chicken (have you guessed?) Paprika. "I got something that I want to show you. *Plus*" — he winked at Herb — "you'll get to park your buns on supersoft Moroccan leather getting there, and go riding in a mighty mean machine."

Herb had seen the car from his bedroom window, when Babbo'd pulled it into the little driveway, right beside his house. He wasn't sure exactly what it was, what kind of car, that is. But you couldn't miss its reason for existence. On both sides of its long, white hood there were three words, in black block letters, big ones: YOUR MANE MAN. On the backside, right across the trunk, was: HONK IF YOU LOVE HAIRSPRAY.

Herb didn't have to call a friend to learn that *Your*

Mane Man™ was one of the (if not *the*) most popular complete home hairstyling systems in America. During dinner, though, he'd learned that Uncle Babbo, nowadays, was way, way up there in the company. As Regional Administrator (Sales), he was one of four; he reported *only* to the Sales Director, who was just a door away from Mr. Big, himself, the CEO.

Babbo Orgalescu had a gorgeous head of hair: thick and glossily inviting, wildly and excitingly adventurous, but at the same time never out of his control. When he first started out at *YMM* selling store to store, he used to ask the beauty products buyer to go wild, to do a total number on his hair, dishevel it in every way she could.

"Make me look the way I would if I'da spent ten hours in the sack," he'd say, and then he'd wink and add, "with, like, a real close friend." The buyer often was a prospect in more ways than one.

Well, nine times out of ten she'd take the challenge, and she'd do a muss-job on his head that made him look as if they'd left him staked out in the barnyard, back in Kansas, at tornado time. But all that Babbo'd do, when she was done, was smile and raise one pointer-finger and one eyebrow, and then give his head the slightest little . . . toss. Like that, just . . . *toss*. And — *schvipp!* — a hundred thousand hairs or so would first leap up, and then dive back into their rightful places in such perfect order that you'd swear they'd got the word from someone like the Chinese People's Army's calisthenics leader.

Babbo's hair was beautiful, but also *trained* — make no mistake about it.

* * *

"There's only two things in the world that hold my interest, nowadays," Babbo said to Herb, as they pulled out of the little driveway. "Other than the way I look, of course." He laughed and turned his head to look at Herb, made sure that he was laughing, too.

"Chicks," he said, "and buckarooties. Do you follow me?"

Herb believed he did. "Buckarooties," he was pretty sure, meant "money." So he said, "Sure," and nodded. In a way, this sounded promising.

"*Right*," said Babbo. "So. Now let me ask you this. Are you the same as me, in this regard? Or, wait — instead, let's put it this way — I'll make the question slightly broader by rephrasing it." He laughed again. "Are broads and bread, like, two of *your main interests*, too?" This time, he turned and winked at Herb.

"You see," he said, "I know a smart young guy, such as yourself, is apt to have a lot of interests, still. That's only natural. *My* world, however, it has shrunk a little, interest-wise — which happens, as a man gets older. Like, take, for instance, cars. I used to be fanatical about my cars. *Fanatical*. Tell you the truth, I used to *love* the cars I had. But nowadays, although I still insist, as you can see, on having decent-looking wheels that handle good et cetera, et cetera, cars are not like something that I put a lot of time and effort into, anymore. In other words, *they didn't hold my interest* in the way that chicks and dough have done. You follow me? So, tell me, Herbie, anyway. *Are* chicks and bread, like, two of *your* main interests, too?"

"Well, I guess they *are*," said Herb. He thought

that sounded cool and "with it," two qualities that he was pretty sure his uncle would be looking for, would want to find, in him. He also thought he spoke the truth. He guessed that "chicks" and "bread" *were* two of his main interests. Weren't they the same as "love" and "money"?

"Okay," said Babbo, sounding pleased. They were heading out of town, already on the outskirts, whizzing past the car lots and the fast-food places and the outlet stores, past the drop-in plastic surgeons' clinics, like *McSvelte*. Herb wondered where they might be going to. Straight ahead were, mostly, just the hills.

"Okay," his Uncle Babbo said again. His voice got serious and thoughtful, his tone the one Herb's teachers were disposed to use when they were setting out to show the class some stuff they thought was difficult to follow. And important. Reflexively, Herb straightened up and seemed to pay attention.

"Suppose I told you," Babbo said, "I know a way for you to get — I mean *have access to* — a huge supply, a *mothuh* lode" — he snickered — "of the both of them?" He sat back in the driver's seat and seemed to push against the steering wheel. He looked as if he might be holding something in; he also looked as if he might be pushing something out.

"Well, I guess I'd say 'That sure is interesting,' " said Herb. He rolled his window down and paused. He thought that maybe sounded *too* cool, almost flat. He tried to flesh it out a little, warm it up. "I suppose I'd say 'What is it?' "

That wasn't much of an improvement, Herbie thought. Why *was* he being so laid back? Wasn't this, perhaps, the knock of opportunity? Wasn't it a fact that "*who* you know" was *everything*, when you were looking for a job, something to do? Why *couldn't* Uncle Babbo be the genie from the lamp? He *could* be. Shouldn't he start drooling?

"Hubba-hubba," Herbie added.

The car was climbing now, gaining elevation in the hills outside of town. Uncle Babbo started shooting glances to his left, as they kept climbing. It also seemed to Herb that they were slowing down.

"The *way*," said Uncle B, "involves a job that's more than just a job. Because the way involves . . ." He swung the car sharp left, going all the way across the road and into this small Scenic Lookout on the other side.

". . . a *territory*," Babbo said. He shut the engine off and killed his headlights.

Below them was — what else? — the valley, miles and miles and miles of it, every bit as far as you could see. More or less straight down from where they were, there were the lights of town: streetlights, house lights, stoplights; these had a certain symmetry and order to them. Away from town the lights were much more random, widely spaced, most of them along the major highways, but also many others here and there, around the countryside. In the northern distance you could see the City Airport, lighted up, and the City, too, beyond it. The City sort of *glowed* out there, crouching in the distance, letting off its rays.

"You see that, Herbie?" Babbo said. "You *see* all that?" He lifted up his hand and moved it in an arc from left to right, horizon to horizon, and then back again, but lower down this time.

Herb followed Babbo's hand. He saw it, and the

view behind it. He'd seen both things a lot of times before.

"All of it, everything you see, is yours — or will be yours — if you say 'Yes' to me," said Uncle Babbo.

"What?" said Herb, instead — although he had a pretty good idea of what was going on. His mother had been right. Babbo's thoughts about his future were *extremely* tempting. *He* could have, like, all of that, for nothing?

"This area we're looking at is called a 'territory,' " Babbo said. "*You* can be the 'Mane Man' in that territory, Herb. You know how come I know that, Herb? I know *that*, and more, because I am in charge of much, much more than that. It's mine to offer, yours to take. All you have to do is just say 'Yes' to me." And Babbo struck the steering wheel a good one with his fist. "Yes! And yes! And *yes!*" he said.

Herbie said, "To what, exactly?" He could feel himself becoming nervous. That was quite a string of 'yeses' Babbo'd just reeled off.

"Why, to the work," his Uncle Babbo said. His tone of voice was one of mild surprise, as if to say: Who wouldn't know *that*? "To all *Your Mane Man*'s products: to our shampoos and our conditioners, and to our styling sprays and gels and holds and spritzers. To *Your Mane Man*'s dryers, scalp conditioners and brushes, combs (both hot and cold) and curlers. To what hair *means*, to all the *fun* it is. To waking up and thinking hair, the first thing in the morning. To treating your own hair with reverence, to working with it, letting it be all that it can be, to making sacrifices for it."

"Sacrifices for it?" Herbie said. A friend of his

named Luther Bates had tried out for the football team, and he'd told Herbie he was prepared to "make the necessary sacrifices." Herb hadn't really known what Luther meant — he didn't think that he was talking sandwiches and shakes — but he hadn't liked the sound of it. Hair, however . . . hair would be a less demanding god than football, wouldn't it? Or would it?

"Of course," his Uncle Babbo said. He turned his upper body all the way around, so he was facing Herb. He tucked a leg up on the leather seat.

"Any person who succeeds at this — I mean *succeeds*," said Babbo, "has to regard the care of hair as fundamental. Hair is, after all, a gift of nature and a part of one's creation. I'm asking you to make a deep commitment to the care of hair. Not nine to five, five days a week, and then forget about it, might as well be bald. Even when you aren't talking hair, or working with a product or a customer, you are still a witness, right? You understand what I've been telling you? This isn't something that you only *do*; I like to feel it's something that you *are*." He stopped and took a deep, deep breath.

"It isn't walking on the beach without a hat on," he explained. "It isn't walking on the beach *with* a hat on, either — supposing that the hat is any one of all the kinds that *stifle* hair, don't let it breathe, enjoy itself. It also isn't swimming in salt water at the beach, except when you can rinse with fresh, like, right away. It isn't letting someone *touch* your hair who's just been reading, say, the Sunday *New York Times*, or eating with nomadic desert tribes, or making model airplanes. It isn't staying in a room where there are onions cooking, or people smoking anything that's thicker than a pencil, or women named Delilah. It's letting it grow out, *your* hair grow out, to where it makes a statement, Herb. And it's putting one of these on, every night," and Babbo leered, "for . . . *business's* sake, you know?"

He'd reached into his pocket, found his wallet, reached inside of *it*, and tossed what he took out of it right onto Herbie's lap.

"You really shouldn't keep these in your wallet," he told Herb. "They say it isn't good for them at all. But what the hell."

Herb looked down at the little packet. Yes, it *was* a hairnet — black, one-size-fits-all.

"Get outa here," said Herb, agreeably, before he'd even had a chance to think about it.

"Hey?" said Babbo. He gave his head a little shake, then tilted it and struck himself above one ear with just the heel, like, of his open hand, as if he'd gotten water in that ear. "Wazzat?"

For just an instant there, Herbie thought that what he'd heard was *qué?* and that his Uncle Babbo was a dryback, not his mother's brother after all. But then he knew that wasn't right, that he had seen too many pictures that his mother had of them both growing up, first over in Romania and then right here. Even at the age of eight and twelve and seventeen, Babbo had had memorable hair.

"I just can't do it, Uncle Babbo," Herbie said. "Call it immaturity, stupidity, whatever. But I just can't do it."

Of course he didn't think that it was any of those things.

"But what about the *chicks*?" his uncle said. "The *bread*? The schools of eager lovelies, skinny-dipping in a huge, unchlorinated pool of dough?" He slouched back in his bucket seat. His head shook back and forth again, as he threw question after question, not at Herb, but up into the empty evening air.

"What kind of guy is this, I'm talking to?" he said. "What kind of relative of mine, with hot ambition throbbing in, *engorging*, all his veins? What kind of son of apple pie, and amber waves of grain?" He stopped and shook himself, then turned to Herb, again. "Wait, wait. We aren't blood-related, right? Is *that* it, huh — is *that* it? My sister found you on her doorstep, or maybe on an airport runway, in a ladies' room."

"Whatever," Herbie said. He didn't feel related, not to Babbo, not to *Your Mane Man*. He didn't want to talk about it, either.

Babbo started up the car. He looked like someone in a state of shock.

"It seems to me that I remember Lena being pregnant, though," he muttered, talking mostly to himself, it seemed. "Or was that Anna, or Maria? Look," he said to Herb, "suppose I leave it open for a while? I don't need a yes or no *today*."

"I just said 'no,' " said Herbie. And he leaned back in the seat and closed his eyes.

Monday, he'd try Castles in the Air again, he thought.

16
HOMETOWN, USA

Herb found his second trip to Castles in the Air was about half the hassle and twice the fun that his first one had been. Instead of *groping* around the northwest part of town, *hoping* to bump into a street called Sunset Strip, he was able to stride confidently along in the proper direction until he got to it. And, rather than encountering unpleasant creatures such as Private Buford "Buddy" Road along the way, and having to exchange sharp jabs with some pretty nasty pickets near his destination, he was whisked along the Strip and up the Castles driveway in a panel truck that stopped and offered him a ride.

The truck was driven by a friendly-looking, paint-bespattered man, and had *Pigments of Your Imagination* written on the sides of it. Inside, behind the seats, there were a lot of different cans of paint, and brushes, jars of turpentine and drop cloths.

"Seven-eleven?" said the man, as soon as Herb had clambered in the door and told him where on Sunset Strip he hoped to get to. "So it's Castles in the Air that you'll be visiting, I guess."

"Exactly right," said Herb. "And looking forward to it. Do you know the place, yourself? Or Ms. deBarque, by any chance?"

"Ses?" the painter said. "Hell, yes. I've done a lot of work for her. And I'm heading up to Castles now, to do some more — so you're in luck. She wants the lady-in-waiting's room done over in a beige, I think. Or, was that the ladies' room beside the wading pool, and she was in a rage when she called up?" He made a clucking sound and scratched his head.

"But maybe it's the waiting room for pages to the ladies in the car pool," he went on, and gave a small, self-deprecating chuckle. "Hell, I can't remember. Wants *something* painted, anyway. And I'm a painter, so I'll see to it. I'm pretty sure my name's John Jaspers, anyway. And what might your name be?"

"Well," said Herb, infected by the man's good humor, "it *might* be Peter Falconer, I guess. But if it was, the chances are I wouldn't be here, and I'd know exactly where I'm going, what I'm going to do and where the snows of yesteryear are now. In fact, I'm Herbie Hertzman."

"It's a pleasure," said John Jaspers, dealing out a hand for Herb to shake. "If you're a friend of Ses deBarque, I want you for a friend of mine. And if you haven't met her yet, you've got a treat in store for you."

Herb nodded and admitted that he knew and liked the lady very much, and so the atmosphere inside the truck was one of warmth and cordiality, as it pulled up to Castles in the Air. And there, outside, was Ses deBarque herself, wearing pale pink pedal pushers and a black Hawaiian shirt, while gamely pitching horseshoes on the lawn.

"Hey, John Jaspers, good to see you," she cried out, speaking to the truck, the way one's apt to do, before she'd even seen its occupants.

"You've come to do the baby's spool bed in the weight room, I assume," she added. "In that nice, light sage we talked about, correct?"

The painter climbed down from the truck and tapped his temple, wisely — as if to say he'd known that all along. Meanwhile, Ses deBarque caught sight of Herb.

"And look who else you brought along," she said. "Welcome back to Castles, Herb. I'll be with you in no time at all. Just watch my smoke, you'll see."

Herb nodded cheerfully and thought about the way that Don DeLillo's novel *End Zone* started. ("Taft Robinson was the first black student to be enrolled at Logos College in west Texas. They got him for his speed.") John Jaspers picked out all the painting gear that he would need from back inside his truck. And Sesame deBarque resumed her game.

She had two horseshoes left, a gold one and a silver, both gleaming brightly in the sunshine, and in spite of what she'd said, she didn't rush her throws. She first got set, then concentrated fiercely on her target, this black metal stake, no thicker than a crowbar, driven deep into the ground. At last, now squinting, with her tongue between her teeth, she threw — first one and then the other shoe.

Each of the two throws she made, however, was

completely different from the other — that's in every way except for outcome. The shoes spun crazily, in two peculiar arcs, tumbling and twisting. They looked, to Herb, like two "wild heaves." But at the end, both shoes had wrapped themselves around the stake, and she had made two ringers. Two more ringers, Herb could see.

"Wow!" said Herb as she approached him, dusting off her palms. "Two on top of two!"

"Yeah," she said. "Just luck, I guess. But all the bending over *must* be good for me." She laughed. "And how was Uncle Babbo?"

"Good," said Herb. "Pretty much the same as usual. He had a proposition for me, but I didn't take it. Maybe I was foolish, *I* don't know."

"Mmm," she answered, noncommittally. They started strolling toward the castle's door. Ses dug out a bag of salted peanuts from her pocket, and she poured them each a heaping handful. As they got onto the drawbridge, Herb saw that there was someone swimming in the moat, really motoring along, way down and to his right, and almost out of sight. He couldn't tell what kind of someone, just that he or she could really handle swimming on a curve.

"There's someone swimming in the moat," said Herb. "Someone really *good*."

She glanced in the direction he was looking, at the disappearing swimmer.

"Yeah," she said, "it's probably the maid. She's got good form, all right. But don't start thinking that she's perfect. She won't do windows on a bet, or polish armor, either." She opened up the huge main castle door.

"So, now you think you'd like to take another spin," she said.

"Yes," he said. "I really would."

"Well," she said, "you've got a lovely afternoon for it."

Riding in the Upwardlimobile was more pleasant and less stressful, Herbie thought, now that both the van itself and the whole . . . process were a bit familiar. He also was amazed — intrigued — by what he'd spun: Public Service, Including Government. He had to wonder if there maybe was a reason that he'd gotten it. Was T.K. *with* him or *against* him on this deal? First he'd gotten Crime — Organized or not, and *that* had not been right for him at all. But while he was involved with it, back there on Wince 'n' Wails, he'd come to some conclusions, one concerning *politics*. That *it* was a career a real *dumb jerk* could prosper in. So, what does he spin next? Public Service, Including Government — or politics, in other words, you *could* say. Was this going to be a different kind of test? If he *liked* what happened next, would he have found out something he was *glad* to know? Herb touched the child-sized wristwatch that he'd shoved into his pocket as he left his room that morning, the first timepiece he'd ever gotten, his old "TicK-TocK."

When the 'mobile settled to a stop this time, the door did not fly open and a blond guy jump right in. In fact, for just about a count of ten there was no action whatsoever. Then the door *eased* open, real informally. And when he rose and looked on out, he saw that he was in . . . a parking lot.

Well. Herb thought that over, and he had to smile. The van had had the sense to come down in a parking lot, this time; it had landed in its native habitat! And when Herb stepped outside and looked around, he saw that he was also not on hostile, unfamiliar ground, like permafrost. It seemed that he was in a town about the size and shape of his hometown, with more or less the same degree of homeliness. There beside him was a building that could only be a nice, brick, ugly City Hall.

He stretched and strolled a short way from the van to look around. Running left to right, in front of him, was — hey, what else? — a Main Street, which of course was wide and had on it, beside a bunch of stores, the post office and library. Prospect Street crossed Main Street, looking left, while Church Street crossed it on his right. Both Church and Prospect looked like Main, except they might have been a little narrower, and Church Street had some steeples on it. Almost all the buildings in the town were more or less four stories high.

Herb next checked out the stores. Shops could tell you quite a lot about a town; their names, the different storefront styles and what they sold were all significant. He thought this town seemed sort of average. He saw Bull's China Shop, Take a Gander Opticals, One Great Danish Bakery. There was a Kitty Hall, which he assumed to be a pet shop, and a Bear's Din that appeared to be a record store. On the corner was a drive-in feed store. Its sign, at first glance, looked familiar. It had a likeness of a white-haired gent on it, with mustache and goatee, a string tie 'round his neck. But underneath it said that this was Kernel Jimmy Leghorn's, "Cracked Corn You

Can Care About." Herb made a shrewd deduction: If there was a feed store in the heart of town, the chances were he wasn't in New Jersey.

At just about the moment after he thought that, Herb had another thought, more like a feeling, actually. He felt as if he might be being . . . well, *observed*. He looked around and, sure enough, behind him was a man, a small but speculative man, who looked at Herb with narrowed eyes, and one arm crossed, his sharp chin in his hand.

When he saw Herb looking back at him, he gave a kind of start and trotted in the boy's direction, saying, "Hertzman? Herbie Hertzman, is it?"

"Yo," said Herb. "I'm Herbie. In the fellow flesh."

"Danville Pine," the small man said, and offered Herb a slender hand held backside up, the way a dog would, or a noblewoman. "I'm the M.O.S., the Mayor's Official Spokesman. Welcome, welcome, welcome. That's one for her and one for me and one for all the rest of good ol' Hometown, USA."

Herb liked the sound of all of that, but still he didn't rush to judgment on the man. Greenfield Hill had come across as Mr. Cordiality, at first. Danville Pine, by contrast, seemed more *shrewd* than anything: curious, and sharp and maybe even slightly devious. He looked to be a man who'd find a way to get things done. With his copper-colored hair and mustache (both neatly parted in the middle), and his slight and narrow-shouldered build, he probably could slip quite nicely through a door, just before it closed, or any sort of loophole. He was dressed in clean white shirtsleeves on this pleasant, sunny day, but he also wore a bright red bow tie and a

sporty vest, a tattersall. Herb guessed his age to be
. . . oh, forty-eight.

"*Her*?" said Herb, hoping to show sharpness of
his own. "The mayor's a woman, here?"

"Well," said Danville Pine, "the mayor's a *female*,
sure enough. But not a woman, no. I guess you don't
take *Time* or *Newsweek*, do you? 'Cause if you did,
you'd know that she's a chicken. The elected mayor
of all us folks in Hometown is a Big Red Chicken."

"Wo!" said Herb. "Time *out*!" He took a blink or
two, digesting that. "That's pretty darn unusual, I'd
say. Or are there lots of, like, . . . *elected fowl*, out
here?" Wherever "here" was, it seemed to Herb that
it was really out there.

"Not so far as *Time* and *Newsweek* know, I guess,"
said Danville Pine. "Years ago, I read about a La-
brador retriever winning an election out in Idaho, I
think it was. But I'm pretty sure that this one is
the only full-fledged chicken to succeed in politics.
Stand-up comedy, of course, would be a different
story."

"But," Herbie had to ask, "what happened with
the other candidates? I mean, were there, like, any
people in the race? Or not?"

"Oh, sure there were," said Pine. "Both the major
parties put up people, same as always. The Big Red
Chicken was an independent, like you'd think. Part
of it was that the folks around this area were looking
for a change. They were tired of the same old two-
faced candidates, the fat cats and corrupt machines.
They felt that with the Big Red Chicken, what they
saw would be exactly what they'd get."

"I see," said Herb. "And you're the Mayor's Official Spokesman. You must have lots of, well, *re-*

sponsibility — being spokesman for a Big Red Chicken." Herb made sure he didn't smile. He felt that it was possible his leg was being pulled. Given Mr. Pine's appearance, that *certainly* was possible. But yet, Kentucky Fried Chicken had been moved — or driven — out of town, and there was cracked corn in its place. He decided just to play along, and try to get a handle on the situation, be prepared, be cool. More so than he'd been on Wince 'n' Wails, for all that it was way above the Arctic Circle.

"Well, the thing is this," said Danville Pine. "I understand her perfectly. That helps. Few people can. But me, I understand the things she says in chicken talk, and then I say them to the people — but in English, naturally. They, of course, are looking just to hear the things they *want* to hear. That's the way that people are. They have their needs or interests in their minds and not much more. Other than the things that they're against, of course. If they think a politician's *for* those needs or interests, and *against* that other crap, then they're going to be for her. The Big Red Chicken understands that pretty good, I'd say." He chuckled.

"You mean," said Herb, "that everything the chicken said in her campaign, and everything that she says now, as mayor, is clucked to you, a sentence or a paragraph at a time, and then you say it to the people?"

"*Exactly*," Danville Pine replied. "What we do in public is just like all those speeches at the airport on TV. Soon as Gorbachev gets off the plane, they take him to the microphones, him and some short guy with glasses, right? He goes: '*Najdee sposseeyay dubnoyet . . .*' and then he pauses and the short guy says:

'People of my favorite country in the whole wide world . . .' We do just like that."

"Boy," said Herb. "It sounds as if you've got a real hard job. On top of all the time you've got to spend with her, it also seems fantastically *complex*. Like, our Spanish teacher told us that a lot of jokes in Spanish can't even be put in English, word for word. She said they aren't even funny, that way."

"Right," said Pine, "The same thing's true of chicken jokes. I'll throw in a line sometimes that isn't hardly like the one that she just said. But if it gets a laugh, she doesn't mind."

"Wow," said Herb. "The two of you must have a great relationship. *She* may be the mayor, but hey, without your willingness to do the job you do for her, the Big Red Chicken would be nowhere, nothing."

"You catch on quick," said Danville Pine. "So let's go meet Her Honor."

The Big Red Chicken was, for sure, imposing poultry, Herbie thought. When Danville Pine ushered him into her office, she was pacing up and down her desk muttering to herself and, from time to time, pecking at the different piles of paper that surrounded her. He guessed her feathered weight to be a hefty ten–twelve pounds, her height at least a foot from claw to comb; her color was a lustrous reddish-brown. She sure was Big, all right.

Clearly, Herbie thought, this was a working bird who liked to stay on top of things. A sign, inscribed THE CLUCK STOPS HERE was the only frivolous, or personal — unbusinesslike — appurtenance on her entire desk.

As soon as she caught sight of Danville Pine, she stopped her pacing, faced the man, and started in to squawk and cluck. This chicken is a rapper, Herbie thought, for sure.

The Mayor's Official Spokesman gave an almost simultaneous translation, this time.

"She says she's really glad to see you, and she hopes you had a pleasant trip," said Danville Pine. "She has nothing but respect and, more than that, affection for Ms. Sesame deBarque and her entire family and all her friends, and she only wishes they could get together much more often. She hopes that you'll enjoy, and profit from, your stay with us in Hometown, and that the plan that she's drawn up for you — a five-year plan you can accomplish in a week, heh-heh — will prove to meet your every need. Said plan, as presently envisioned, calls for you to spend a little time in each and every main department here in City Hall, starting with the Office of Assessment and continuing right through to the Zoning Board. She feels that this will give you some real basis for a judgment as to whether what she sometimes calls 'this Public Service bullbleep,' is the ideal field for you, or not."

As the Mayor's Official Spokesman said all that, Herb looked back and forth, from man to chicken. He'd never needed an interpreter before, and so he didn't know, for sure, how many nods and smiles to give to *him*, beside the ones he felt he *owed* the Chicken. One peculiar thing, it seemed to him, was that the mayor's expression — the anger in her eyes, the sharp emphatic gestures with her beak — didn't really match the words that Pine was saying. And right there at the end, when he'd employed that

. . . barnyard epithet, she'd let out a sound that seemed to him to be a squawk of outrage.

"And now," said Pine, concluding, "she says she'd like for me to run and fetch the Chief Assessor, so's she can introduce you. For obvious reasons," he said to Herb in a different tone of voice, "her office, here, don't have a phone."

"Hey, fine," said Herb. "I'll just wait here till you get back." He produced another round of nods and smiles. "That sounds *terrific*," he assured the mayor, and he sat down in a chair, prepared to go on looking affable and grateful for as long as they were left alone together.

But, no sooner had the Mayor's Official Spokesman left the room, than Her Honor started acting very weird, it seemed to Herb. She seemed to be a chicken in a frenzy. She didn't *say* a word; instead she shut her beak and used it to seek out, from underneath a pile of records and reports, an ink pad. This, she first flipped open and then, much to Herb's surprise, she started to *dance up and down* on it. After that, she jumped upon a sheet of plain white paper, seemed to think a moment, and then began to run across it, taking quick and careful steps, the way a ballerina might. When she'd finished doing that, she pushed the paper *off* the desk, in Herb's direction. It fluttered to the floor, of course. Between them.

Herb looked at it. He looked at her. She was staring at the paper, and she bobbed her head at it and clucked. Then she bobbed her head at *him*.

"You want for me to pick the paper up?" Herb asked the Big Red Chicken, feeling something of a fool. He'd had a dog who understood some words like "out" and "dinner" and "cryonics," but he'd never posed a question to a chicken.

She nodded, and her eyes were locked on his, and very bright.

He picked it up. There was a line of chicken scratchings on the page. He leaned to put it back on her desk.

The Big Red Chicken had a minor fit. She shook her head; she also shook her neck, her wings, her breast, her thighs, her drumsticks. It's fair to say she shook all over. After that, she danced a bit, jumped up and down. For her closing number, she then jabbed her beak in Herb's direction — one time, two times, three times, four.

"You want for me to keep this?" Herbie asked her, holding up the sheet of paper.

The Big Red Chicken nodded.

"Well, I will," said Herb. "I'll keep it."

The Chicken nodded, and then stretched her neck, like, "And . . . ."

"And something else," said Herb. "But what?"

The Chicken's head went left to right, a little herky-jerkily. She stopped and stared at Herb. When he did nothing, she went left to right, again.

"You want that I should *read* it?" Herbie asked, sounding maybe just a bit incredulous.

The Chicken nodded.

Herb went along with it. He was, as has been said, a trained good sport. He focused on the paper. The "writing" on it looked like chicken scratchings — naturally. But that reminded him of something. All through school, his teachers had described *his* penmanship in just that way. "This paper looks like chicken scratchings!" they'd exclaim, holding up some work of his for public ridicule.

And so, he looked down at the Big Red Chicken's paper once again, and . . . read it!

Her claws had surely not produced a perfect Palmer method script, but it was *legible*, all right, to him. *This isn't all that bad*, he thought.

What it said was: "Thairs a rotten fox in this heer henhouse. Help!"

No sooner had he finished reading that, than Herb heard someone at the door. He just had time to tuck the paper in his pocket, flash a thumb's-up at the Chicken, and lean toward the desk and whisper "I'll come back tonight." The Chicken gave him one quick final nod, and Herb sat back and crossed his legs, and got real busy with a hangnail.

"Well, well, well," said Danville Pine as he came in. With him was a tall and very skinny man who looked as if he might be smelling quite a bad potato.

"This," said Mr. Pine, "is Mr. Bon Ballou, our Chief Assessor. Bon, our young friend Herbie Hertzman."

"Hoy," said Mr. Bon Ballou to Herb. He looked the young man over carefully, no doubt including any hangnails.

"It don't appear to me that you'd be worth much in a tug-of-war," was his assessment.

"Heh-heh," said Danville Pine. "Now what the mayor was hoping, Bon . . ."

Danville Pine, thought Herb, looking at the crafty little man again, but in a different light. Of course! *He's* the fox "in this heer henhouse." Say the name a little differently and Danville Pine becomes . . . well, *Damn Vulpine*!

As Herb politely listened to the Mayor's Official Spokes . . . *fox*, he also checked the Chicken from the corner of his eye. She seemed a lot less agitated. She'd closed the ink pad noiselessly, and slid it out of sight, again. Then she opened a report and seemed to settle down to read it. She looked, to Herb, like one relieved, and even hopeful, fowl. She looked the way a prisoner might look who'd gotten word that her appeal was being heard.

17
SCRATCHING UNDERNEATH THE SURFACE

It didn't take young Herbie all that long to convince the Mayor's Official Spokesman that he'd rather spend his nights in the Upwardlimobile there in the City Hall parking lot than in the AKC-approved and color-cabled Sleeping Dog Motel, which was way the hell and gone out on the edge of town. For one thing, Danville Pine could not care less about our hero's comfort. For another, he was sure that, seeing as he owned the place, he could collect and also pocket one fat refund on the motel room (which Castles in the Air had paid for in advance), and then proceed to rent the room again to someone else. Double his profit, double the fun, was pretty much the way he looked at it. And for a third thing, this meant that chances were he'd never have to see the kid past 5 P.M. Pine often hung around the motel lounge at night, playing strip Parcheesi and a little chamber music with the guys and gals who'd holed up there (for this or that immoral purpose) and who'd told their wives and husbands they were out of town. As Danville Pine had planned when he had built, and named, the place, the Sleeping Dog attracted lots of liars.

In any case, by being in the van at night, Herb got exactly what he wanted most: a place to stay right close to City Hall, from which he could . . . *invade* it, after hours. "Public Service," it appeared to him, now included doing all he could for this deserving Big Red Chicken.

His task was made a good bit easier, initially, by Hometown's easygoing hometown way of doing things. No one locked his door, or hers, at night in Hometown and so, therefore, it followed that no one locked the City Hall. Herb waited until after 2 A.M. to creep out of the van, assuming he might have to break a window to gain entrance to the place, but first he did just *test* a door, almost as a might-as-well. It swung right open, gladly, though, and so he slipped inside it fast and skittered up the stairs and to Her Honor's door.

That one didn't yield so easily. The Big Red Chicken was what Hometown seldom had in its small jail, a prisoner.

Her office wasn't maximum security, however. Let's face it, when the person that you're holding is a chicken, you don't need a lot of fancy locks and dead bolts. In fact, all Herbie had to do was lift the little hook out of its eye, and go on in.

A lamp was lit inside the Big Red Chicken's office,

and when her eyes snapped open and she saw that it was Herb, she started in to cluck, at once, but in a soft, enthusiastic tone of voice.

The boy decided this was not the time for small talk and amenities. He walked right to the desk and got the ink pad, flipped it open. Then he found a pile of plain white paper, put a few sheets in a clipboard that was there and set that down before the mayor.

"So, what's the story, here?" he said.

The Big Red Chicken hopped up on the ink pad right away, and in another minute she was writing, just as fast as her two feet could carry her. As she finished every page, Herb would pick it up and read it and then stuff it in his pocket. Her tale was really quite a simple one — the age-old tale of Trust Betrayed.

When Danville Pine had put her up for mayor, she'd gone along with the idea, quite willingly. Things were not exactly copacetic in the coop where she'd been perched. Although she was a top producer, she was getting only chicken feed, by way of a reward; there was an awful lot of wrangling about who got to peck ahead of whom; and sisters had a way of "disappearing" just before a yellow van with the mysterious license plate, FPRDU, was seen near the barnyard. Finally the rooster she'd been living with was an impossible chauvinist, loud-mouthed, self-important and (she told the boy) "if yoo want to no the trooth, a louzy lay." She'd taught herself to write (if not to spell too well) to combat henhouse boredom, and although in her early weeks in office she'd tried to send Pine memos, he had clearly felt that they were only "chikken skratch-ingz."

"So, Danville Pine is not aware that you can write, or even *understand* the spoken word?" asked Herbie, rather grandly.

"I dont beleve so," scratched the Chicken.

She then went on to "say" that she'd believed, at first, that Danville Pine was an authentic Hometown hero, interested in good, but not intrusive, govern-ment, an end to machine politics, and the restoration of such traditional values as honesty, integrity and father-knows-best. She was pretty sure, she said, that Pine had had a phone call from the President, telling him he was "hiz kind uv guy."

Shortly after that, she'd come to see that her Of-ficial Spokesman was a crook. It hadn't been that difficult.

"Becauze he thot — he *noo* — that I wuz just 'a chikken,' " wrote the Big Red Chicken, "he didden make the slitest effurt to, like, cuvver up wot he wuz dooing. He did hiz dirde deels rite in this offis, rite in frunt uv me, and hede put the munni that he got — the bribez, paola, kikbaks or wotever — rite into my offis safe, thair." She flapped a wing in the direction of this huge cast-iron vault that took up one whole corner of her office.

"In that safe," she wrote, "is all the evidents wede need to hang him hier than a . . . *wethervane*." She paused to cluck, morosely. "If we cood only get to it." She shook her head. "To think that wunce upon a time, a meer too weeks ago, I had the combi-nashun."

"What?" said Herb, although he'd read her perfectly. "You *had* the combination to the safe? Why don't you have it now? Or, wait, just *tell* me what it is, and I will . . . do the honors." He made some twirling motions with his fingers, trying to be a little sensitive in bringing up this thing that Man, not because of any great intelligence or virtue of his own, could do, and Fowl could not. Herb was very conscious of the fact that Man could not lay eggs.

"O, I dont *no* it," wrote the Chicken, "and he got it bak. Tho not befor I led him kwite the mary chace. Dyuring wich I also rote it down — that iz to say I coppied it."

"You *did*?" said Herbie, all excited once again. "That's *great*! So all I have to do is get the copy — right? — and. . . ."

But the Chicken wasn't listening. She was writing, fast and furious. She had another tale to tell, a tale of courage and adventure, of one bird's ability to improvise and to show the kind of grace under pressure that is the hallmark of a . . . well, as Herbie read, he found out for the first time in his life what it really meant to be a *chicken*.

"The furst thing that yoove got to realize," wrote the Chicken, perhaps to justify — explain — her lack of recollection, "iz that a big olefashun safe haz lotz of numberz in its combinashun. *Ate*, to be eggzact. Danville Pine himself, he haz to keep them ritten on this little pece of paper in a pokket uv hiz vest. Well, this one day, he came in heer in sumthing of a rush. Yoojalee, he makez reel shoor heze clozed the dor tite so I cant get out — az yoo no, I cant do nobs — but this one day, I notissed that it didn latch. So, when he took hiz little paper out, and

110

started opunning the safe, I saw my chantz and took it. . . ."

What the Chicken did, apparently, was to, like, launch herself from off the desk in one great flapping, falling swoop, and seize the little piece of paper out of Pine's left hand. Then, with the paper firmly in her beak, she nudged the door enough so she could flutter through it to the hall and *up* the stairs.

Almost before she'd thought what she was doing, the Big Red Chicken had gone up two flights of stairs and out the fire door the janitor had left propped open for the breeze. She was on the roof!

"I gess wot happend wuz," she wrote to Herb, "that misster smarty chaste me *down* the stairz, at furst, insted of up. So, for a wile, I had a reel good leed on him."

While she had this lead, the Chicken sped across the roof of City Hall and flutter-flew across the wall between it and the roof next door. She said that she was hoping for another open door that she could use to head back down again and make it to the street. Her plan, from there, would be to run down to the corner, to the feed store, hide herself in some old farmer's truck, and disappear into *his* flock of chickens for a while, until she'd hatched a plan. The only trouble was, she didn't find an open door on that roof, or the next one, or the next. By then, the Mayor's Official Spokesman had found out his quarry'd never gone downstairs at all, so he, along with half a dozen henchmen, had reversed his field and run upstairs, and reached the top of City Hall and seen the fleeing fowl four roofs away.

The fifth roof that the Chicken reached was different than the others, though. That roof was . . . occupied. There was a young and comely woman on it, lying on a beach towel, getting rays. She appeared to be asleep. Beside her, was the book that she'd been reading and the thick, absorbent terry bathrobe that she must have doffed before she'd stretched out on her stomach. When the girl had taken off that robe (the Chicken told our boy), there wasn't any more undressing left for her to do. Except for her white terry mules, the woman was completely naked.

"Of corse, at that point I wuz in a total *panik*," wrote the Big Red Chicken. "Not becauze Ide cum upon a female in the nood, but rather over seeing all those raskels cumming after me, and me with no way to get off those roofs. We chikkens, az yoo may *not* no, doo not sirvive for storey fallz too offen, enny mor than peepul doo." The Chicken paused and shook her head, as if in painful recollection.

"Ime shoor yoove herd that reel dizgusting fowlist fraze that peepul uze sumtimez," she wrote. " 'Running around like a chikken with its hed cut off'? Well, thatz probablee the way I woodve looked to enny fowlists in the area. All I cood think, the moment that I landed on that roof, was that Ide better make a coppy of that combinashun — kwik, befor they got me, got *it*, bak again."

So what she did, the Chicken made completely clear to Herb (in spite of her misspellings) was to run and lay the combination down where she could read the thing, and then to quickly scratch a copy with her dancing feet, using . . . well, the first smooth surface that had "cawt her I." After which, she picked the combination up again and kept on

112

going, over to another rooftop, and another, and a third — at which point Pine and Co. caught up with her and grabbed her, and snatched the little paper from her beak.

"Wow," said Herbie, much impressed again, or still — whatever. "You made a copy and they didn't even know it. I'll bet you scratched those numbers in the roofing tar up there. It'd get a little soft on days like we've been having, right?"

"Why, no," the Chicken wrote. "Thay mite have seen it in the roofing tar, and rubbed it out."

"Well, then, where else . . . ?" asked Herb, completely mystified again, or still — as usual.

"Why, on that gurlz behind," the Chicken wrote. "I noo shede get it covered up and outa thair, befor thoze men arrived. And so I put for numbers on her left bun, and the uthers on her rite wun."

"Good *grief*," said Herb, amazed, amused — and acting scandalized — by what he'd heard. "You carved eight numbers into some poor person's . . . *butt*?"

" 'Carved,' " the Chicken wrote, a little testily, "wood be a huje eggzagerashun. 'Litelee scratched' wood be the wurdz Ide yooze. And if yood seen the butt in kwesschun, I dout yood say 'poor person,' eether."

The Chicken then went on to say that just as she had thought, the girl, awakened by the *gentle* scratching on her rear, had sat right up and seen the people coming (and the Chicken going, I'd presume), put her bathrobe on and grabbed her book and towel, and gotten off that roof, posthaste.

When he had finished reading all of that, Herb took a step or two directly backwards, so he could sink down in the chair he'd occupied the day before. He felt he needed just a minute, there, to get this whole amazing story settled in his mind. And then to think about exactly what it *meant*, what action(s) it suggested should be taken by one very junior Public Servant by the name of Hertzman, H.

The thoughts that soon flashed through his brain began to take the form of questions:

—Was the Big Red Chicken now in any danger from the foxy Mr. Pine?

—Did she really not remember any of the numbers she had written on that girl's behind?

—If, indeed, she didn't . . . well, who *was* the girl? and where?

—And would that combination still be where she'd put it, two weeks later?

—And, finally, would the finding and the reading of the combination be the sort of thing that one would call a "Public Service"?

Not really having answers to a single one of those, Herbie stood back up again and put them to the Chicken.

The Chicken said that, first of all, she didn't feel that she was now in any danger. Not *yet*, that is to say. She was sure there wasn't any way — because of all the walls between the roofs — that Pine had seen her put the combination on the girl. And, don't forget — she said — Pine didn't even know that she could write. Her best guess was that Pine had not yet stashed away inside the safe enough illegal bucks to set himself up comfortably for life. She figured once he *had*, that she'd be instant barbecue (she shuddered). But, for the moment, no, she said, she didn't feel she had to fly the coop.

Also, no, "alass," she *hadn't* memorized the combination; she'd just been too shook up. She *thought* that she remembered 8, 19 and 46, but all the other numbers had completely left her mind — and even those *could* be her father's mother's birthday. She said that even at the best of times, numbers and arithmetic were not her "fortays."

But *names*, she told the boy, were quite a different matter. She'd always had a "nak" for names, she wrote. She could, she wrote, still give him everybody's name in her homeflock, the one that she'd grown up in ("Combhed," "Wattleface," "Gizzardbreth," "Geekbeek" were the ones she rattled off before he stopped her). And just before she'd scratched the combination on the girl's rear end, she'd glanced down at the book the girl had earlier been reading, which was right beside her elbow, on the towel. The girl, apparently, had marked her place in it with an old credit card. The Chicken saw her name, as it was printed on the card, and thought it every bit as elegant as her behind had been: Felicity Tantamount. "Gawjus," she opined.

The Chicken then went on to say she didn't *know* if Herb could read the combination still, or not — but that she *assumed* he would be able to. That, of course, was when Herb learned that she expected him to try.

"The gurl was nice and tan all over, if yoo follo me," she wrote, "so even if the scratches are all heeled, thaird still be liter-cullerd . . . *marx* back thair, Ide thnk."

And then the Chicken looked at Herb and wrote a final line, which she then also underlined.

"*Yoor my only hope*," she put down on the page,

and looked again in Herbie's eyes. Quite unexpectedly, the start of Roth's *Goodbye, Columbus* popped into his mind. ("The first time I saw Brenda she asked me to hold her glasses.")

He'd never seen such trust, and also desperation, in a chicken's face, before. In *her* mind, anyway, his finding this young woman, this Felicity, and getting her to let him have the combination would be . . . well, a Public Service of the very highest order. He decided that he'd give the thing a whirl, he really would; maybe he'd be lucky. And even if the combination wasn't there, or wasn't *visible*, at least he would have . . . tried.

Herb smiled and nodded at the bird. "Okay, I'll start to look for her today," he said.

Looking some pounds heavier — he'd stuffed about a ream of paper in his pockets — Herb left the Chicken's office just at daybreak. If he'd been out there at the Sleeping Dog, he might have heard a rooster crow.

18
KITTY HALL

When Herb's alarm clock shocked him out of sleep a scant three hours later, he just lay there in his bunk a while. In his present sleep-deprived condition, our young man felt anything but "up" for Public Service.

He thought about the day ahead of him. He was to spend it in the company of Mr. Bon Ballou, Hometown's Chief Assessor, in (or maybe out of) the Office of Assessment. The idea was for him to "learn the ropes," as he assumed they used to say on whaling ships, or in a Hanging for Beginners class — what ropes you pulled to get which things to happen.

In other words, he realized rather dully, today he'd spend some hours doing just the sort of stuff he'd *hoped* to do in Hometown. He'd be doing research, you could say, on future possibilities. Wasn't that his central purpose, being there? The only trouble was, it sounded pretty deadly, given how he felt, just then.

That other whole involvement with the Big Red Chicken's crisis was a side-light, only — a kind of a *parenthesis*, or a digression. His English teacher, Ms. Katrina Pell, had urged him to avoid parentheses; she said they were annoying to "the reader." He wondered how Ms. Pell would feel if she found out he was knee-deep in one that had the earmarks of a major scandal — a scandal that would come to light *only* when and if he read eight numbers off the bare, allegedly attractive, *derrière* of one Felicity Tantamount. He thought she'd be annoyed. (Most likely.)

Herb pulled himself together and got up. He'd be a sport and take a bite of this assessment world and see how it went down. Furthermore, he'd keep an open mind, at first, and see what it was full of by, say, 5 P.M. that afternoon.

At 4 P.M. he had his answer and it was "not too much." That was the hour Mr. Bon Ballou had called it "one fine d - a - y," saying that he had to meet with Mr. Danville Pine, in order to discuss some "classy-fied" material. Up until then, they had mostly driven here and there, both inside Hometown's city limits and outside them in what Mr. Bon Ballou referred to as "the Greater Hometown area."

What they did was look at property that Mr. Bon Ballou would first assess and then heap heavy scorn on. Herb learned that the average ranch house in the near vicinity "wasn't worth the chowder to fill a cup," while the old Victorians near the center of town mostly "weren't worth a mart in a maelstrom." Nor would Mr. Bon Ballou give you "a slug's tickle" for some renovated capes they saw; he felt the condos going up just on the edge of town were "worth about as much as an iguana in a cuddle contest."

At first, Herb found it impossible to figure out how Mr. Bon Ballou arrived at all the dollar values that he placed on different homes. At one point in the afternoon, the Chief Assessor turned to him and said, "As you can see, this work's part art, part science, part pure quasi-mystical experience." He pronounced that "q" word "kwayzee."

Herb saw none of that, but he decided not to press the point. By late afternoon, however, he *had* observed that Mr. Bon Ballou would often take whatever price the property just sold for, and then add or subtract another number that he'd get from anywhere — the one from off the license plate of the next Cadillac they passed, for instance — and that'd be the new official value, the assessment of the place. As far as Herb could tell, the only reason that they *looked* at any properties at all was so that Mr. Bon Ballou could criticize the way the occupants kept house.

But, no matter. By the time that it was 4 P.M., the assessing day was over, and an exhausted and befuddled Herb was pretty sure that this was not his future line of work. He went back to the van and lay down on his bunk. The big parenthesis was next; he hoped to get a plan of action clearly in his mind.

First, of course, he had to find the building that the girl, Felicity, resided in, the one that she'd been sunning on, two weeks before. That shouldn't be too hard; the Chicken had been sure it was the fifth one down from City Hall. Next, he'd find the door that led to the apartments on the upper floors (he knew there'd be a store below); he'd learn which one she lived in from the nametag on her mailbox. When he rang her doorbell, and she answered it, he wouldn't be that far from what they called (Herb smiled at his ironic wit) "the bottom line."

Just what he'd *say* to her was something of a problem. "Hello. Would you please turn around and drop your pants?" did not sound either "him" or promising. He thought that maybe he'd just wing it, be spontaneous. He'd always heard that it was good to be spontaneous.

The next thing that Herb didn't know, he'd fallen fast asleep.

When he woke up it was near dark inside the van, and he was hungry. He heard a clock chime someplace up on Church Street; it was eight o'clock.

Drat! he thought. He hoped he hadn't missed Felicity. She could have taken out, and gotten home, then eaten in, and gone right out again. Gone to the movies with a girlfriend. Gone to a class in Tae Kwon Do, or Homestyle Cooking. That last reminded Herb that he was really, *really* hungry. Time compression was confusing. He wondered how his body's cells were taking this. Were they aging faster than they should have been? Could he be *losing* time from the future he was trying to make? Would it be worth it? What did "it" mean, in that sentence? How about the other "it"?

Herb knew he wasn't making sense. He stood up, groggily, and splashed some water on his face. Two minutes later, he was standing in a fast-food place called Pig Out. Apparently they specialized in pork to go. A sign said they had hot dogs, ribs, ham sandwiches and sausage rolls and bacon buns, as well as pig's feet and pig's knuckles, even snouts on special order. "We carry everything except the squeal," the sign concluded — rather tastelessly, Herb thought. And so our youthful epicure selected hot dogs (three of them and "all the way") and two large cups of chocolate milk and went back to the van to gobble down his supper.

With that accomplished, Herbie hit the streets again. The time had come to make his move, to "go for it." He felt a pounding and a queasiness inside his chest: excitement, yes, but something more — a touch of heartburn, surely. Covering a burp, he turned the corner just past City Hall and started counting buildings. One, two, three, four, five. And there he was.

The building was the one that all along he'd thought contained a pet shop, Kitty Hall. Before, when he'd first come to town, he'd seen its sign from down the block; it was the kind that stuck out from the building and projected out above the sidewalk. But, now that he was there, in front of it, the place did not look pet-shoppy at all. There wasn't any big glass window, just for instance, behind which you could watch a bunch of cunning little puppies being totally adorable on shredded newspapers. There wasn't any window, *period*. Instead, there was a big, opaque front door, a heavy-looking wooden one, with long, black, metal hinges. In the center of the door was just this painting of a sleek black cat that stretched and arched its back, and had an odd expression on its face. Wise, but still distinctly playful. It almost looked as if the cat were smiling — or it could be singing — showing just the pink tip of its tongue. *Doink*.

Herb stood and stared at it. He wished he'd had some coffee with his supper. He wasn't feeling sharp or on the ball, at all. He'd come this far expecting he would see a pet shop window with its door beside it, and then another door that opened onto stairs that led up to apartments. He wasn't seeing that, at all.

He looked above the one big door in front of him. It *did* appear there were apartments on the second floor, and on the third and fourth, as well. He could see that there were lights in lots of windows. But how did anyone get up to them? He guessed this *had to* be the door.

He tried the handle of it, pushed, but nothing happened. The door was tightly locked. He looked around. The fourth and sixth buildings down from City Hall had the kinds of doors on them that he'd expected the fifth would have, so Herb went into both of them and checked the nametags on the mailboxes. The only one remotely like the one he sought was "Pete Lamonica."

"*Great*," he said, out loud. He was feeling really tired and a little sick. And stupid. Also, angry, in a way. He didn't know what at, exactly.

He decided he would go across the street and see if he could see inside the rooms upstairs. He'd stand in a doorway and observe the building. When people — like, *detectives* — did that in the movies, something always happened.

As it turned out, he couldn't see inside the rooms

at all. They all had shades or curtains, which were drawn. For all he knew, those rooms were full of catnip mice, or tattooed ladies. They could be full of people watching boring slides of someone's trip to Yellowstone. They *could* contain a lunatic named — let's see — *Mordecai*, holding lots of hostages, including Frank Sinatra. Or possibly Felicity was there, in one of them.

"*Wonderful*," he muttered to himself, this time.

But then a movement caught his eye from up the block, across the way.

"Hark," our young man whispered. And, "A *stranger*."

The "stranger" was a man, and he was *sauntering* along. He had his hands thrust deep inside the pockets of his pants, and he was whistling. Herb didn't think he'd *ever* seen a person look as casual as this guy did. The song that he was whistling was "Start Me Up," composed by Messrs. Jagger, M., and Richards, K., a song that, to Herb's mind, was not the least bit casual.

"Naturally I'm trained to notice little contradictions of that sort," our private eye informed himself, to pass the time.

As the man was just about to pass the door of Kitty Hall, he bent, as if to tie his shoe. But as he did so, Herb was pretty sure he saw the man look quickly up and down the block. Seeing only (possibly) a boy detective pressed into the shadow of a doorway on the other side, the man arose and faced the door of Kitty Hall. He knocked: three shorts, a pause, one short, another pause, a long-two shorts-a long. The door swung quickly open and he disappeared inside.

123

"Gol-*lee*," the boy exclaimed. It seemed that Kitty Hall was not, for sure, a pet shop — not, at least, as those two words are understood by normal people. It *seemed* that it was what he'd known — and feared — it might be, the moment he had seen that painting on the door.

"But let's not jump to a conclusion," our young Mister Fairness told himself. "This is America, and every storefront is presumed completely innocent, until it's proven guilty." He tried to think of other things that Kitty Hall might be, other than a pet shop and a . . . *that*.

It *could* (he thought) be, like, a *veterinary hospital*, perhaps. That would account for evening hours, wouldn't it? Conceivably the man he'd seen was there to visit his sick spaniel, or to hold the paw of, say, a convalescent coon cat.

Or, *possibly*, the guy had come to practice the *piccolo*, for instance, on the darkened stage way in the back of this *recital* hall. Hadn't he first thought the kitty in the painting on the door was (maybe) *singing*? There were lots of different kinds of Kittys. Kitty Carlisle Hart, for one example. And *Carnegie* Hall.

In fact — Herb's eyes grew large when he came up with this one — *this* "Kitty Hall" could *also* simply be a woman's name, the way that *Annie* Hall was. **A** woman's name that had to do with fashion and design! The way "Liz Claiborne" did, or "Norma Kamali," or "Coco Chanel." The cat could (merely) be her *logo*! Yes (Herb thought), he'd heard that some boutiques had special evening shows where gorgeous models showed off all the latest and most daring clothes from Paris, Venice, Tokyo, et cetera to wealthy and sophisticated buyers. Such buyers would be *casual* and cool, and they would come by invitation only, and they'd have to knock to gain admittance. The clothes would probably have first been shown in Paris, Venice, Tokyo, et cetera, and after they'd been seen in Hometown, they'd go on to San Francisco and New York, to Minneapolis. Felicity could be a model, easily, he guessed. The reason she'd been sunning naked on the roof was so she wouldn't show a tan line anywhere, when she was wearing daring, latest-fashion clothes. And of course she'd have to have — as the BRC had said she did — a *most* outstanding figure.

Herb crossed the street, as casually as possible. He knocked on the big door of Kitty Hall, using the same tempo that the other "buyer" had.

The door came open fast. A fellow in a butler's uniform looked out at him. The boy was glad the man was dressed that way. If he had had a bathrobe on, or shorts, Herbie would have thought he was a boxer.

"Well? You coming in or not?" the butler said, when Herbie simply stood there, staring at him.

"I'm looking for Felicity . . . uh, Tantamount," he finally said, and stepped inside. The butler quickly shut the door behind him.

"I ain't the lost and found," the butler said. "Tell it to the lady at the desk. Betcha she can fix you up, all right." He'd jerked his thumb behind him, down the entrance hall. Then he opened up what could have been a closet door and disappeared behind it.

Herb took a breath and looked around. One thing was absolutely clear: He was not in any Pets-R-Us, smelling an exotic blend of wildlife odors, hearing yelps and birdsong, chattering and hisses. Nor were there any of the sorts of sounds that you'd expect from music studios or concert halls: no rattles from a drum machine, no synthesizer's whine.

No, he was standing in a stylish, gracious entry-way — a *foyer*, if you please. It was a place that looked a lot like many he had seen, in passing, on TV, on *E*TV to be exact, on shows that had a lot too many episodes for him. Close at hand, there was a bentwood coatrack, just beyond it an umbrella stand. On the other side there was a table, like a sideboard, with a dish of mints on it, and flanked by straight-backed chairs, upholstered in a deep red velvet.

A little farther down the hall, and facing him, quite near the foot of curving stairs, there was a little desk, an *escritoire*, behind which sat a woman, old enough to be — but not — his mother. She had on a long, full, flowing, silken high-necked gown. Way up on the left side of her bosom there was pinned an orange plastic card that read: "Hi, pilgrim, and *bon soir*! I'm Madame Marguerite, Marquise de Marinade."

"Good even-ing, *m'sieur*," she said to Herb, and smiled.

"Good evening," our young man replied, politely. Having taken Spanish, he'd never met a madame in his life. Up ahead, beyond the woman, in a sort of formal drawing room, the boy could see some younger females, dressed in evening clothes. Though Herb was not well qualified to make such judgments, it appeared to him that some of them were dressed for evenings in the home, like, in their own . . . *boudoirs*, was it? while others wore the sorts

126

of gowns you'd see at nightclubs, or the theater, or at a dinner party at the Hefners', or in a James Bond movie. In other words, in every case Herb thought those younger women looked sophisticated, stylish . . . *daring*.

Although he knew darn well he shouldn't, Herbie gawked. Face it, this was not a scene he'd ever been exposed to in his life, so far. Nor was it one he'd been prepared for by the ambiance of Hometown. It didn't really go with feed stores in the heart of town, and restaurants named Pig Out and a mayor who was a Big Red Chicken.

But while he gawked, he also had to face the fact that he was *scared*. Being on this spot, the spot that he was on right there, right then, was scary. Sure, he understood — if just a little vaguely — what sorts of things went on in places of this sort. But knowing what goes on somewhere is not the same as going on yourself. He knew what happened in a play-off game in Boston Garden, but still he wouldn't want to play in one. Not that very day, at least. Later on? Perhaps.

"Felicity?" Herb tried his magic words again. "Felicity . . . uh, *Tantamount*?" He arched both brows this time, at the Marquise. Unfortunately, he looked to be in pain, instead of merely curious. "She's here?"

"But, yes," the woman said. "Ub gorse," her next words sounded like.

"Well, may I see her, please?" said Herb, feeling that politeness knew no social borders.

"Oh, absolyou," the woman said. Reaching down, she slid the most discreet small drawer imaginable just slightly open. "Wi' zat be cash or charge?" She said the last three words completely undemandingly, but also most distinctly.

"Cash or charge," repeated Herb, as if deciding.

"*Oui*," the woman said. "Mamzelle's retainer is one hundred dollars." She said *those* last three words, "wan hondraid dough-lars," but there was no mistaking that she meant $100.

"Retainer?" Herb was stalling, now. "One hundred dollars?"

Back in junior high, the boy had known some kids whose parents made them go to orthodontists, and who (therefore) had to *wear* retainers, yukky plastic things with wires on them that they stuck inside their mouths at night. What these retainers did was help to straighten teeth. But he was pretty sure he wasn't being asked to buy a thing like that right now, a sort of kinky souvenir of Madame What'sherface's place. The "retainer" that Madame was speaking of was like a fee for services, he knew. But even if he wanted to employ the girl, he didn't have a hundred bucks.

"Well," the boy said slowly, "well, I mean, if I could *see* her for a minute, and find out — "

He cut it off, himself. Amazingly, he'd gotten through to the Marquise. She was nodding at him now, and smiling, once again.

"Ub gorse," she said, once more. "You weesh to *see* her first. Can be arrange." She gaily punched some buttons on her fancy telephone. "Felici-*tee*? Can you come down *un moment*, dear? A gentleman would like to *see* you. Yes. *Mare-see*." She put the phone back down and said to Herb, "She come. You see. You won' be disappointment."

Herb smiled and stepped back from the desk to wait, leaning up against the newel post at the foot of the staircase. This possibly was working out, he thought. For sure, it was a fact that he was getting closer. He was going to see the girl, perform that public service — and that was the whole point, the thing that *had* to happen. If he was going to do his *job*.

A minute later, he heard footsteps, coming down. And so he turned his head to say hello to this Felicity, at last.

Luckily for him, he wasn't chewing gum.

Technically, perhaps, Felicity was "dressed." She did have on a little lacy wraparound, belted at the waist, but it was shorter than the shortest mini Herb had ever seen, and *totally* transparent. Herb confirmed, at once, she didn't have a tan line, anywhere. And it's fair to say that although he experienced a whole *thesaurus* of emotions, "disappointment" wasn't one of them.

You see, our Herb had never seen a real, in-person, female's hypogastric region — all of it — in his entire life, before. The place he swam at in the summertime was not, let's face it, Sweden.

So *this*, he thought, is Tyree Toledano, in the total flesh.

"Oh, hi," he said, when he was able to. He tried to say it just as if she wore a down-filled parka over a floor-length Amish woman's housedress. By then, he'd wrenched his eyes away from *terra incognita* and was staring at a point right in between, and just above, her lovely, long-lashed, hazel eyes.

"Okay?" she said — to him, Herb thought. She was asking *him* if she was, like, *Okay*? She had a pleasant, cultivated voice. It made him think of words like "Williams College," "music lessons," "drama club" — and from his own real life, "Forget it." She moved her eyes from Herb to the Marquise.

"All set?" she asked the woman. Then, she sounded like the same girl, still, but clerking down at Grenville's Pharmacy — working at a summer job, perhaps.

"No, no, not yet, my dear," the Marquise said. "The young m'sieur has not yet pa — "

"Oh, well, the thing *is*, Miss Felicity," the boy began, talking without thinking, without *breathing*, actually. His ears were ringing and his eyes were watering, his nose was running, but his mouth was dry as ashes. "All I need is just five minutes of your time," he babbled *sotto voce*. "Or even less, a *lot* less, really. If there was someplace we could *go* and — "

"Sure," she told him, sticking to that same agreeable tone, "I understand. I really do. Truthfully — it might be only fifteen *seconds*, mightn't it? But all the same, you see, you have to pa — "

"But I don't *have* a hundred dollars." Herb's whisper sounded desperate, even to himself. "And I promise you, I won't do anything but *look*. I've got to see if . . . well, if — "

But he had to break it off, again. This clearly wasn't working. The girl had sighed, and shook her head and started up the stairs. Herb could plainly see the Chicken's . . . notepads; they *were* beautiful. But not, of course, what had been written on them. Not in *that* light, anyway, or through the little mist of lace she wore.

"I'm sorry, really," floated back to him.

The next thing Herbie knew, the butler had him

by the elbow and had moved him out the door and to the sidewalk, where he left him, once again.

Herb, perhaps reflexively, looked up and down the street, and then turned left, toward City Hall. He started humming something, "Can't Buy Me Love," by Messrs. Lennon and McCartney. He didn't even know that, so confused — and warm — was he.

It was hard for him to get his feelings straight — again. Back there on Wince 'n' Wails, he'd reached for Zippy, sure he had, when she'd whipped off her shirt like that. He hadn't known — expected — she would do it, and his reaching out for her had been a reflex, you could say; he'd *wanted* her. *Naturally* he had. And vice versa, so it seemed. And she *had* started it. If Greenfield Hill had not come in the room, they would have crossed each other's stop lines and each other's goal lines, too. If it wasn't for that murderer, he would have *scored*! Which would have been all right, he thought. It had to happen sometime.

But seeing as it hadn't happened *then*, he had these worries and confusions *now*. It almost seemed like it was just his luck to keep on finding gorgeous and exciting girls on these excursions out of Castles in the Air. Zippy had been simply uninhibited but, well, with this Felicity . . . scoring was her *business*, you could say. Could a person make the argument that he was *meant* to do it on some trip or other, such as this one? That *that* might be a part of his good fortune?

But trip or no trip (Herbie told himself) he still, presumably, could exercise free will. What he did would always be his choice; he didn't have to "do," like, anything (except, perhaps, eventually, some "something" with himself). So let's suppose, on some occasion at some place he could not presently imagine, Felicity was willing. If not for love, perhaps, at least, for money. What would he do then?

He simply didn't know. The turmoil in his mind, which seemed to have to do with what "love" meant to him, somehow, just wouldn't go away. There were some things — Am I really just another Dartmouth guy? — that he could not get straight.

The trouble in *this* situation — as compared to what had happened there on Wince 'n' Wails — was that he had the time to think about it, first. Or so Herb told himself, right then.

19
NUMBERS GAME

Herb walked straight back to the van, seeing almost no one on the sidewalks and few cars in the streets. That figured. Hometown was a real dull place; it always had been, always is, and always will be. They roll the sidewalks up real early, there in Hometown.

Lots of kids maintain they just can't wait till they're adults so they can bug on out of there and live someplace where something happens, sometimes — where there's something, like, to *do*. A few of them go on and do that, too. But adults, as a rule, speak well of Hometown. Its nowhere-ness and nothingness appeal to them; they call it quiet, peaceful, homey and affordable. So, if you're going to get out of Hometown and live somewhere else, the best time to do it is after you've stopped being a kid, but before you get to be an adult. You have to move real fast.

It was still too early to go to the mayor's office, Herb thought. Plus, he didn't much look forward to telling her he hadn't got the combination. Or that there was a . . . what? *bordello*, right there in the heart of town. He was sure the Big Red Chicken didn't know that fact already; she would have a fit. Or would she? Who was he to say where chickens stood on sex, free enterprise, or feminism? Herb decided that perhaps a little sleep would make him both a better bearer of bad tidings and, in general, a smarter, more resourceful public servant.

He sat down on his bunk and reset his alarm clock. His stomach rumbled, and he realized he was hungry. Not for hot dogs "all the way" awash in chocolate milk, however. What he thought would really hit the spot would be a plate of mom's home cooking, of Paprika Chi- . . . uh, whoops! A nice plate of *linguine*, but with tomato sauce, not clams.

Herb shook his head, and then got up and went outside and walked back to an Arco station, where he had some Hometown-type excitement getting cheese-and-peanut butter crackers out of a machine. He put his money in the proper slots, and — bingo! — the machine delivered. Talk about a grand old time! He walked back, munching, to the van again.

The alarm was set for 2 A.M. already, so the boy lay down and soon was fast asleep and, later, dreaming. In his dream he was back in the great hall at Castles in the Air, but Ses deBarque was nowhere to be seen. Instead, Felicity was standing by the wheel, dressed as she had been when he last saw her. She spun the thing, and when it stopped, the arrow pointed right at . . . *her*!

"All right!" This dream of a Felicity said that to Herb. "You're just a hundred dollar bill away from heaven."

"But how about good government?" the dream-state Herb inquired.

"When winter comes, can spring be far behind?" she asked.

Of course, he didn't have that kind of money (even in his dreams), and he wasn't sure he understood the saying, so he awakened, sweating in frustration, very close to tears. It was a quarter after one, so he got up and brushed his teeth and tried to get his act together. He knew he wanted to get something from the girl, all right. Was it more than just the combination to that office safe? Now that he had *seen* her in that . . . habitat.

This "Public Service" deal was turning out to be a lot like "Crime—Organized or not," he realized. Or, at any rate, it had that side to it. There were people in the field who had an eye and both their hands out for big bucks. And who would break the law to get them, gladly. Break both the law and anyone who showed up in their way — a boy, for instance.

He had to wonder how his values were surviving this experience. Were *love* and *money* still the things he wanted most in life? Or would he settle for a night with someone like Felicity, a decent meal, and, maybe, peace and quiet? For *benefits*, in other words.

Herb walked across the parking lot, into City Hall, and up the stairs, heading for Her Honor's office. Right now, he thought, he didn't seem to have a choice.

The mayor was snoozing when he stepped into her office, but as soon as she woke up and saw that it was Herb, she started clucking loudly in excitement, just as he had feared she would. And of course she next flipped open and jumped on the ink pad, too, wild to fire off some loaded rockets in the form of Good News-seeking questions.

The boy held up his hand. He figured he could save her tread-wear.

"I didn't get the combination," he admitted. And so learned, to his regret, exactly what the word "crestfallen" meant.

"But I found the girl, all right," he said. "The fifth place down is Kitty Hall. I'd thought it was a pet shop, but it's not — not even close. It's a . . . well, a house of ill repute."

The Big Red Chicken looked, first, puzzled, then aghast. Before he'd finished, she was writing, madly; there was no way that he could have stopped her, short of chickicide.

Herb once again read every page as it rolled out from underneath her feet. It seemed the Chicken was *extremely* pleased that there was not a *second* pet shop, here in Hometown. She had, in fact, this *thing* against the one she knew about already, a place called Katz's Meows and Bow-wows, which was down on Prospect Street. Apparently this Mr. Katz had chicknapped half a dozen youngsters from the Big Red Chicken's former coop one Easter season, years before, and had even dyed them different colors in his shop before he sold them off to families with children, there in town.

"Sum peepul still indulj in stuff like that, u no," she told the boy. "They dont think uv it as slaveree, uv corse."

And then she wrote, "So whatz a howse of ill repewt?"

As Herb explained how it, too, tended to promote a sort of slavery (which he described, but not in great detail), the Chicken's eyes grew round with horror, once again. Soon she started stamping back and forth, from one side of her desk back to the other. Herb didn't think he'd ever seen a more disgusted fowl.

"Boy," she finally stopped and wrote, "peepul ar scrood up, u no that? How can u treet each uther so uncaringlee?"

But she wasn't letting moral outrage blind her to her central purpose.

"Wot yule hav to do — thatz if ur game to take anuther shot at this — iz try the roof. *If* that dorz still opun, mabee u can get down to the gurlz room after ourz — when sheze finished . . . wurk," she wrote.

Herb thought that over. He supposed he *could* do that. House of ill repute or no, this was Hometown, still. People wouldn't keep late hours, even in the bawdy business, probably. But still, no matter when he saw the girl, or which door he came in by, there was still this central problem he had. He was lacking any *leverage*, any means of gaining her cooperation. To put it bluntly, any money. Like, $100.

He said as much, succinctly, to the bird.

She scratched her head and thought it over. Then she rummaged in the mess atop her desk until she found a nice clean piece of Town of Hometown stationery. Taking lots of time and care, she wrote on it the following:

IOU $100
Town of Hometown
Big Red Chikken, Mare

Of course! Herb could have kicked himself for . . . well, not having been the first to think of such a Neat Idea. Never in his life, again, would he call someone "birdbrain." He did, however, feel that given this Felicity's well-educated style, it might be worth the risk of hurting mayoral feelings to request a rewrite of this little document with all the words spelled right.

No problem. The Chicken wasn't in the least offended, just amused.

"U say u spel Mare 'Mayor'?" she wrote. "Thatz dum. But not ur fallt Ime shoor," she finished, gracefully, and started on the copy.

Before the clocks struck three, young Herb was climbing over rooftops, like a burglar in Paris.

When the boy arrived on rooftop number five, he tried the door he found on it with mixed emotions, truth to tell. Having it be locked could save him quite a lot of trouble and excitement and confusion. Or at least postpone them for a while. Sometimes it was easier if you *couldn't* do anything with yourself (he thought), if you could put the blame on circumstances that were clearly out of your control. ("All doors were closed to me . . ." et cetera.) Then, in that case, you could simply lie, or wallow, where you were, safely in a rut (you'd *never* call Self-Pity). He tried the door; of course it opened, easily.

Herb crept down a flight of narrow stairs and found they ended in a lighted corridor with doors on either side of it. It was the sort of hall you find in cheap small-town hotels, or older dorms in less demanding colleges. He listened, left and right, and to his great delight and real relief, he heard no sounds of any sort, from anywhere. He began to reconnoiter and discovered all the rooms had names: "Annabelle," "Babette," "Cherie," "Dolores," "Eloise," "Felicity," he read. And went no further up the hall, or alphabet.

He turned the knob and slipped into "Felicity."

Like the mayor herself, his quarry kept a nightlight on, and by its gentle glow our boy could see a shape like hers beneath a sheet, but turned toward the wall. He looked around the room. In style, it was Victorian, with heavy wooden furniture, mahogany perhaps, and velvet drapes, and prints and paintings on the walls. Tacked above the bed, however, was an Amherst banner with a college playbill pinned to it; apparently Felicity had once been in *A Doll's House* (too). And, yes, there was a mandolin, leaning up against her dressing table.

While Herb had still been up there on the rooftops, he'd thought about what method he might use to wake the girl — assuming that she'd be asleep — but not alarm her. The Big Red Chicken's Hometown IOU would surely be a help, or a necessity, at some point in the conversation they would have, but maybe there was something better he could flash at her, at first. It seemed to him the first few seconds would be critical; if she were to scream, he might be sunk — *deep*-sunk, and possibly for good. What he had to do was *somehow* find a way to let her know, *at once*, that he was harmless. Weird, perhaps, and needy, but quite harmless.

He tiptoed to the bed. First, he took the bellpull that was hanging by the head of it and got it hooked onto the Amherst banner so that she couldn't reach it easily. Her having gone to Amherst was a plus, in light of what he'd planned. Then, he put a hand down on her sheeted shoulder and began to shake it, very gently. And, as he saw her coming to, he whispered this:

"Felicity! Felicity! Could you help me with my *Hampshire* application, do you think?"

Her eyes snapped open, and perhaps in horror, but not in fear at least, or even loathing. More like horror mixed with pity — condescension, maybe.

Herb kept on with his whispering. "Please. I only want to talk to you. It's a matter of life and death, I promise you. I'm just a kid; I'm absolutely harmless."

The girl looked puzzled, now, also just a bit annoyed.

"Look," she said. "It isn't *really* a matter of life and death; it only *seems* that way, right now. There are a *lot* of first-class colleges out there, some of which aren't even *in* New England. And as far as Hampshire is concerned. . . ."

It took Herb another few minutes to explain to the groggy girl that there was something other than his college application on his mind. He sketched the story in the sort of big bold strokes he favored: a Simple, Honest mayor held Captive and against her will by Crooked Underlings; the records of Corruption locked inside an office Safe; the need to get the Combination to that safe so Righteousness could Triumph over Evil.

"Hmmph," Felicity replied, when she had heard all that. "All well and good. But where do *I* fit in?"

"Well," said Herb, "do you remember — sure you do — about two weeks ago? A little incident when you were lying on the roof and, well, a chicken came and . . . ?"

"You're damn well tootin' I remember!" flared the girl. Her hand moved, underneath the covers. "Talk about fowl play! I got your 'little incident,' all right. I still get *flashbacks* from it! How d'you think *you'd* like to be just lying on your roof, asleep, and have a chicken come along and *sink* her nails into your . . . body? I'm a vegetarian, myself, but still — if I'd had a knife right then, believe me, I'd have cut that chicken into serving pieces *long* before you said *'Bon appetit*, my little *cacciatore.*' "

It took a lot of "I don't blame you"s and a bunch of "That sounds really, really *awful*"s before Herb got the girl calmed down again and listening to reason — and the facts, the full facts of the case.

This time he went into detail: how the Chicken was the honest, simple mayor that he'd been speaking of, and that what Felicity had gone through on the roof was not the mindless piece of pure brutality it might have seemed to be. That, in fact, the scratch marks she had "suffered" were, he was quite sure, eight numbers, and the combination to that office safe.

When Felicity had heard all that, she looked reflective, and she didn't answer right away. She moved her hand again, back out from underneath the covers, and she nibbled on its thumbnail.

"I never even knew there *was* a mayor of Hometown," she began — and then went on to say that she and all the other girls in Kitty Hall were prisoners in there, forced to do the "jobs" they did by threats against their persons and their reputations, both.

Herb didn't know exactly what she meant by that — the "reputations" part — but he kept right on talking anyway, and when he said that perhaps when Danville Pine, the mayor's . . . well, puppeteer and chief tormenter, got his well-deserved comeuppance, maybe lots of things in Hometown would be changed, it turned out that he'd used the magic words.

"Danville Pine!" the girl exclaimed. "Why, he's the lowlife scum who owns this place! *He's* the one who . . ." And away she went.

Her story was an ugly one and all too commonplace, I fear. Danville Pine had somehow laid his rotten paws upon some photographs "a roommate took in college — silly things," and had (of course) threatened to send copies to Felicity's mother, aunts and fiancé, if she didn't . . . you can just *imagine*. What she realized *now* was that those pictures, in all likelihood, were sitting *in* the safe that Herbie and the Big Red Chicken hoped to open with the combination she'd been sitting *on* the last two weeks.

In another minute they had cut a deal: Herb could look for numbers on her bottom, here and now, but if he found them, *she* would get to go with him and be there when the safe was opened, to regain her "property," and so her freedom and respectability.

One moment, Herb was shaking the hand on the

end of the bare arm Felicity had slid out of its hiding place beneath the sheet, and they both were saying "It's a deal," and the next moment she was out of bed and turning every light on in the room — all the lights that possibly might help him see what he was looking for.

And that illumination — all those watts or lumens or what have you — also helped him see that all the rest of her, just then, was just as bare as that one arm had been.

"There!" Felicity exclaimed. "How's that?" She'd just rigged up her desk lamp so that, turned around, it threw a beam of special brightness and intensity directly on the bed.

Herb looked from girl to bed to girl again. If this be Public Service, make the most of it, he told himself. It seemed a pity that this job was going to end — that he couldn't just do *this*, this sort of thing, as a career, forever.

The more he got accustomed to . . . well, looking at the girl, the more he loved to do it — the more he was attracted by, and dazzled by, excited by, the sight of her. Herb wished he *knew* her better, wished that they were friends. Then, perhaps, he wouldn't feel so weird about the feelings he was feeling. If only he could tell her that he *loved* her. . . .

"Great," he said, out loud, at last. And she flopped down, face forward, on the bed.

"Oh, I've got a magnifying glass," she said. "It's on the dresser, there, I think." She wiggled her butt a bit as she said that, perhaps in her impatience and anxiety, he thought. He wondered if he might pretend that he was having trouble finding it — the magnifying glass, that is.

Of course he didn't, though. He got the glass and went to work. In the beginning, it appeared that he was going to get the combination easily. The first four numbers, on the left cheek of her round behind, were clear to what is called "the naked eye": 8, 46, 19, 15. But the others, on the other side, were no-where near as easy.

The boy leaned forward, framed the well-healed scratch marks with his hands. 38 — that was the first one. The panicked Chicken had been scribbling by then, for sure. 23 — that was the second one, no doubt about it, but he'd had to take a hand away and use the glass.

The last two were the hardest. The Chicken must have been, like, slipping off the girl's smooth rump, by then. Herb was kneeling on the bed, his eyes just inches from the . . . information. 4, he thought, and . . . 12. He traced the last two numbers with a finger. He was sure of them; he had it! 8, 46, 19, 15, 38, 23, 4, 12.

And, just as many great explorers all through history supposedly knelt down and kissed the ground they'd landed on, so did our boy (spontaneously and joyfully) bend forward just a little farther and . . . yes, *kiss* this great discovery of his!

"Hey!" the girl cried out. "What's going on back there?" She lifted up her head and turned a bit around to try to see. "Did you get, like, what you need?"

It was then that Herb remembered what he had in his back pocket: the mayoral IOU. He closed his eyes a moment, thinking, contemplating; when he opened them again, she was still there, this gorgeous naked girl, and lying on a bed. He fished the paper out and thrust it toward her face.

Felicity looked puzzled, looked at it, and then at Herb.

"Well — how about it?" croaked the boy, his voice not equal to the question, its momentousness.

"Yeah, how *about* that?" said the girl, either misunderstanding it, and him, or not; he'd never know.

She bounded off the bed. "So. You got it, right?" she said.

"I guess," said Herbie with a sigh, in heat — and some confusion.

It didn't take her long to dress. She put on a rugby shirt, some baggy yellow pants, a lime-green unconstructed jacket with the sleeves turned up and sandals.

This was a *really* odd relationship they had, Herb thought. He'd realized that up till then, he'd never seen her with her clothes on. He thought about the way *Green Mansions* started. ("Now that we are cool, he said . . .")

20
GRAND OPENING

When Herbie had unhooked the Big Red Chicken's office door, he motioned to the girl, Felicity, to go on in ahead of him. Her Honor was awake this time, so naturally she focused on the girl at once, and then her bright round eyes went darting back and forth from girl to boy and back again, alight with eager curiosity.

"We *got* it!" Herb exclaimed, excitedly, before the bird exploded, or could even ink a claw. Then, remembering his manners, "Miss Felicity Tantamount, I'd like to introduce you to our mayor, the Big Red Chicken."

"Your Honor, it's my pleasure," said the girl — sincerely, Herbie thought. She made a little half a curtsy, instead of holding out her hand. A nice touch, that, Herb thought. Like, *sensitive*.

The Chicken nodded cordially, and then she

started scribbling away. When she had finished, and the boy had picked the paper up, the Chicken jerked her head toward the girl, as if to say, "For *her*. Just hand it over."

Herb caught a glimpse of what she'd written, anyway.

"Ime *reely* sorry that I had to uze ur epidurmus for a postit pad," she'd written, showing sensitivity, herself. "Buhleve me, it wuz nuthing pursonul."

"Please, think nothing of it," Felicity replied. "From what I understand, you did us both a favor." And she chuckled in a natural, and friendly and unvengeful way, Herb thought. The fact that she could read the Chicken's writing but did not get rude about the spelling showed the boy two other pluses, too.

Herb then explained exactly why Felicity was there: how Danville Pine had cruelly bent her to his will, and how she hoped to find her property inside the safe, along with all the other evidence of Pine's misdeeds.

While he was laying all that out, Felicity just stood there with her head down, and her hands deep-buried in her jacket pockets, the picture (thought the boy) of both humiliation and . . . a certain high resolve to, well, go on from there to future, finer things.

"Wel, letz get to it," wrote the Chicken, with a head-swing toward the safe.

Herb hadn't written down the numbers, back in Kitty Hall. He felt that they were deeply etched in both his long- and short-term memories. Years from now, he thought, he'd see them still: 8, 46, 19, 15; then 38, and 23, 4, and 12. And even if he didn't

147

see all eight of them, he'd surely recollect the fundamental features they'd been written on. Just as you remember, say, the shape of, well, the Eiffel Tower or your favorite baseball glove, long after you've forgotten what the writing on it may have said.

He rubbed his fingers on his shirtfront, took the dial and twirled it once, for practice. Then he fed the combination into it, slowly, carefully; he was glad to put this aspect of his high school education into useful, real-life practice.

The huge doors opened on his first attempt. That almost made him think that darned old safe had not been locked at all. As big and heavy as it was, it might have been a Hometown native, and so have had a lifelong, deep-dyed prejudice against all you-know-what-ed doors.

"Boy!" said Herb, when he beheld the quasi-mess inside the safe. "It's a good thing Mr. Bon Ballou's not here."

Most of the shelves were stuffed with money, stacks and stacks of the stuff, piled this way and that, with different colored rubber bands around them; they were sorted by denominations, yes, but these were not in any order. Fifties lay on top of twos (yes, twos!), on top of twenties, fives and singles. Herb took out a big fat wad of fifties; tucked inside its rubber band there was a note: "Hot digs! A new Ford Ranger, here!" Clearly, crook or no, this Mr. Danville Pine had kept his Hometown tastes intact.

On the topmost shelf there were some three-ring binders of the kind that younger children sometimes take to school, with cutouts of a lot of Disney characters glued onto them. These were labeled on their spines, as follows: *Protection $*, *Vice, including Rock & Roll*, *Narcotics/Vending Machines*, and *Trash, other than Manure*. And next to the notebooks was a folding file that had the label *Letters, Photographs and Useful, Silly Things — Plus other spreadable Manure*.

The girl looked over at the Chicken and then gestured at the file.

"May I?" she inquired. And the Chicken nodded her assent. Herb shifted slightly in the girl's direction, and he craned his neck a little.

"Hmm," she mused. She was looking at a letter. "Whoa!" She blushed and turned a scrap of parchment over, fast. "I *see*," she nodded at another item in the file.

When she got to the first photograph, she bit her lip and folded it real fast; she did the same with both the next one and the next, and that was all of them. Herb saw enough to know that they were hardly Mother's Day material. The person in the photos with Felicity was possibly another roommate or, if not, a real close friend, as well as something of an acrobat. The folded photos went into her inside jacket pocket.

Herbie had expected that the girl would just relax and look delighted, then. He'd imagined that a clubby little scene, quite possibly, would follow, one in which the two of them — the ones who happened to have hands — would organize the evidence against the foxy Mr. Pine, while Her Honor clucked around and listened to the juicy bits they passed along to her, while writing memos that were full of witty, wise suggestions. Once everything was organized and counted, packed in cardboard boxes that they'd get from somewhere, they would carry down the evidence and lock it in his van.

After that, the three of them would head out to the homey Hometown Diner on the edge of town. There, they'd have a huge and satisfying breakfast that included lots of homefries, and a plate of steaming cornbread for the mayor. Then, stuffed and satisfied, they'd drive the contents of the safe down to the Hometown county sheriff's office and accept his heartfelt and astounded gratitude for about the best-done exposé of governmental crime since Whatsitsface and Whatchacallit.

From that point on, things (meaning, Herb's imaginings) were somewhat vaguer. *Probably*, they'd drop the Big Red Chicken off somewhere, and then the two of them would . . . maybe take a little trip? Like, to the *shore*, or somewhere? Someplace, *any*place, that everybody knew was fun, relaxing, with a lot of privacy. Herb imagined them beside the hotel/motel registration desk. "Mr. and Mrs. Herbert *Hansen*" he'd put down in the register, in case his mother ever stopped there — just dash it off, as if it were a thing he'd done a thousand times. Hopefully they wouldn't bump into a former . . . client of Felicity's. "Dream on," Herb told himself.

". . . hate to do this to you two," the girl was saying when he left the world of fantasy and came back to the present moment, *now*.

Herb stared; he gaped. Felicity had used the gun before; he could just *tell*. She didn't seem afraid of it at all; it didn't look too long or heavy for her hand. She must have had it in her jacket pocket, all that time.

Now she shrugged, almost apologetically, Herb thought.

" *'Carpe diem'* — seize the day," she said, "as our old friend, the poet Horace, said. 'A woman's time of opportunity is short. . . .' That's from the *Lysistrata*. But, either way, this here is dirty money, and I'm a-gonna take it with me. Here's how I excuse myself: It isn't Danville Pine's, nor is it yours, or Hometown's. Maybe, someday, *some* of it would find its way back to a rightful owner, but a lot of it doesn't even *have* a rightful owner. *Some* of it is really mine, in fact. Money that I earned for Pine, the hard way." She made a little gesture with the gun.

"What I'm saying is," she said, "this money is a springboard to a brand-new life for me, a long, long way from here. And so it's going with me, almost all of it. And you two aren't going to stop it."

Herb didn't get a lot of pleasure from the next half hour. Some, a little bit, but not a lot. First, she made him pack the money, most of it — she left one wad of fives and one of singles — into plastic liners of the sort you put in wastebaskets. While he did that, she composed a note that said *about* how many dollars had been in the safe when they had opened it, and also said that she, "Miss X," had "liberated" almost all of it. That was so, she said, the cops and IRS would know how much that "rotted Pine" had stolen and extorted and evaded paying taxes on, she'd bet.

Then, she made Herb cut a length of cord from off the office blinds. She used that, swiftly and convincingly, to tie his hands behind his back, *and* to the handle of the massive safe's main door.

151

"Those notebooks and the file, together with my note, are evidence enough to put that swine away for good, and then some," said the girl. "And, having firsthand knowledge of her . . . well, *dexterity*, I'm sure Her Honor will be able to untie those knots I made before the janitors — or Pine — come in. I'm really sorry, both of you; I know you'll be all right."

She looked over at the mayor. "I never had a Chicken for a friend, before," she said. "If I can get a ballot — absentee — I'll vote for you for reelection, that's a promise. Assuming that you want to run again, of course. I kinda hope you do."

And then she came right up to Herb, where he stood cinched against the safe.

"I don't even know your name," she said. "But if you tell me what it is, I'll write to Hampshire for you. I'd like to tell them you're a hero, *and* a gentleman."

"Herbie Hansen — *Hertzman*," Herbie muttered. He didn't even know if he'd apply to Hampshire, but he didn't see how it could hurt to be a hero in a file in the Admissions Office there.

She made a note of what he'd said, and put a hand on Herbie's cheek, then leaned and kissed him on the mouth, letting all her attributes press up against his body for a moment. It was, he thought, a meaningful occasion, in a way.

"*Ciao*, now," were her final words to them, and she was out the door, the plastic bags in hand. They heard the little hook drop into place.

21
BUMMERS

"I can't get *over* Kitty Hall!" said Ses deBarque. She shook with glee, as usual, and smelled, perhaps, of frangipani, which might have been the flower on her black Hawaiian shirt. "I mean, I've been around forever, but I've never heard of any cat house with a *sign*, before. Not on any *Church* Street, in a *Home-town*, anyway." She fluffed her dark blonde curls above one ear, and seemed to think about her last remark. "Nevada, *maybe*," she appended, "but Nevada can't be blamed for being different. They're always testing nuclear devices there."

"I just didn't want to think about it," Herbie said. He shook his head and laughed, remembering. "Having it be what it was just seemed like such a bummer." He and Ses had talked about "the Home-town caper," as he'd dared, just once, to call it in his mind — but not out loud, of course. He'd given her a lot more details, this time. And he'd shown her the small silver-plated loving cup with *Hometown Hero* on it that the Chicken had presented to him, once the sheriff planted Pine inside the local lockup.

The two of them were sitting on the second floor of Castles in the Air, in Ses's living quarters. When Herb had gotten back from Hometown, and she had asked him if he'd like to come on up, "for figs and flummery," he'd been delighted to accept. The figs turned out to all be members of the Newton tribe; he didn't know if "flummery" was what they washed them down with. If so, it was a fairly nice cold drink that tasted sort of like cream soda, only flat.

Herb had never been on Castles's second floor before, and he'd been knocked darn close to sockless by the room that they were sitting in — her living room, he guessed it was.

The space was huge and circular, the ceiling very high; what they were in, in fact, appeared to be a canvas *tent*, suspended from the castle's ceiling. In shape, it would have been a half a sphere, or slightly more, except that it had walls that came straight down, the last eight feet. But the most amazing thing about it was: The inside of the tent was *painted*, not just in a single color, like off-white, but as if it were a scene, and you were looking out at *landscapes*, *vistas* and *horizons*, topped by an enormous bright blue dome of sky, with just a few white, puffy clouds.

The overall effect was very much like sitting on a lovely mountaintop; all around were these delightful views, views of other mountains, rolling hills and valleys full of groves, with rushing rivers running through them and, on one side in the distance, dark unfathomed ocean with, he thought, some islands in it. They were sitting in the center of the room, where nice, low furniture was grouped for conversation, relaxation and enjoying sweet, refreshing drinks with cookies (Herb was thinking), and the views. It had also crossed his mind that Ses deBarque was much — *way* — farther out than any of his parents' friends, and that John Jaspers, if he'd done this paint job, simply had to be a modern master.

"You know what else I still don't want to think about?" Herb said.

"Maybe." Sesame sat back and smiled, her head just slightly tilted to one side.

"There's *two* things," Herbie said, and smiled himself. Mysteriously, he hoped. More or less above it all.

He'd noticed something in the last half hour. He was more relaxed, right then, with Ses deBarque, than he had ever been with any woman, maybe any *person*, other than his mom. When he was ten-eleven, right in there, he'd been bosom-roughhouse-buddies with one Harvey Parker, Junior, better known as "Porksome." That was different, though. It seemed to him that he could really *talk* to Ses, that he could tell her *anything*.

"Maybe I'll tell you one of them," said Herb.

"Only if you want to," she replied.

"Well," he said, "remember when Felicity pulled out the gun and said that she was going to take the money?"

"Yup." She nodded.

"I don't think I would've stopped her if I could've," Herbie said. "That's the kind of person that I am."

"Oh?" said Sesame.

"Uh-huh," said Herb. "It really sucks, but that's the truth. People never hesitate to do minor damage to school property when I'm around. You know what else they do? They over-claim insurance when their cars get broken into, and they tell me all about it."

"Hmm," said Sesame. "How come?"

"Because they know I'll say it isn't any of my business," Herbie said. "Like I said — that's the kind of person that I am. *I'll* say they aren't really hurting anybody. And of course they know I want all of them to like me. Which, of course, they don't."

"But now you realize all that really *bothers* you," she said. "That stuff."

"Right," said Herb. "*I* bother me. And you know who'd never go along with stuff like that? Who never would have, ever?"

"No, who?" said Sesame. Possibly she did, and possibly she didn't, Herbie thought.

"The Big Red Chicken," said the boy. "Need I say more?"

"She's a plucky one, all right," said Ses.

Herb looked at her suspiciously, but Ses deBarque just stared straight back at him, the picture of a wide-eyed, friendly innocent. When he didn't go on talking, she took a big deep breath, and sighed.

"No man is an island, eh?" she said. "Not even Simon and Garfunkel." The boy looked puzzled, so she said, "Just kidding."

Herbie nodded. "Sometimes I wish I *was* an island," he opined. "Islands never have to worry. Islands have girls crawling all over them. They don't have to think about . . . well, *anything*."

"Let me guess, like — what?" said Ses, and she

was smiling. "Let me guess the *second* thing that you don't want to think about."

"Feel free," said Herbie. "Be my guest." He wondered if she would. He didn't think she would. Or, actually, he thought she maybe *could*, but wouldn't.

"You don't want to think about what *didn't* happen with Felicity," she said. "Correct?" She let out one of her most juicy chortles yet. "How you *didn't* end up at the luxurious Elysian Fields Motel on the virtually uninhibited Ecstatic Isles with her. How you *didn't*, as they used to say, get your ashes hauled."

She paused and looked at him; he kept his face as straight as possible.

"Come on. Provide a one-word answer, please," she said. "Is the teacher right or wrong?"

Herb had to laugh. Laugh and nod and sort of gurgle "*Right*." She had said it, after all, not him; *he* didn't have to be embarrassed. But were they going to talk about it? Apparently they were.

". . . don't get, then," she was saying, "is why you didn't go for Uncle Babbo's deal. He was promising that kind of stuff, galore."

Herb tried to think. Had he gone into all of that with Sesame, everything that Babbo'd said? He guessed he must have.

"That was different, though," he said. "The girls that Babbo meant, they were into surfaces, like *hair*. Chances are, they wouldn't even get to know me, first." He was staring at the floor between his feet.

"Well, it doesn't seem to me," said Ses, "that either Zippy or Felicity were what I'd call 'old friends.' "

Herbie made a small, despairing gesture with his hand. "I know, I know," he said. "But both of them at least had, like, a little reason to look up to me — for who I *was*, I mean. Before, with girls, it's been as if I didn't . . . well, *you* know, *exist*."

The boy looked up at Sesame, again.

"Maybe this is crazy," he continued, "but what I keep thinking is that once I've *done* it, and I know about that kind of thing, then maybe I can just relax, have a normal life, like other guys. Have *girlfriends* that I do it with, the way that everybody else does. Now, I seem like such a total *doofus*, usually. . . ."

Sesame deBarque stood up and did a kind of little dance, all by herself — dipping, swirling, pirouetting, just around a quarter of the room, singing softly to herself. When she stopped, she was behind Herb's chair; she touched him on the shoulder.

"I think I understand the way you feel," she said. "But let this wise old woman tell you something, possibly important. The danger of your plan is that you end up thinking *doing* it is most of what there is *to* do, with girls. That was the Big Red Chicken's barnyard boyfriend's problem, of course. I've known a lot of guys like that, down through the ages; I even married one or two of them, you want to know the truth." She sighed, and then she laughed. "Luckily for me, they died," she said. "Of course."

"Have you had kids, yourself?" asked Herb, looking for a minor change of subject. He wasn't in the least surprised to hear that Ses had been a widow, more than once. Somehow, she *looked* as if she'd had a lot of husbands.

She roared with laughter at his question, who knows why.

"Hell, yes," she said, "a ton of 'em. And every one a treasure. I'm the only mother in the history of the world who's never had to worry. That's the junior member of the clan, right there — destiny's tot, herself." She pointed at a photo on the table, next to her old seat.

Herb had noticed it, before. It was a photo of a girl about his age. She looked a lot like Ses, take away a lot of confidence and much experience, especially around the mouth and eyes. Of course Herb liked her . . . general appearance (as he put it to himself).

"Does she live at Castles, here?" he asked, off-handedly.

"Sometimes," said Ses. "She travels quite a lot. E.T., I call her, sometimes. Her father is, or was, a Spaniard of some sort." She didn't sound as if this was a subject she would welcome further questions on.

Herb nodded. "Oh, I see," he muttered. He didn't know what else to say, at that point.

Ses did, though. She was the type who always would, he thought.

"Well — how ya feeling now, about another spin?" she asked. And winked.

"Oh, I really want to take one," Herbie said. "But maybe not right now, if that's all right. I'd like to more or less digest this one another day or two. But how about on Thursday? Would that be possible? Another spin on Thursday?"

"I don't see why not," said Sesame. "You can come right after school?" He nodded. "Perfect."

When he stood up, she slipped a hand under his arm again, and held it as they strolled toward the door.

"You know," she said to him, "I think I'm going

to send that Sandy Rex a five-pound box of truffles."
She nodded to herself. "That little cutie."

When Herbie got back to his house, on that late
afternoon, he found that preparations for a cookout
were in progress. He knew his father had, as usual,
begun the process with a small wood fire in his rustic
fieldstone grill, and had added charcoal later. The
coals were close to cooking-ready when the boy arrived, and steaks were on a platter, close at hand.
Ben Hertzman liked to say he was a "purist," when
it came to outdoor cooking. He only used old-
fashioned hardwood charcoal, no briquets, and
wouldn't touch those liquid firestarters. "I may eat
a peck of dirt before I die," he'd say, "but no one's
gonna make me wash it down with distillations of
petroleum. You tell me you can't taste the stuff in
food, and I'll tell *you* you need to get your buds
examined."

"Hey!" he called to Herb that day, when he
caught sight of him. "Come say hello to Mr. Gardenside. I promised him a piece of beef so tender,
tasty and delicious that he'll think he's at Four Sea-
sons — or Five Spices, anyway. Ira, this is my son
Herbert. Herbie, tell him what the relatives all say
about my steaks."

"Hello, sir," Herbie said to the legendary Mr.
Ira Gardenside, who was eighty-seven and his father's boss. He knew that this was some occasion.
Mr. Gardenside had never been to Herbie's parents' house before, but he *had* been to the White
House — fourteen times, spread out through nine
administrations.

"Dad's steaks are famous from here to Wissahickon," Herbie said. "He's a legend in his own time. Indisputably the best."

"I like that in a man," said Mr. Gardenside, dapper in a double-breasted blazer and white flannels, an ascot at his neck. He was absentmindedly (or not, perhaps) pouring bourbon whiskey in a squatty glass that also had three ice cubes in it. When the glass was almost full, he stopped and said, "Oh-oh," and put the bottle down.

Herb already knew, thanks to his father, that when Mr. Gardenside was *his* age, he'd held down six jobs at once. He was a newsboy and a milkman in the morning, driving his own horse-drawn cart at 5 A.M. In the afternoon, he mowed a bunch of lawns, or raked some leaves, or shoveled walks — *while* exercising different people's dogs. And in the evening he both baby-sat *and* tutored either French or long division. Now, he was president of his own company, a director of eight others and, the year before, had played the lead in *Fiddler on the Roof* and goalie on a local water polo team. There were rumors that he planned to run for Congress; Herbie's father thought that was a neat idea.

"So, young man, I understand you're in your senior year in high school. Good for you," said Mr. Ira Gardenside. He filled his mouth with bourbon and said, "Ahh!"

"Thank you very much, sir," Herbie said.

"You have a game plan, yet?" asked Mr. Gardenside. "I'd say you're at about the most exciting time of life there is. All those possibilities in front of you, for you to pick and choose from. Real estate, investment banking, mergers, acquisitions, energy — there's untold fortunes still, just waiting to be

161

made." He did a little further whistle-wetting.

"Yes," said Herb. "It's an exciting time, all right."

"So — what direction is your thinking running in?" asked Mr. Gardenside. "What plans and schemes, what dreams, are yours, young man? Oh, how I'd love to be in *your* shoes, at this point in history." Pause. Ingestion of libation. "Ahh!"

"Well," said Herb, feeling for the first time in his life that he had something he could say, in answer to that question, "I'm toying with the possibility of public service."

"Public service?" The old man's eyes were clear; his speech, however, might have been a little slurred. "That wouldn't be too bad, I guess. But let me make a small suggestion to you, something that you maybe wouldn't think of, otherwise. You want to know what I would go for, supposin' I was in your shoes, right now? The best idea that I could give you, free of charge? C'mere."

He pulled Herb two-three steps away from where Ben Hertzman stood, long fork in hand. The boy looked back and saw his father beaming; they'd watched a movie called *The Graduate* together.

"I'm only going to say this once," whispered Mr. Gardenside, a merry twinkle in his eyes, now. He licked his lips and Herb could see that he was concentrating very hard, making sure he got what he was going to say exactly right. Then, with a rush of bourbon breath, he whispered once again, and quite distinctly: "*Mixed nude synchronized swimming.*"

After which, he suddenly sat down — ker-plunk! — the victim of a *massive* heart attack, from which he died, in seconds. Bummer.

When the hubbub occasioned by the phone calls

and the ambulance and having to take the steaks off and then, later, adding a lot more charcoal before putting them back on again had subsided, his father asked the boy what Mr. Gardenside's last words had been.

Herbie looked at him, all blue-eyed innocence.

"He said that I should follow, like, my *bliss*," he said.

"Whatever *that* may mean," his father said, sounding, Herbie thought, quite disappointed.

22
THURSDAY

The Thursday Herbie headed back to Castles in the Air had started pretty well, as Thursdays go. The shock of Mr. Gardenside's "untimely coronary accident" (as Herbie's mother chose to call it) had worn off by then, and all three Hertzmans had resumed their (so-called) normal lives.

Herb's father'd moved into a different office with a much, much better view, and original artwork on the walls instead of photographs of factories and beavers. His mother'd finally bought the breakfast food that had, in laboratory tests, improved the hang-time of a group of adolescent male orangutans. And Herb himself had stopped blaming himself for *not* blaming himself for being in some way responsible for "I.G." 's death.

In school that day, Herb had handled seven tricky academic fungoes flawlessly, and helped a girl whose name he didn't know retrieve a Nerf ball from atop a row of lockers.

"Wow, you're really *tall*," she'd said to him, and smiled in such a way he had to wonder if she meant much more than that.

Later on, when he had barely started on the walk to Castles, he'd come upon two grade-school kids about the age of nine or ten, both busy writing on the sidewalk with some sticks of orange chalk. Just as Herbie reached them, they finished writing this:

Pee on Omalley

"Hey! Be nice, you guys!" he said to them. Much to his surprise, they dropped their writing tools and ran.

Herb picked up the orange chalk and looked again at what they'd written. With the help of crossings-out and carets, he made their message read:

PÉe ŏn THE Ø'Ħalley

and continued on his way.

At the four-way stop where Sunset Strip and Ginseng Lane collide and cross each other, though, Herb found some items he was sure had not been there before. First of all, there was a large white Cadillac, sitting on a patch of public lawn. And leaning up against its shiny side was an instruction: TAKE A CHANCE — $5! Next to *that* there was a round white metal table with a striped umbrella, open, sticking out of it. Behind the table sat a red-faced man. He wore a wide-brimmed planter's hat, a red bandanna knotted 'round his neck, dark trousers and a light gray frock coat.

"How you doin', sonny?" he asked Herb. And, "Isn't she a beauty, now?"

"I suppose," said Herb. He laid an honest stare right on the car. "Though frankly, for myself, I'd rather have a compact. They're a lot more fuel-efficient, plus I think I'd look a little foolish dressed like *this*" — he gestured at his jeans and western shirt and leather vest — "driving in a car like *that*."

"Please-please-please-*please*," the red-faced man replied, holding up a palm. "Let's not be dull, all right? You win the car, you *sell* the car. You take the money and you get yourself a decent suit of clothes, and any sort of *compact* car you want, some fancy luggage and a pinky ring. Of course if you feel foolish *then*, riding in your little Yugo or whatever, don't blame me." He laughed, but not unpleasantly.

"So, take a chance, why don't you, sport?" he said. "I've only got one left. Later on today, we'll have the drawing and — hey, hey! — *you* could be a *winnah*!" The man appeared delighted by that prospect.

Herb didn't really mind it, either, but he still was cautious.

"How many chances are there?" he inquired. "Five bucks would darn near clean my wallet out, right now. So, what's the odds against my winning?"

The red-faced man said, "Well, uh, not *too* bad at all. I mean, really pretty good, in fact, as these things go. Or maybe even better." His face had gotten slightly redder.

"I believe," said Herbie quietly, "you *have to* say. I'm pretty sure that there's a law about that. It was put in to protect the consumer from his own irrational hopefulness — or that's my understanding, anyway."

"All right, all right, I'll tell you," said the red-faced man. "If you buy this last remaining chance, you only have one chance in three of winning. I've sold two other chances to four other parties — one to me, myself, and I. So, chances are you *wouldn't* win. The *odds* are that you wouldn't. *Probably* the other buyer or myself will win."

"What?" said Herb. "You're telling me you're going to raffle off this twenty-thirty-thousand dollar car by selling just *three* tickets? You're going to risk that car for fifteen dollars?"

"Hell, why shouldn't I?" the man replied. "Possibly I'll win the raffle, which'll mean I get to keep the car *and* all the money that I got from you (if you decide to play), and from my other customer. And even if I don't, I've got no great affection for this car. I've never had the time to learn to drive, and once you've sat down in the back of one block-long white Cadallic, you've pretty much sat down in all of 'em."

"You mean, you actually don't *want* this car?" said Herb. "Then why not sell it, like you said?" He gave a little chuckle. "You could get yourself some jeans, a nice new pair of running shoes, and possibly a business of your own — a little candy store, or something."

"*Please*." The red-faced man held up his hand again. "I used to own a candy store. And then eight *hundred* candy stores, in fact. I made a fortune selling candy. Then I made another more enormous fortune selling candy *stores*. Now I'm into something new: acting like a damned old fool — or so my children say. Tomorrow I may give someone a year's supply of Christmas trees, or build some natives-only, low-cost housing in Vermont, or Northern California, so that local people can afford to go on living there." He shook his head. "Now, please, go on and take a chance. Think how good I'll feel if I can put a total-stranger kid behind the wheel of his first car."

"Well, if you're going to put it *that* way," Herbie said. "And anyway, Mother's Day is — what? — next month? I'll bet my mom would be surprised to get a Cadillac instead of candy."

He gave the red-faced man five singles.

"The drawing ought to be in maybe half an hour," said the man. "Just tell me where you'll be, and if you win, you'll find this baby parked out front, with all the necessary papers in the glove compartment."

Herb explained that he'd be at Castles in the Air for probably at least an hour, but he also gave the man his home address, in case of any foul-ups. In turn, the red-faced man made Herbie take his card, on which he'd written: "Rec'd, from Herbert Hertzman, Esq., 5 simoleons for 1 great chance in the Big Caddy raffle."

His name was printed on the card, but he also signed the thing, quite clearly, with a flourish: *Francis Farmer*.

* * *

When Herb arrived at Castles in the Air, Sesame deBarque was out on the front lawn again, but sitting on a folding stool, this time, before an easel, with a palette in her hand. From the way that she was facing, Herb assumed that she was painting Castles's portrait, and that proved to be the case.

"Boy, that's really *great*," he said, when he was close enough to see what she had done. "I didn't know you were an artist!"

In fact, the picture that she'd made looked mighty like a masterpiece, to him. Not only had she gotten all the shapes and colors right, but also she had managed to reflect the *spirit* of the place, its enigmatic joyfulness (as Herbie thought of it). Clearly, she was almost finished with the painting. There was only one small section left to do, just where the driveway curves up to the drawbridge, right outside the big front door.

"Yes," she said. "It came out pretty well." She cocked her head and looked at what she'd done some more, and smiled. She had a black beret on, worn at quite a jaunty angle, and a yellow smock that didn't have a single dab of paint on it.

"Maybe it's beginner's luck," she added. "Thing is, I saw this hat and smock right in the window of an art store, and I had to have 'em. Don't I look great? I got this other junk to go along with **th**em." She gestured at the easel and her paint box and the palette. "And I thought, well, what the heck." She'd gotten up, by then. "But, anyway, let's go," she said. "I got some peanut brittle on the same excursion, and I'm looking forward to your spin."

"Hey, wait," said Herb. "Why don't you go ahead

and finish, first? I'm not in all that big a hurry."

"No, no," she said. "I've got some time right now. Fact is, that I *can't* finish, yet. I want to get the car in there, and it hasn't been delivered."

"Car?" said Herb, suspiciously. "What car?"

"It's a humongous, big, white Cadillac," she said. "You saw it coming over, right? The raffle car?"

"Sure I saw it," Herbie said. "*I* bought the other chance. But you're already sure you won?"

"Not *sure*," said Ses deBarque. "Especially not now. But, yeah, I had a feeling, like you get, sometimes. What I figured was, that Upwardlimobile of mine has got an awful lot of spatiotemporal miles on it. I thought I'd kind of like to let it end its days as just a normal car, going on real roads, getting into gridlock, taking trips to concerts, rubbing fenders with some other vans. Then, I could modify the Caddy, turn it into 'mobile II." She shrugged. "But now, with you a player — well, I just don't know. Maybe I won't win it, after all. Maybe you will — or the geezer. I guess we'll have to wait and see."

"Well, I don't really *want* it," Herbie quickly said. "I'd love it if the Upwardlimobile could just take it easy and enjoy itself. So, maybe if *I* win the Cadillac, I'll give the thing to *you*!" That thought made Herb excited. "You've been so great to me, and anyway, my mom's already got this real nice Pontiac."

"All right, all *right* already." Ses laughed and dropped a hand down on his shoulder. "Leave us not forget what we are here for, right? I've got a wheel in there that needs a spin, real bad. That's more important than some silly status symbol, right?"

They crossed the drawbridge and went into the

castle. The peanut brittle, in a bowl, was right there in the hall; they both had some, Herb quite a handful. He also looked around. He listened, hoping that he'd hear some rock and roll, or something.

But there weren't any sorts of sounds.

"Um," he said, and "Well." He shrugged. "Just wondering. Your daughter home from school? I was thinking . . . I've been taking up a lot of time — *your* time — when she might want to talk to you, or something. So, I was thinking, maybe if I just said 'Hi,' and told her that I didn't mea — "

"Oh," Ses cut him off, "*she* doesn't mind. You kidding? She likes it when there's something different going on, a little action. Like your trips and all. She eats all that stuff up."

"So — I shouldn't try to talk to her?" said Herb, pausing by the door to the great hall. If this daughter was enjoying hearing all about his trips, his "action," he wasn't sure that meeting her would be a good idea at all. Probably, she'd bust out laughing at the sight of him.

"Maybe not right now," said Ses, but not as if the whole idea was hopeless.

They reached the wheel, the Winner's Circle. Herbie put his hand on it, and looked at all the different categories. It struck him that they *all* were *interesting* — even Crime — Organized or not, which he had learned he didn't want to do. He had a thought (a flash, an inkling) that he could work in any one of those careers, *or any other one*. And that what he was *really* trying to find was which jobs would be *fun* for him, the only Herbie Hertzman in the universe, a guy that he was still discovering, and possibly (new thought!) *creating*.

171

Herb gave that wheel a healthy spin.

It came up Health Care. Fascinating.

Ses deBarque agreed, apparently. "Now there's *another* doozie," she opined. She started pushing buttons on her console.

Herb wondered if this meant he'd be involved, somehow, with AIDS, which he had heard described as Public Health Care Problem Number One. Getting AIDS would be about the biggest bummer he could think of. But so would *having* AIDS, he thought. People who had AIDS were people like himself, he thought, but more unlucky. That was the only way to think about it. It really was that simple.

"Hmm," said Sesame, looking at the little card that the machine provided her. "This should be a *very* interesting turn."

Herb felt he shouldn't ask for information at this point — for any sort of preview. What was going to happen, would; better just to let events unfold. Health, both good and bad, was everywhere (like Crime, he guessed). He might go anywhere and have to do with anyone, even Tyree Toledano, if there truly was a person by that name. So be it. They started walking toward the tower, he and Ses.

"There's something that I want to ask you," Herbie said. "Not about this spin. It's more of a general question."

"So, ask away," said Ses. "Liberty Hall, and all that rot."

"Well, I've been wondering," said Herb. "How many trips do clients take? Like, on the average."

"I really couldn't say," she said. "I don't pay attention to that kind of stuff. You know what I mean:

like scores, and medians, and averages. That's all a lot of bush-wa. Everybody's different, thank the Lord, so why compare so much? And everybody's got a magic number: One. That's the one they get it on. You see?"

"Um," said Herb. He laughed. Get it? Get *what*? He thought he *maybe* got it, but he wasn't sure.

He climbed into the pleasantly familiar van. It had a certain fragrance he would miss, when he stopped taking trips (he thought). When he was sure he'd gotten it.

23
"SHALIMAR SLOAN,"
SHE SAID . . .

When the Upwardlimobile had settled to a stop, Herb stretched and yawned and looked expectantly across the van, waiting for the door to open, or *be* opened, either one. It didn't and it wasn't; time dragged by. He sat and fidgeted for at least a half an hour. It was like when he was eight, and waiting for his mother to get off the phone and take him to the pool, or — who knows! — *Disneyland*, or *Europe*. At last he couldn't sit there any longer. There were discoveries just waiting to be made, he thought, falling trees that needed him to hear them, unseen blossoms that might never bloom without him.

He raised himself up off the seat and, crouching, took the steps that brought him to the sliding door. Then, after a last small hesitation, he reached out and opened it.

Of course it was a different setting, not the tundra

or a parking lot. They, the 'bile and he (he'd right away jumped out of it), were in a pleasant, yet exotic, courtyard, parked on one side of a flagstone walk that went around the space. Neatly tended flower beds were in the center of the court, bordering a statue; they also ran along outside the walk, between it and the building that surrounded everything. On one end of the courtyard was an arch that seemed to open on a street; at the other end, a big, red, wooden door gave access to the building. Straight overhead, the sky was very blue.

From an open window on the second floor there came a rhythmic drumbeat and the sound of something being chanted, not in English or in Spanish, not for fun. And, from time to time, as if to serve as punctuation, or to keep the chanters mellow, there was a gong sound.

Shuffling along the walk in front of him were half a dozen very senior individuals, all men. They all were dressed alike, in dark red robes and sandals, and they muttered to themselves — a little whiningly, Herb thought — while moving in the same direction, clockwise. Herb was pretty sure that these were monks, or priests, or devotees, who had their minds on higher things. None of them had any hair to speak of, and their concentrated calm suggested to the boy that stuff like sex was not a big concern of theirs. They were living in a zone that Herb was not familiar with, in terms of personal experience.

From time to time, one of the old men would stop and face the statue in the middle of the court, and bow, and whine a little louder. The statue kept on sitting; it was of a man — clean-shaven, empty-eyed and poker-faced, bare-chested. It could have been

Lee Iacocca, younger, without glasses, add a funny hat, but Herb was pretty sure it wasn't. Given the religious atmosphere, the chances are the statue was a Buddha. It paid the same attention to the boy as everybody else did.

Adaptable as ever and anxious to fit in — and also to leave the courtyard — Herb stepped out into a gap between two monks. Under his breath and just a bit complainingly, he spoke the first twelve words of Bellow's novel, *Herzog* ("If I am out of my mind, it's all right with me . . ."), while he shuffled at the speed of traffic till he reached the open arch that led out to the street. Then, with a small, respectful nod, he exited the courtyard. He was in the open, on the street.

Herb looked around, but *all* around, not totally surprised, considering the sorts of things he'd seen and heard inside, but totally agape, impressed. He was standing in a town, or possibly a tiny city, built on a small, treeless knoll on a large treeless plain, surrounded by the highest mountains he (or *anyone*, he'd bet) had ever seen.

"Chomolungma, Kangchenjunga, Nanda Devi." Herbie rummaged through the mental knapsack where he kept his Himalayan word supply. *When in Rome* . . . and all that jazz. He felt like President Kennedy at the Berlin Wall. "Levi Strauss," he added, knowing those two words were understood, and spoken, everywhere.

He decided that the street he was on was Market Street. On either side of it were shops and stalls; some vendors had their goods laid out on blankets on the ground. Herb checked his pockets, found a dollar thirty-five, American; he figured that made him a browser, only. And so, hands clasped behind his back, he started strolling down the middle of the street, hoping that his face reflected any three of these: ease, good humor, admiration, only modest means, a total lack of chauvinism. All in one neat package called "experienced adventurer."

At once he saw he was a great deal taller than the local people all around him, but that didn't seem to matter much, to anyone. No one gawked at him, or tried to sell him goods or services, or relatives. A lot of men and women, both, wore running shoes, not always in their size, or in real great condition; by and large, they smiled and laughed a lot, particularly the ones who hung around the stalls where cups of something could be bought and drunk. Herb smiled at everything they had for sale, and said "Real *nice*!" a lot of times. He looked at bolts of different-colored cloth, woolen socks and woven belts, straw placemats and badminton sets, felt shoulder bags and wooden bowls and backscratchers, beads of many different sizes, and some silver jewelry that certainly included nose rings, going by the noses of some women that he saw.

When he'd gone the length of Market Street, he turned onto another, wider thoroughfare. Here, clearly, were the local tourist traps, the shops and businesses that catered to whatever foreigners might be in town for any arcane purposes. Many of the buildings here had signs on them in English, such as Bank and Barber, but the grandest of them was The Great Couloir Hotel, which Herbie thought was almost equal to the monastery, size-wise. Next to it was the Because It's There Cafe and Restaurant, while right across the street there was a clothing store (Darjeeling Traders) and an Abida's Fitness Center — Running Shoes and Croissants Fresh Hot Daily Ice Cream.

Herb headed for Abida's, fingering his change, like worry beads.

Three local youngsters, boys who looked to be no more than ten, were right outside it, eating gooey-covered ice cream out of paper cups with plastic spoons. As Herb approached, he noticed they were staring at his Reeboks in the way — adoringly — that kids back home would stare at, say, their parents' credit cards.

"Man, you American?" squeaked one of them.

"Sure am," said Herb. Then, diplomatically, "You speak great English."

"Be cool," the second boy chimed in. "Peace, love, good vibes, nonviolent change."

"Oh, wow," said Herb, adaptably.

"You know our teacher?" said the third boy. "Mister Dhubi-dhubi-dhu?"

"We all good deadheads, man," said number one.

"That's great," said Herb, who'd never figured out what deadheads *did*. Once again, he touched the money in his pocket. He wondered if he possibly might change the subject.

"So, here's a question for you," he continued. "How much might a sundae be up here — in dollars *or* piasters?"

The three boys looked at one another. They conferred among themselves, speaking very fast and mostly not in English. Herb was pretty sure he caught a "sundae" jammed in there, along with "might," and (he was pretty sure) "piaster." Finally, they all nodded; general agreement had been reached.

"Nixon fulla blooey," the third boy said to him, and smiled delightedly.

Herb nodded vaguely, muttered, "Thanks." He could go along with that, all right, but thought he'd be a little cautious when it came to speaking out on politics. After all, he didn't even know the *name* — not to mention the alignment — of the country he was in. Clutching his small bunch of money, still, he started toward Abida's door.

Before he reached it, it flew open. Someone came rushing out, but stopped in front of him, as if he were a traffic light. It took him just a moment to be sure; she was a girl. She was wearing an eclectic outfit if he'd ever seen one, and she held a large vanilla cone.

Her lower half was purely western, starting from New Balance running shoes and working up to baggy painters' pants. Above the waist, most of her was covered by a sort of tablecloth she'd draped around her head and shoulders and which hung down to that waist, where it got belted. This was a shorter version of the robe that all the local men and women wore, except that theirs just started at their shoulders. Perhaps to hold this shawl of hers around her head, the girl had on a well-worn cowboy hat, jammed over it, and her eyes hid out behind a pair of glacier glasses, real dark gray ones.

For all of that, she looked, to Herb, in some small, unspecific way, familiar. Apparently that went both ways.

"Herbie Hertzman," was the way she greeted him.

179

"Yes," he said, not totally surprised.

"Shalimar Sloan," she said, and changed the cone from one hand to the other. Then she wiped the empty one on her right thigh and offered it to him. They shook.

"I'm pleased to meet you," Herbie said. Her name set zero bells a-ringing.

"We've still got quite a trip ahead of us," she said. "Our final destination's way up there." She pointed toward the set of mountains to the right. "And time is of the essence, as they say. We'd better get ourselves in gear and hit the yak-track."

Herb was looking where she'd pointed. He couldn't tell, of course, just where on "way up there" she meant. It looked as if they'd have to first go down a ways, and then back up, and then repeat that sort of thing again, another time or two. In other words, they faced not just a "walk," or even, as she'd said, a "trip"; it seemed to him that she was talking "major expedition."

"Why?" he said. "Why *are* we going way up there? And what's the rush?"

She pressed her pointer finger to her temple, wiggled that same thumb a time or two. "Idiot," she told him, speaking of and to herself, he was quite certain. "How *could* he know?" And then to him, "I'm sorry."

She touched him on the forearm. It was a little, gentle, pacifying touch that more than did the job. Herb smiled and nodded: Hey, okay. She took a couple real quick hits on her vanilla cone. He thought that she had one terrific-looking tongue. A woman's eyes might be the windows of her soul,

Herb thought, but her tongue was like the maitre d' of her entire restaurant.

"We're going there to meet a man," she said. "A teacher and a scientist of sorts — some say a saint, but that's debatable. He's weird, all right. He runs an ashram way up there that has a modern lab in it, and if our information's right, he's made a major scientific breakthrough. Something on the order of a cancer cure, or possibly an AIDS vaccine; we're not exactly sure, except we know it's big and that we want it."

She tilted her head to one side and took a big, long slurp around the top rim of the cone, to keep the thing from dripping.

" 'We'?" said Herb. "You don't mean you and I."

"Well, yes," she said. "I *hope* you want it, too. You're into Health Care, right?" He nodded. "But lots of other people, too. We're acting on behalf of . . . well, of certain agencies that'd like to see this stuff — whatever it may be — become available to everybody everywhere who needs it. Without regard to who or where or what they can afford."

"That sounds terrific," Herbie said. It seemed to him that maybe Ses had punched him in a winner, this time. "And you want to hurry up and get this stuff, so's the people that we're acting for can start alleviating untold amounts of human misery as soon as possible!"

"Well, that, too," she said. "But there's a second reason we should ditch the dawdles — two of them in fact. We're pretty sure there are a pair of other expeditions, either in the area or soon to be. One of them is Japanese, the other is American. Both of them are representing huge consortiums, major corporations who would hope to share enormous profits from this product. If our information's right, they're both prepared to lay at least a billion on the table — cash, small bills, no plastic." She licked across the summit of the cone, from one side to the other.

"While we," said Herb, "will offer . . ."

"Nothing," said the girl. "Or nothing in the way of that which men call cold and hard. Our appeal will be to Baba's . . . reputation. To his better side — his saintliness, his spirit of fair play, his love of all mankind." She grinned. "Although we may remind him of Pearl Harbor and the IRS."

Herb wrinkled up his brow, not wholly sure that he was following.

The girl bit off a chunk of ice cream, and then sucked on it a bit, before she swallowed. Then she took a last, long lick across the slightly flattened top of it and held the cone toward Herb.

"You want the rest of this?" she said to him.

Herb felt his heart race in his chest. He knew that that was silly — kids often share an ice-cream cone with other kids — but there you are.

"Sure," he said. And, "Thanks a lot." He took the cone from her, and right away he ran his tongue from one side to the other of it; then he gave the thing a quarter-turn and took a second lick covering, that way, the whole entire surface of the ice cream. It was, to him, a little ceremonial that made the two of them (don't laugh) . . . saliva brothers.

She nodded, either noticing or not. If he only could have seen her eyes, he might have known.

"Baba Malomar is an American," she said. "His real name's Sidney Drexel Arthur. Like most Americans, he's very dual about the Japanese. Much as he admires them, and *loves* his four-wheel-drive Toyota truck and his whatever stereo — including CD player, probably — and VCR, he also fears them. Not the *stuff*, you understand, the people, some of them. He doesn't really *trust* them; they're, like, too much of a threat. Not to bomb another naval base, perhaps, but possibly to buy . . . Montana. And the IRS is why he came here in the first place. *He* called it a small, correctable misunderstanding. *They* were thinking more in terms of ten-to-twenty and a million dollar fine. Negotiations still continue, I believe."

"Yes," said Herb. "I see. And you are also hoping we can get there first and make the opposition more or less . . . superfluous."

"Exactly," said the girl. He wondered if he should bring up the van. In a moment he decided not to. If he'd been *meant* to get to this guy Malomar's in the Upwardlimobile, he'd have gone direct, he figured. And, too, he'd no idea how they could start the thing, or steer it. Plus, if this girl had been expecting him — as she so clearly had — she also knew both Ses deBarque and how her clients traveled. So, it had to be that he was meant to just shut up and take this monster trek with her — the two of them alone for countless miles and days, he reckoned — and go through whatever *that* entailed.

Herb began to nibble bits of cone and ice cream, going 'round and 'round. Let it be, he thought.

24
YAK TRACK

The first part of the trip to Baba Malomar's turned out to be a mingling of pain and pleasure such as Herb could not remember having known before, at least not since his birth, about which there is still uncertainty.

To begin with, Shalimar Sloan had made all of the arrangements, using what for money he had no idea. It must have added up to quite a bundle. She'd bought them packs and freeze-dried food and one-man tents, as well as extra clothes and boots and sundries, all at the *Giant Warehouse Sale* going on behind Abida's Fitness Center — Running Shoes and Croissants Fresh Hot Daily Ice Cream at Abida's Super-Discount Barn — Prescriptions Travel Agency. At that same location, she had also gotten places for the two of them in a trading caravan led by someone by the name of Pookie Woodchuck, going by the way Herb heard it, anyway.

"This is definitely a break for us," she told the boy as they confirmed their reservations just before the caravan pushed off. "I've asked around, and everybody says that Pookie is the best — for speed and safety, both. He isn't into booze or drugs, and he even doesn't mind Americans; he says that they're a lot like yaks: you're going to get some good ones and some bad ones. So, if it's true that we're ahead of those two other groups right now — as I believe we are — there oughta be no catching us. The airstrip here's the closest one to Baba's by three hundred miles, and Pookie's yaks move right along on trails and — um — *terrain* no other vehicle would last an hour on."

She'd said that he could call her "Shali," if he wanted to. She'd also said she hoped he didn't have flat feet or hate to walk on "sort of — well — uneven ground."

They left just after dawn: fifteen loaded yaks, two assistant trainers, the indomitable Pookie Woodchuck, and the "honored guests," Shali and himself. As such, they had the right, or privilege, to walk beside a yak and hang onto its coat, a horn, or even — in an emergency — its tail, for balance on the sort of — well — uneven rocky stretches, which were almost all of them. The yaks seemed not to notice much of anything. They could have passed for '60s oxen, being long-haired types whose mien suggested they had done a lot of downs that day, and possibly for days before. They just went along, bearing Herb's and Shali's luggage in addition to their loads of woven belts and nose rings and the other sorts of goods that the owner of Abida's Import-Export — Spices Concrete Intimate Necessities believed that people in the valley would go crazy for.

Before their trek began, Herb would have said he was in "not that bad" condition, physically — meaning that he wasn't overweight, could run upstairs at home without distress, and that if looked at naked, in a certain kind of light, he had some muscle definition, here and there. But after about a third of the first day of this expedition, "pathetic" was the only word that came into his mind about himself as, say, a specimen of manhood (*genus* Young American). While everybody else trudged manfully and girlfully and yakfully along, their faces showing minimal discomfort (to his eyes), it seemed to him he panted like a St. Bernard in the Bahamas, conscious every step of both the altitude and of the message that his legs and feet were sending him: "Why us?"

But still, if djinn or fairy godmother, the chairman of the State Lottery Commission, or Mrs. Quigley (who, if you recall, once read the stars for our First Lady) had come to him and told him that he really didn't have to do this anymore, that all good things would happen in his life in any case, he still would certainly have kept on going. Indeed, Shalimar Sloan *did* say something of that sort to him, in camp, the first night out, minus guarantees, of course. Clearly she'd observed his sufferings.

"Look," she said, in that direct, unornamented way she generally expressed herself, "why don't you do yourself a favor and head back to town, tomorrow. Get a nice room at The Great Couloir and just

186

hang out till I get back. It's not your fault you're not acclimatized, or used to the terrain. And it isn't as if you have some particular *skill* we'll need to help us get ahold of what it is that Baba has, up there."

"Tell me about it," Herbie said, more in deep regret than bitterness. Bitterness was not his kind of thing — not bitterness, self-pity or anchovies on a pizza.

"Well, you're not a trained negotiator," Shali said, willing, it appeared, to do so. "I don't believe that you're a hypnotist, either, and you're not like Albert Schweitzer or Mother Teresa — someone he'd be, well, *embarrassed* to turn down. In fact, those last few miles you looked like someone in an extra-strength Excedrin ad, or ready for the fifteen-day disabled list."

Herb stared at her. This clearly wasn't any ordinary girl, the kind that he'd grown used to, back in high school. He hadn't thought she'd answer his rhetorical request at all, but she had done so, not just calmly, but in a tone of voice that didn't seem at all insulting. It had been the tone of voice you'd use to tell a friend the ball scores, or a recipe.

"You're right, of course," said Herbie, mildly. "But in a way, that's why I'm going. Or why I'm not *not* going, anyway."

That seemed to puzzle her. When they'd made camp, she'd taken off her shawl and shades for the first time, and he'd found out she had blue eyes, about the same electric blue as his, and light brown hair with just a glow of reddish light in it. She still kept on her cowboy hat, but tilted back, and Herbie thought that she was gorgeous — her entire, open, friendly face, not just her tongue. But, looking in her eyes, he saw that she was puzzled, too. He'd seen that same look in his own blue irises enough, while looking in a mirror.

"Why you're not *not* going," she repeated, slowly. Then, with a little head shake, she appeared to change the subject. "Can't you finish this? There's just about two bites, is all."

She was offering him the pot that they'd been eating out of; Herbie took it. Their dinner had been freeze-dried Tuna Something, to which she'd added curry powder, and then had heated on their little Coleman stove. And though they had a lot of plastic plates and extra spoons, she hadn't gotten any of them out. Instead, they'd simply eaten from the pot, taking alternating mouthfuls, using just the one big spoon. Herb had been reminded of the way they'd shared her ice cream cone, except that this was even better.

So, now he scraped the pot and ate the last two mouthfuls, saying "Yum." The dinner *had* been good, and using the one spoon had been an *extra* reason he'd decided he was going to make this trip, and not turn back, regardless. He'd come to that decision earlier, while walking right beside — and talking to — a yak, that afternoon. Now he said the same things to the girl, repeated them.

"If I quit now, and wait for work I'm good at, or that isn't hard for me," he'd told the shaggy beast, "I might have quite a wait."

The yak had just accepted that, in stoic silence; it *was* doing something it was good at, fair to say. The girl, however, nodded her agreement, and affirmed it.

"Sure, that's absolutely true," she said. "Except for a few odd prodigies, no kid is good at *anything* that matters much in life. Getting A's in subjects, or being all-state soccer, doesn't guarantee you squat."

"Also, I don't think that having to be great at everything you do is quite the *point*," he said.

"Um," she answered, neutrally. From the yak he'd gotten some digestive sounds.

"Everything I do with any point to it will probably be hard for me," he said. "But that's okay. I think that's the way it is for everyone."

"Almost everyone," she said. The yak had audibly chewed cud, or maybe something from between its teeth.

"I guess I also think that if I didn't go, this time, I maybe never would," he said. "Go anywhere, for any halfway decent reason."

The yak, for reasons of its own, had chosen just that moment to relieve itself. The girl was much more positive.

"You know," she said, "it sounds as if you've really thought this out. I never did. I just *do* whatever it might be." She shrugged, perhaps apologetically. "And it works out, somehow."

"You're one of those," said Herb. "One of those fine feathered few."

"A-yup," she said, and grinned.

He couldn't get too mad at her. Her kind of honesty was so completely uncontaminated. She just said whatever she thought and let it lay there, didn't try to stand on it, so she'd seem taller.

"Well, let me ask you this," he said. "Is what we're

doing now" — he made a rolling gesture with one hand, signifying *everything* — "like, just a *cinch*, for you?"

"Hell, no," she said. "Of course it's not. I'm going to be a tortured mass of aches and pains tomorrow morning, same as you. It's just that I think about it differently, the whole *idea* of hardness."

"I get it," Herbie smiled. "You're a . . . whatcha-callit? — *masochist*."

"Uh-*unh*," she said. "It isn't that." She stood up and stretched. "Hardness is to things I want to do as eggshells are to eggs. I don't even *think* about the shells when I eat eggs. They're just a part of something that I love, so I don't sweat 'em." And she grinned again and turned to rummage in her pack, came up with toilet articles in hand.

"But now I've gotta get some sleep," she said. "Those yaks, they look like early risers. I'll go a little ways upstream to do my teeth and stuff."

Pookie, his assistants and the yaks had bivouacked downstream from them, their choice. Herb hadn't heard them talking for a while, and he supposed they were asleep, already. He watched his fellow honored guest until she disappeared around some boulders. She wasn't headed for a scented bathroom in a nice warm house, but for some other rocks, "a little ways upstream." Apparently she just was "doing it," as usual.

Later on, when they were both in their respective sleeping bags in their respective tents, their heads perhaps ten feet apart, he heard her whisper, "Herbie?"

"Yes?" he whispered, too.

"I would have hated it, if you'd gone back," she said.

"Me, too," he said. "I'm really happy to be going on. With you." The last two words were said a lot more softly, less distinctly, muffled by the pounding in his chest. There was silence for about a minute.

"I'm not as brave and philosophical as how I sounded." She spoke very softly, too. "I should be, but I'm not. But even if I was, I'd still want you to take this trip." A minor pause. "With me." And then, "Good night."

"Good night," said Herb. He tried to tell himself he shouldn't make too much of it, this conversation.

Before he fell asleep, he tried to classify what he was feeling, when it came to Shali. So, what things were there that he *didn't* like, about her looks or personality? As a rule, that was an easy one for him to answer. Most real girls were much too *this*, or really short on *that*. But, that night, the question didn't seem to hold his interest.

25
GETTING BALMED

Herb woke up hearing noises from downstream. Pookie and his men were clattering around, and talking to each other in their mother tongue. Herbie, only half awake, a little bit disoriented, semi-panicked. He thought they sounded like three guys who'd had their showers and their second cups of coffee, and were just about to leave the house. At any moment, he might hear a yak start up, he thought. So hurriedly and thoughtlessly, he reached around his shoulder for the zipper on his sleeping bag.

"UMfff," was more or less the sound he made, his quickly muffled groan. It seemed as if the muscles in his back had been replaced by Sheetrock, overnight — Sheetrock with a lot of *wires* in it, through which currents bearing *pain* could pass — and did, and did, and did.

Slowly, slowly, Herb began to semi-crawl and semi-wriggle — to creep out of his envelope of down.

"Ta-ra-ra-boom-de-yay," said quite a cheerful voice from real close by. "This should be *quite* a day. For those of us who seek enlightenment through suffering, that is." She laughed, perhaps not all *that* heartily.

Shalimar was sitting on the ground, fully dressed as usual, her left leg stretched straight out in front of her, her right leg bent and pulled around to one side, sort of in a hurdling position. As he watched, she slowly reached way forward with both hands, until she touched her pointed toe. Then she bent her hat brim to her knee.

"Egad," said Herbie. "How did you do that?"

"Easy," Shali said. "First, I took a sauna at my health club, followed by a deep massage. Then I kept on trying for about ten minutes. It took me all of five to get my clothes on, bubba."

Her saying "clothes" reminded Herb that he was much too close to naked to be comfortable — with her. He'd gone to bed in just his underpants, an older pair of boxer shorts; at the moment they had left him pretty well exposed, all things considered. He quickly grabbed at what he'd taken off the night before and, making sudden jerky movements (nicely synchronized with sounds like OOh-ah-ooh), he managed to put on his sweatshirt, jeans and running shoes, and socks. Then he limped a little ways upstream for just a minute.

"Perhaps you'd like to try some stretches?" Shali said when he came back. "I know a bunch of different ones. Here, for instance, is my favorite. . . ."

She showed him one after another. In between each demonstration (followed by Herb's repetition), they put together and prepared a pan of scrambled powdered eggs, which they then ate with local bread, chapatis and big mugs of sweetened tea.

Although nobody said to anybody else how glad she was to be with him while packing up, the two of them worked well together. Or so it seemed to Herbie, anyway.

The first mile out there on the track passed painfully, but uneventfully. Herb would have said it was a mile, in any case — say, twenty minutes worth of walking. But then he heard some bursts of laughter, *foreign-sounding* laughter, coming from behind him. Naturally he had to look around and check it out.

Mistake.

What he saw was one of Pookie Woodchuck's helpers, Pema, doing an exaggerated — *much* exaggerated — imitation of the way *he*, Herbie, walked. This little limp that he'd been using.

It never had occurred to him he might look *funny*. Actually, he'd sort of hoped the thing would be *respected*, as a flare-up of an old, old football injury, or conceivably a war wound. He tried to walk more normally.

Pookie Woodchuck, though, had caught him looking.

" 'Avin' us a spot of pain this mornin', guv?" he called out in a cheerful tone of voice. So far as Herb could tell, he was the only English-speaking yaksman. He surely was the only one with real long hair and granny glasses, who spoke English like a native of, say, Liverpool.

" 'Fraid so," said Herb, good-sportingly, adding on a rueful head shake. "A touch of Osgood-Schlatter's. It kicks up from time to time," he added, pulling out the name of a disease some neighbor's kid had said he had, when he was in his early teens. Herb thought it sounded serious.

"But I won't slow us down," he said. "Don't worry; I'll keep up. I *promise* you."

He smiled and shifted gears into a faster hobble. He'd just remembered different tribes had different ways of dealing with the aged, or infirm, or wounded — the ones who couldn't keep up with the rest. Who knew what customs Pookie and his gang observed? He wouldn't want to find himself dropped into some crevasse with, say, a can of deviled ham, a book of poems by Robert Browning and a yo-yo.

"Coo," said Pookie, "where's the bloody rush? Our customers ain't goin' nowheres, that's for sure."

This Pema guy, a grizzled little man who sported J.C. Penney running shoes and a Denver Broncos woolen cap, then had to get his two cents in, speaking to his boss in that strange language Herbie only knew to be not-English and not-Spanish.

" 'E says our customers is nowheres now, already," Pookie said, and everybody laughed, including Herb and Shali just a beat behind the others. Pema's eyes went back and forth between them, sopping up approval like the curtain-raising act at Mr. Laff's. Herb wished he'd pull the woolen cap a little lower on his head; half of his right ear was missing.

By that time, everyone, including yaks, was standing still.

"Pookie," Shali said. She walked toward him,

whipping off her Ray-Bans, looking blue-eyed up into his grannies. "You know, it *would* be great if, just today, we possibly could take some extra rest stops? Like, maybe every hour, even? My legs and back are really killing me, and that'd make a big, big difference. Then, tomorrow — or the next day, certainly — I know that I'd be fine. I realize that it'd be, like, an *enormous* favor. . . ."

Herbie watched the yaksman melt. He was sure that all through history girls from everywhere had gotten guys to answer "Sure!" "You got it!" and "My pleasure, babe!" by using tones of voice like that.

Pookie grinned at her.

"Don't even think about it, ducks," he said. "And 'ere" — he reached inside a yak pack — "every time we stop, the two of you can rub on some of this. . . ."

He gave the girl a wide-mouthed jar, its top draped over with Saran Wrap held on by a bright red rubber band. She took it, looking much the way that cancer patients look when someone's handed them their chiropractor's name and number.

In fact, the stops that Pookie ordered came at more like every *half* an hour. At the first one, Shali pushed the jar at Herb.

"You try it first," she said. "I want to see if it grows hair, or anything." She smiled. "Want me to come and rub it in for you?"

Herb was pretty sure she wasn't serious.

"No. No, thanks," he said. He looked around. "I guess I'll just slide over there. . . ." There were — there *always* were — large rocks not far away.

Shali shrugged and off he went. The stuff was slick and warming, with a pleasant piney odor.

When he came back and handed her the jar, he said, "It's nice." She nodded, headed for the place he'd gone to. Pema, pantomiming rubbing motions, made as if to follow her. Pookie grabbed him, and the guys all laughed, including Herbie, nervously.

The salve turned out to be not merely good, but unbelievable, miraculous. Herb had always thought that Eastern medicine was mostly getting punctured here and there by needles, and drinking different herbal potions with an empty mind. This stuff made him think again. By early afternoon, he and the girl were telling Pookie that they didn't have to stop that often. By evening, they were just a little stiff, about the way you get from walking in a mall all afternoon. Moved by more than *heart*felt gratitude, Herbie promised Pookie quite a splendid gift, his Reeboks, just as soon as his new boots were broken in.

If Baba Malomar possessed a health care product better than this salve, it really must be something, Herbie thought.

26
YAKSMEN

For the next six days the caravan moved right along, running like a roller coaster, up and down, from ridges into valleys and back up again. Every day, the boy and girl felt more like yaksmen, less like supercargo, tourists. By the third day, they were pitching campsites right beside the men, tasting one another's food and sharing one another's cultures. ("Take out the papers and the trash, or you don't get no spending cash . . ." sang Pookie and his boys, before too long, ". . . Yakety-yak. Don't talk back." "Regard as one this life, the next life, and the one between . . ." recited Herb and Shali.) On the morning of the fifth day, early-rising Pema stuck a lizard into one of Herbie's boots.

Herb didn't know exactly what to make of their relationship — not the one with Pema, his with Shali. Sometimes the two of them would share a pot and spoon, and sometimes not; that seemed a good deal less significant, as time went by. They talked a lot, both walking on the trail and with the heads of their two tents pitched close together, lying down at night. Mostly they just stuck to everyday occurrences, like weather, food and washing socks, or the birds and views they saw, the personalities of different yaks, and how much hot sauce was about enough. She still did not repeat that line about how glad she was to have him with her, although from time to time she'd say or do some little thing that made him think she might be.

The most surprising and direct remark she made along those lines was what she said the sixth day of their journey, on a sunny morning. Herb had dared to put on hiking shorts, instead of trousers, and he'd even taken off his shirt.

"I *like* looking at a guy who has your kind of body," she had told him. "The long and lanky type."

Herbie'd blushed and almost said, "Me, too," instead of what he meant, which was that he liked looking at *her* kind of body, too, or would if he were ever given such an opportunity.

So far, he hadn't been, for sure. She always changed her clothes some place where she was out of sight, and perhaps to show respect for local customs, perhaps for other reasons of her own, she kept herself as covered up as all the native women Herb had seen in town. But still, from just the indications that he'd had, the generalities of size and shape that even *spacesuits* can't entirely hide, he was sure she had a lovely body. *Of course* he hadn't dared to say a thing like that, not yet.

In fact, he hadn't dared to say or do . . . well,

anything. Not any of the things like telling her he liked her, holding hands, or kissing — all the stuff that he was sure that almost anybody else would certainly have tried to do, by then. He'd told himself that was because he didn't want to maybe *ruin* it, the real nice way that everything was going.

At least he got some confirmation of the fact that he did not *repulse* her. She *touched* him all the time. Not on any of the *zones*, of course, and not . . . carressingly, exactly. But it *was* true her fingers *lingered* on his shoulder, arm, or neck, sometimes, or on his knee if they were sitting down. He'd made up his mind that he was going to start to touch her, too, offhandedly, but not until they'd left the caravan, and it was just the two of them. Then, in case she slapped his face, or stabbed him in the gut with some jeweled dagger she kept hidden in her sleeve, he wouldn't have to hear old Pema giggle at him.

That day, the day that it'd be the two of them, drew closer all the time. Soon, they'd reach the sacred river in the final valley, the place where Pookie and the boys would stop, unload and set up shop.

"Yop, they're wot you might call pilgrims, like," said Pookie Woodchuck, leaning back against a rock and slurping at his after-dinner drink, yak butter tea. "Blokes come up by the thousands, all year long. As soon as ten goes 'ome, 'ere comes another twenty."

"It is a *very* sacred river," Shali said, in tones of great respect, "from what I understand."

The five of them had finished eating and were sitting in a group around the little fire that they'd made, yawning and digesting in the twilight.

"Bloody right it is — top five," said Pookie. "Some'd say top *two*. This 'ere's the virgin river: sacred, pure and undefiled. No boats allowed on 'er, no bridges over 'er. You want to 'ear 'ow sacred? Bloody river's so damn sacred, 'er ain't even got a *name*!"

"Wo!" said Herb. "That's just about as sacred as you get, *I'd* say. Even Eric Clapton — "

"An' there's more," said Pookie, talking right on through the interruption, in the way old friends are apt to do. " 'Er be so sacred, *they* don't even put 'er on their maps! Lots of foreigners come up to it an' think they must be bloody *lost*!"

Pema had some things to add to that. He spoke to Pookie, in their native tongue, but looked at Herb and Shali. It had become entirely clear he understood *all* spoken English, never mind what accent, perfectly. But though he'd learned the words to certain songs, he didn't seem to *speak* it.

" 'E says that you should know the river's on *our* maps," said Pookie, with a thumb-jerk at the half-eared man. "But bein' such respectful sods, we don't give it a real name, neither. No," he shook his head, "the Leh-ze River does *not* have a name." It seemed he'd finished speaking.

Pema shook his shoulder, looking cross. Then he made a gesture that, in any language, means "Go on."

" 'Leh'ze' meaning 'that which is too sacred to be named,' " said Pookie, and old Pema and the silent one, named Sendup, cackled merrily.

"So, when the pilgrims come, they stick around

and paddle in the sacred waters," Shali said. "And they also *shop* a lot?"

"Yop," said Pookie. "Some of 'em 'ang out for *weeks*, sometimes. Just dip and shop, and shop and dip — like that. Some learn 'ow to swim while they're about it. Try to catch themselves an eel or two."

"An *eel* or two?" said Herb. "To *eat*?"

"Bugger, no," said Pookie. "Catch 'em for the *slime* they're covered with. Them pilgrims, they scrape off the slime and put it in a jar; then they toss the bloody eel back in. Them eels are sacred, too, y'know."

"Gross," said Shali. "I hate eels."

"Not this lot, you don't," said Pookie. "Eel slime's part of wot you rubbed on you, before. Wot took your aches away? It's full of 'ealin' properties. Even *we* believe in eel slime, ducks."

"Well, eels or no eels, we have got to swim across that river, Herb and me," said Shali. "To get to where we're going." They'd never talked about their destination with the men before.

"You better plan to 'ead upstream, then," Pookie said. "Twenty miles, or better thirty. Get up where she's narrower, you know? 'Er's just too bloody wide, where we'll be 'ittin' 'er."

But Shali shook her head. "We don't have time," she said. "It's Baba Malomar's we're going to. You know his ashram, right? We've got to beat some other people there, get there just as soon as possible. *Up*stream would be *way* out of our way."

Pema had some more to say, at that point. He had a funny sort of *naughty-boy* expression on his face. That seemed peculiar, strange.

" 'E says Baba Malomar's too much," was Pookie's terse translation. "Of course, there's some believe's that 'e's a saint," he added, moments later.

Shalimar decided she would head for bed, on that.

"Let's hope they're right," she said, rising rapidly and taking off, with toothbrush.

27
COMPETITION

The next day, Pema went ahead alone. His assignment, Pookie said, was, first, to find a good location for their caravan to park, where they would set up their boutique. Its name would be Abida's Secret Sharpest Image, Pookie said. Then, having found some kids to work as counter help, Pema'd hustle back that evening and report.

When he did, he also brought back local news, one piece of which was passed along to Herb and Shali by his boss.

" 'Member wot I said about the river bein' left off all their maps?" said Pookie. He then laughed, self-satisfiedly, the way that prophets often do. "Well, yesterday, 'ere comes this bleedin' bunch of foreigners, five or six of 'em, all Japanese, an' drivin' supercharged Suzukis, four-wheel drives. An' when they see wot-all they got in front of 'em, an' not a bridge or boat to cross it on, they like' to puke, from wot ol' Pema said. An' 'e said even if they *could* swim over 'er, they can't, 'cause one of 'em, 'e's got 'is wrist, like, chained to this big bloody steamer trunk. A thing the size of some young yak, wot Pema said, but not as smart by 'arf, I'll bet." He broke off into chuckles.

"So, looks as if *that* bunch is gonna 'ead upstream, all right," concluded Pookie, "goin' by wot Pema said."

Herb and Shali looked at one another. It seemed her information had been incorrect; the Japanese *had* been ahead of them. And now they'd soon be heading upstream — possibly they'd started up, already — where eventually they'd reach a place where they could ford the river in their vehicles. And then race on to Baba's.

Shali sighed, and licked her lips, then spoke.

"I can tell you what they've got there, in that trunk," she said, in an *extremely* offhand tone of voice. "Those Japanese."

"Wot's that?" said Pookie, sounding equally uninterested. The other yaksmen looked off into space, as if they had their minds on other matters altogether.

"A billion dollars cash, American," said Shali. "It's chained onto that fellow's wrist because it's his responsibility."

"That so?" said Pookie, and he yawned, enormously. Pema and the silent Sendup also yawned, and shook their heads, and looked like guys about to drop from tiredness.

"Well, time for nighty-night, I guess," said Pookie. "I'll just be checkin' on the yaks before I turn on in." He rose and started toward the tethered beasts, and both assistants followed.

Next morning, Pookie was the only yaksman present at the breakfast rock, and when the boy inquired where the others were, he said he'd told them they could go ahead and do a little early dipping in the sacred waters, if they wanted to.

"We, too, believe the river brings good fortune," he explained.

28
CROSSING

By mid-morning, Pookie's caravan had reached the sacred river on the valley floor, but the two assistant yaksmen still had not rejoined it.

"I guess you'll have to say good-bye for us," Shali told their boss. "We've got a couple of things to do before we make the crossing."

Pookie said he understood. He said that he could not *imagine* where those two " 'ad gotten to." But he also was a proud and happy man. Herb's Reeboks were a *little* narrow, but they basically felt great, and when it came to looks, they *really* did the job. When he had led his loaded yaks between the rows of pilgrims' tents, a lot of almond eyes had widened at the sight of them and words were softly spoken that their wearer found, if anything, *en*couraging. Pookie told the two that if by any chance they made it back to there before this "sales event" was over, he'd offer them real savings on the trip back to their point of origin.

"We'll just pretend you bought a round-trip ticket to begin with," he told them with a wink. "Abida, he don't like it if I 'ave to come back empty."

And so, after a round of hugs, "God blesses" and "Good 'untings," the boy and girl turned left, while yaks and Pookie wheeled off to the right, all of them in hopes of happy days ahead. Neither group seemed bothered by the fact that each faced a fairly major (although very different) challenge: in the case of Herb and Shali, swimming this huge river; for Pookie, finding where the hell it was that Pema'd gotten him a parking space.

Herbie found the pilgrims' "city" to be a real eye-opener. There were people by the many hundreds, all of them in plain white outfits, living in their vari-colored tents, and either walking through the streets with shopping bags, or going down to linger in the waters and be cleansed of lust and greed, and anger, envy, covetousness — in other words the sins that go along with shopping.

Although the people living in the city were all transients, the place seemed very orderly and organized, to Herb. Larger stores, such as the one that Pookie'd soon set up, were grouped in mini-malls, while smaller quik-stops, launderettes and franchised eateries (McCurry's) were scattered here and there and everywhere, throughout the different neighborhoods. You got the feeling that there weren't lots of drugs for sale, but Shali found and bought a bunch of blow-up beach balls: bright idea.

"Boats aren't kosher," she remarked to Herb, "and

so I don't imagine rubber rafts are, either. But I'll bet you we can tie a few of these together, and then float our packs across on them, as pretty as you please. I just hate hiking in wet undies."

"My biggest worry," Herbie said, "is floating *me* across. I mean, this kid can *swim*, all right, but not like here to Pago Pago."

She stared at him a moment, somewhat blankly, Herbie thought. As if it never had occurred to her he wasn't Tarzan.

"Well, I'm a *real* good swimmer," she said, finally. "So, if you have to, any time, you can hitch a ride from me a while — just grab onto the raft and let me pull you. I know you'll be all right. All you have to do is have the proper attitude. You do have that, now, don't you?"

"*Absolutely*," Herbie said, with great conviction, nodding. The river looked as if it would be nice and warm, and it was just as smooth as glass — in all ways very like himself, he thought, ha-ha. And besides, before he drowned, he'd get to see his girlfriend in a swimsuit, certainly a major goal in every young man's life. That was "girlfriend" with a ha-ha *also* after it, of course.

Once she'd had a chance to analyze — assess — the river's current, gentle as it was, Shali knew that it'd be impossible to swim, like, straight across the thing; they *would* get carried sideways, some. And so she figured they should start at least two miles above the city, maybe three. That way, they ought to come ashore a little ways downstream from it.

Herb believed it was a good thing that they had to do it that way. By going upstream they would get away from where the pilgrims congregated; they wouldn't call attention to themselves, or to their raft — in case some people thought it was improper. The pilgrims only swam where they had easy access to the river, where the banks were low to non-existent, and there were a lot of nice, wide beaches. That's the way it was beside the city, and below it, downstream. There, too, the river bottom slanted very slightly out for probably a hundred yards or more, and so they had a lot of room for standing, chatting in the water, and for taking swimming lessons. As Pookie'd said, there were a bunch of different swim schools there, a lot of competition for the doggy-paddle dollar.

But by the time you'd walked upstream a mile — there was a dusty road that paralleled the river — the topography had changed. Your feet were well above the water level, and the river's banks were steep and overgrown with brush. There were some narrow beaches at the bases of these mini-cliffs, but when you waded out from them, the river's bottom dropped off sharply. Herb and Shali spotted one such beach a good ways from the city that looked perfect for their purposes; they slid and scrambled down to it. Partway there, they heard a car come down the little narrow road — fast, and therefore recklessly. Shali thought it sounded like a super-charged Suzuki, four-wheel drive, but being driven in a way no Japanese would ever drive it. "Aston-Martin. That'd be James Bond," said Herb. And Shali smiled.

Once on the beach, they first took out, and then blew up, the dozen beach balls that they'd bought; they both got spots before their eyes before they'd finished doing that. And then they stuffed the balls, in groups of three, into these big mesh laundry bags they'd also found for sale. When they tied the bags together, there it was: a colorful and useful raft. Herb christened it *Con T.K.*, showing off his knowledge of both Spanish and mythology, drawing from the girl a look he didn't choose to analyze. Now all they had to do was put what they had on — or most of it — inside their packs and load them on the raft. Then: Swimmers Take Your Marks, Get Set and Go.

They started to undress. Herb couldn't help but notice Shali hadn't pulled a swimsuit from her pack, although she had dug something out of it. That was a length of sturdy cotton rope. He didn't think that it would be in character for her to tie him up, when he'd undressed, and torture him or something. And so he guessed it was a towrope for the raft.

Ahem. Herb dawdled. He decided he'd undress one article behind (or after) her. That way, when she was taking off her socks, he'd be on his boots, still. He'd know exactly when to stop, and when — how far — to go. He'd go as far as she did, and no farther.

Shali was a fast undresser. Before Herb's conscious mind had dealt with anything beyond that fact, she'd both whipped off and stowed away her cowboy hat, and shawl, and long-sleeved shirt, and painter's pants, and boots and socks. That meant she still had on an undersized (it seemed to him) green cotton camisole and matching underpants. Only those; that's all. Not much, quite little, hardly anything.

Because he'd stuck with fierce determination to his plan, Herb was in the act of rolling up his blue jeans at that moment, standing there in just his T-shirt and plaid boxer shorts. He took his eyes off her to open up the zippered pocket in his pack, the one he planned to stow the jeans in. And as he did so, Shali spoke to him.

"There," he heard her say. "They say it's good to have the absolute bare minimum of drag, on swims as long as this one."

Herb froze; he didn't think he moved a muscle for a minute. He was pretty sure he knew what he was going to see, in general, when he turned back in her direction. Yes. Oh, yes. He'd heard kids, swimmers in his school, telling one another how many hundredths of a second they could "save" by buying such-and-such a swimsuit, which had much less "drag." Oh, yes. But no swimsuit could provide "the absolute bare minimum of drag." What Shali meant was something altogether different, he was pretty sure.

He almost didn't want to look, but also knew he would-would-would, regardless of the consequences. He pivoted and stared.

Oh, yes. For sure. It was just as he had guessed, known, hoped and dreaded. Shali'd taken off her camisole and underpants and made them disappear inside her luggage, somewhere. She'd also put her pack onto the floating raft. That meant Herb had to watch her bend and pick up that soft cotton rope and tie one end of it around her waist, the other to the raft. And then look straight at him and smile.

If anything (he thought) she looked more naked with the rope on than without it; don't ask him why. But, either way, she was . . . oh, yes: big-shouldered, pink and honey, but still sleek as any

212

otter, with that swimmer's build and swimmer's ease (he just assumed) with having it exposed. Her body parts were not exactly like Felicity's, he didn't think, but they all held his interest to the same degree. She was waiting for him, standing there, her arms just hanging at her sides, her weight more on her left leg than her right, that small smile on her lips.

But *he* was in a fix. He lacked her . . . social confidence (you *could* say). Or maybe her experience. That probably was it. She'd been in situations of this sort before. She could remember times and places it made sense to strip right down and tie a cotton rope around her waist to drag a raft and possibly a boy across the widest river in the world. Times and places where a boy had looked at her the way she was right then.

She could probably remember all that happening before, but he could not. He had no experience and, worse than that, no confidence. What he did have was a mind awash in negativity. What was the worst thing that could happen? He imagined it right then. Shali taking one long look at him, and laughing.

So, desperately, he seized his pack, a nerdy (he was certain) smile on his own face and, holding it in front of him, he took the three short steps that got him to the raft. That solved exactly nothing. He couldn't simply stand there, playing Statues.

"Hey, it's okay," said Shali, suddenly. "It really is. Come on."

So, Herbie put the pack down, mumbling "God help me." Herkily and jerkily, he pulled his T-shirt up and off his head, and then with equal haste but also carefulness, maneuvered those plaid boxers down and off his feet. Trying unsuccessfully to make his mind a blank, he jammed both articles into the pocket of his pack and, very much avoiding looking anywhere but straight across the river, he then sprinted pell-mell into it. ("Eels, meet your master," was the line that galloped through his head, insanely, as he dove beneath the surface.) When he came up again, as far away from her as one held breath would take him, and looked back, he saw that she was also almost totally submerged. All her points of interest, other than her comely head, were hidden by the muddy water.

"You looked *great*," her shapely mouth informed him casually, offhandedly, as if she'd seen him (for the first time) in a bow tie. "Even greater than I'd guessed." And then she laughed, a pure enjoyment sound, without the smallest trace of mockery.

"You, too," said Herb, exhaling those two words in more than just relief — in exultation. He felt the same as when he'd seen his favorite band: U2 . And then he turned and started swimming toward the other side.

Before he'd gone a quarter of a mile, Herb had made a number of decisions, all pertaining to this feat he was attempting. One, he wasn't going to try to talk too much, while swimming. Two, he was mainly going to use the restful, but effective, breast stroke, even at the risk of looking wimpish. Three, he wasn't going to offer to help out and pull the raft, part-time. Four, he wasn't going to keep on looking at the other shore, and noticing how very far away it was.

He did, however, notice certain other things. The river's temperature was comfortable — warm

214

enough, but still not soupy. There *was* a current, but it didn't seem like any problem. Swimming naked — which, in fact, he'd never done before — was definitely the way to go. Shali *could* swim like a fish; most of the time she used a lazy crawl, and even with the raft to pull, she stayed right up with him, with ease.

They swam about ten feet apart. Herb felt safe, but not in any fear of bumping into her. He tried to stay relaxed and glide as far as possible with every kick. Stroke-kick-glide. He let his face go slightly underwater on the glide. He was more of a *torpedo* than a lumpy frog (he thought), cutting like an arrow through the water.

"How you doing?"

Herb was almost startled by her voice. He stopped his rhythmic stroking and looked over at the girl, made a little cranky by the interruption.

He discovered she'd rolled over on her back and now was lolling in the water, barely moving. Compared to him, she was extremely buoyant. Herb felt himself become less cranky, more a social being.

"Okay," he answered, treading water.

"Want a rest?" she asked. "A tow?"

"No, let's keep going," he replied. "I'm fine." More than ever, then, his mood was *do* it, *make* it, get it over with.

She nodded and rolled over and resumed her stroke. She had to work a little harder, right at first, to get the raft restarted. Herb got glimpses of the muscles in her shoulders, shiny when they broke the surface of the murky water. She really *was* a swimmer; her leg kick was an engine, pushing her along.

He took a peek ahead. They'd come a ways. He looked back where they'd come from. They sure had. They were really out there, now; there *was* no nearby shore — either way was just a huge expanse of water. Herb felt a little fear, a tiny panic bouncing in his chest. For the first time, it seemed very *deep*, the river.

He asked himself how he was feeling — honestly. The answer was: Okay. He really was okay; he hadn't tightened up or anything. He got back in his rhythm: stroke-kick-glide. He was pretty sure that he was going to make it, sure he was. If he ever needed help, it was ten feet away, but he was pretty sure he wouldn't. He was going to make the crossing on his own.

He thought at least another half an hour passed before she stopped again. This time he was glad she had. He paddled over to the beach-ball raft, and got both elbows up on it. His body now admitted to his mind that this was much the longest swim they'd ever taken — by a factor of some five or ten, already, maybe even more. His legs were starting to feel heavy. They always had a tendency to sink, but now they didn't seem to want to kick the way they had before, with that same snap and drive. His lower back felt tired, too, and his shoulders, slightly, just a little. But he still could go. He saw that they were much, much closer to the other side than to where they'd started from. That was a boost. He bet they were three quarters there; he said that to the girl. He thought about how good he'd feel to reach the other side, to make it. This had really been hard work. Making it would be a real accomplishment.

"You're looking good," she told him. She, too,

was hanging on the raft, across from where he was. "You feel okay?"

"For sure," said Herb. He wanted to say something to encourage *her*. "A piece of cake. You want to do some eeling when we get there?"

She laughed at that.

"Sure," she said. "It won't be too long, now."

It took another thirty minutes, though. Herb found he couldn't glide the way he used to. His stroke got choppier, and he was panting. He didn't know whose fault it was, but Shali and the raft were always closer than they'd used to be. He couldn't keep himself from looking at the shore. It made him mad the way it stayed so far away. The current over here seemed stronger, so that for every body length he'd swim — like, *forward* — he seemed to drift one, to the side.

When they were, *finally*, forty-fifty feet from shore — which was another little beach, deserted, brown, with hardly any bank behind it — Herb saw the girl stop stroking. He thought she must be treading water, maybe checking out the depth. But then she gradually stood up! The water was no deeper than the middle of her thighs. They'd made it!

Herb stood up, too, of course. And promptly fell right down again. His legs had turned to stilts made out of cardboard tubes, with maybe melted butter in them. He knelt there in the water, feeling foolish, helpless, grateful, lucky, proud. Knowing he could not get up.

She waded toward him, moving very stiffly, smiling, picking at the rope around her waist. Herb saw how it had chafed her skin, and when she got the knot undone and took it off, she had this fat red line around her middle, and a big red scrape mark on one side from where the knot had rubbed against her hip. Probably he also noticed she was naked, but it didn't register except as something that just happened to be so. It didn't have a thing to do with him. He didn't think about himself, in that regard, at all. Everything was kind of spacey, dreamy.

She helped him up and got his arm around her shoulders.

"This happens," she explained. "Don't worry. In a little while, they'll feel like legs again."

They staggered forward, onto the small beach, she still pulling on the towrope. When the raft was beached, and couldn't float away, she dropped the rope and kept on walking with the boy, up onto the riverbank to where there was a fat, round log, a major piece of driftwood. Herb sat down, and it was then he noticed he was naked, too. He didn't feel embarrassed or, like, anything except *of course* he was, so what.

He was very, very tired. He didn't think he'd felt this kind of tiredness, before. He didn't think he could get up, but that was fine; he didn't want to.

Herb watched the girl walk back along the riverside and get their packs, and then the raft, and set them all down near where he was sitting. That was fine with him.

"I guess I'll take the raft apart," she said.

He nodded, perfectly agreeable, watched her systematically reduce this useful vehicle, the *Con T.K.*, to one small pile of limp, striped rubber blobs and four mesh laundry bags. One of those she folded twice and put by Herbie's feet. Then, from out a little pocket in her pack, she pulled that jar of Pookie's salve, the eel-slime stuff and, kneeling on the laundry bag, began to rub it on his legs. He watched her breasts move, as she did that.

"You're really something, you know that?" she said. "For someone not in training that was one enormous swim."

Herb could feel his legs begin to feel like legs again. But still, he didn't want to jump right up and test them. Actually, he felt much more like lying down than jumping up.

"I wasn't sure I'd ever walk again," he told her, looking at his palms. His finger ends were still quite shriveled, prune-ish.

"Tomorrow will be soon enough," she said. She turned her head to check the setting sun. "It must be seven, eight o'clock already. Morning, you'll be good as new." She tapped his knee. "So, there." She scrambled to her feet and turned back toward her pack, the jar still in her hand. She shifted weight from one leg to the other; Herbie watched her bottom move.

"Wait," he said. He didn't want her to begin some new activity before he'd told her something. They'd just accomplished this great feat together. She was proud of him. They both were naked. Tomorrow she would disappear again inside those layers of clothes. Opportunity, it seemed to him, had knocked *and* maybe even shouted out "Hey, Herb!" Would he ever be in love like this, back home? He'd never been before, except with Tyree Toledano.

"In my younger and more vulnerable years . . ." he thought, the seven words that were the start of *The Great Gatsby*.

"Come here," he said.

She bent and put the jar away, and then came back to where she'd been. "Where?" she said. "I *am* here, aren't I?"

"No," he said, "right *here*." And he patted the big log that he was sitting on, and then leaned forward, scooping up the laundry bag and spreading it for her to sit on. That made her smile. She settled down beside him.

"Yes?" she said. "What is it, now?"

"Shali," Herbie said, and he was stuck. So what he did was take her by the shoulders and a moment later he was kissing her, with one hand coming off her shoulder, dropping down to touch, and then to cup, her breast, holding it like something precious and . . . *sensational*. His hand was doing that.

"Herb," she took her mouth away from his to say. "Oh, absolutely, Herb." And then she kissed him back, her fingers buried in his curly hair.

"*I love you*," Herbie said, soon after that. He took his hand away. It seemed to him that touching her had let the words out, made it possible for him to say the thing that he'd decided that he *had to* say to her right then. The thing that made it perfectly okay for him to want the rest to happen, now. He was sure that this must be the time for it, that he'd be able to, in just a little while. For sure. It wouldn't be too long; it never had been.

"I know," she said. "You sort of do." She laughed. "And me, I sort of do you, too. I have for quite a while. In fact, before we started with the caravan, I went and got some . . . intimate necessities, you know? From old Abida's warehouse? Blush if you believe you know the kind I mean."

Herb blushed. This wasn't any kid stuff they were talking, now.

"Well, I *did*, too," he said. He felt responsible, mature. "I've got a . . . intimate necessity myself. Right over in my pack."

"What?" she said. "Just one? I feel insulted." But he could tell her outrage was a fake.

"I only *had* a dollar thirty-five," he said, sticking with the total honesty.

"Boy," she said. She touched the top of Herbie's nose, with just the tip of her left forefinger. "You *are* a schemer, aren't you? And pretty *confident*, I'd say. Here you'd barely met me, hardly knew a thing about me. Never seen me in your life, before." She paused. "Or had you?" Now she had one hand on his shoulder, the other on his knee.

"No, of course not," Herbie said. What kind of question was that, anyway? Of course he'd never seen her. She wasn't any Tyree Toledano. And she had never seen him, either. Which meant that when she bought what *she* had bought, back at Abida's, *her* set (collection? carton? *ton?*) of intimate necessities, she must have wanted not so much himself, specifically, but more just anyone who was a boy, a man. He'd heard guys talk about such girls, at school; he'd *never* heard guys talk about what wasn't happening.

"And you didn't know *me*, either," Herbie said, feeling sort of swept along. "And that makes you a schemer, too, but worse than me because you planned to do it *lots*, regardless." He hardly knew what he was saying.

"Uh-uh," she said. "Or, well, I *am* a schemer,

maybe, but I had my reasons. It's not the way you think, at all." She'd brought her hand up to his cheek, and then she kissed his mouth again, but not with heavy emphasis, he didn't think.

"I don't understand," said Herb. "How is it?" He was feeling funny, hurt. He didn't know what by, exactly. There was something wrong, he knew that much. He noticed then that she was looking pretty beat. She'd done that long swim, too, and she had had the raft to pull, as well. But she had got him into this. Well, hadn't she?

"I can't tell you now," she said. "I can't tell you anything. It's a sort of promise that I made. Besides, I'm awful tired now. I really am about to drop." She got up on her feet.

"I can tell you this much, though," she said. "It's you, specifically — you, Herb — I'm loving, time compressed, right now. I promise you. Let's not make love unless you totally believe that. And unless you really still believe you love me, too."

Herb sat there nodding, looking at the ground. The pace of all these speeches, and events, and non-events, had been too much for him. He was afraid that if he spoke right then, he'd start to cry, which was absurd. When he lifted up his eyes, he saw that she was laying out their sleeping bags. She hadn't put on any clothes, still.

"Come on, you," she said to Herb, holding out a hand as she approached him. "It's time for beddy-bye."

Herb might have been asleep before his feet had made it to the bottom of that sleeping bag.

* * *

When Herb woke up, the sun was well up in the sky, already. He heard some birdsong and some splashing sounds, and he turned over in his sleeping bag to look. Amazingly that didn't hurt at all.

Unbelievably (thought Herb) Shali had been *swimming*: hair of fifty thousand dogs. She'd just picked up a towel, and she was walking toward him from the beach, fluffing out her auburn hair. She still had that red mark around her waist. He didn't have to think to know he loved her more than anyone had ever loved a woman since the dawn of history. Oh, yes.

"I want to tell you," he called out, "I *totally* believe you and I *absolutely* love you, not just *still*, but more, and. . . ."

He'd got the bag unzipped and started crawling toward his pack, trying to remember if there was *another* thing he had to say, and where he'd put. . . .

But she was trotting toward him, grinning.

"Look, look, look," she said. "Beside your pillow. It can't have been the *tooth* fairy . . ." And — bingo — she was kneeling on his sleeping bag with him, their arms around each other in the friendly morning sunshine.

"Oh, Herbiferous," she said.

And thus did Herbie Hertzman, if indeed there ever was a person by that name, come to have (by great good luck) a taste of what he always *thought* he needed most in life, in order to be happy.

29
FAR-OUT ENCOUNTER
OF SOME KIND

In the next few days, some words of Ses de-Barque's kept sneaking up inside of Herbie's head and saying "Boo!" Each time, he jumped a little. The way you do when you remember that you're going to the dentist's pretty soon, a week from Friday, say. Just before he'd started on this trip, she'd said, quite enigmatically, he thought, "Everybody's got a magic number: one. That's the one you get it on. You see?"

At first bite, he had thought that "it" was something cosmic, like "the point" — the whole darn *story* of the way it is. But almost right away he doubted such an explanation. Ses deBarque was down to earth, a steak and baked potatoes sort of person. Maybe "it" was, like, a *job*, the thing you end up doing with yourself.

But then, beginning on that morning by the sacred

river, and continuing for three more days, he wondered if "it" simply was what guys meant when they asked each other if they'd gotten any lately — namely, sex. Sex sure seemed magical to him.

Herb, typically, did *not* feel he was what you'd call a *natural* at sex, in terms of being *great* at it, the second he came flopping on the field. But what he *did* feel was this worshipful commitment, not just to the act, but her — to Shali, *aka* his "partner" — that allowed him to be *there* for her, with her, and so *enthusiastically* that she would have to laugh, and also gasp, for joy.

Herb knew the setting helped. It didn't rain; there wasn't any smog, or corporation odors. The scenery was beautiful, and there weren't any other actors anywhere around who might pop up and scream, "If you don't stop and get some clothes on by the time I count to ten. . . ."

On top of that Shali was as much involved as he in not just *making* love, but also in discovering and shaping it, permitting it, and using it in ways that had to do not only with their bodies but also with their spirits, their whole attitudes. Herb knew he'd never had such friendly feelings toward another person as he felt toward her — this big, broad-shouldered, easygoing girl. Except for what she wouldn't tell him, she allowed him total access to her being, to her here-and-now. Both of them were so darn glad to see each other, every morning, that the past and future, both, seemed more or less irrelevant.

But on the day before the day they started up the massive snowcapped ridge that was the last high barrier between the two of them and Baba Malomar's, Herb wondered if perhaps the "it" that Ses had talked about was not sex, after all. Feeling older, more mature and philosophical, he wondered — *mused* — if maybe "it" was that man's highest goals and aspirations, such as perfect love, could never be attained except in fleeting moments, little "nows." And that only other sorts of things, like baseball cards and money, could be worked for, saved and kept.

The thing that put those rather cynical and sad ideas in Herbie's mind was realizing he and Shali — perfect lovers, the ideal — would not, no matter what, go on and on. Once this Health Care business finished, so would they be finished. He'd go back to Castles in the Air, and she'd return to either central casting or his own imagination — or *wherever* — and hang out there with chicks like Zippy and Felicity, and older hens such as the Big Red Chicken.

Herb wondered if the *basis* for the love that he and Shali had for one another *now* was that the two of them, at both the conscious and unconscious levels, knew that what was going on between them was ephemeral, unreal. They could love each other unreservedly, holding nothing back, and saving nothing for a rainy day. They didn't have to cling, or worry that the other one would change — or start to make demands, or find somebody else, or die or take up the trombone. Not just because there wasn't *time*, but for another — maybe better? — reason: that it wouldn't really matter if they did. Everything would soon be over, anyway.

When Herbie thought all that, he also thought: But if what happens doesn't matter, how can there be love like this at all?

226

And then he thought: Being in love — if this be really love — is making me peculiar.

And then he thought: The only thing that I want now is something I can't have — just like before — which is for Health Care to go on and on forever, and to hell with baseball cards and money. Is that the way it always is: You can't *ever* get what you want?

When he looked at Shali, hiking happily along in front of him, he felt himself get furious. How can she be so carefree, so oblivious?

Shali stopped and turned around. She had an ice ax in one hand.

"You're walking funny," she informed him. "What's the matter?"

"Walking funny? You can *hear* me walking funny? How?" said Herb. He knew he wasn't going to tell her what the matter was — that nothing really mattered, which included how he walked or didn't walk. He *loved* her, after all. Why make her sad or grouchy? There wasn't anything that anyone could do about the situation.

"Just funny," Shali said. "What is it?"

"I was thinking that I didn't want to die," said Herb.

"Oh, that," she said, and turned around and started hiking toward the ridge, again.

Herb thought he heard the whistle first. Quite possibly, the sound of it was in his head a while, while he just clomped along, thinking of a lot of things, including Shali's butt. He remembered Malcolm Lowry's start for *Under the Volcano*: "Two mountain chains traverse the republic roughly from north to south. . . ."

227

When he recognized the whistle, he also had to realize, *admit*, it was a special kind of whistle, blowing in a special kind of way. It sounded like the kind of whistle British bobbies use, rather than the kind that Coach blew at P.E., and it was going "beeep, beeep, beeep," then "bip-bip-bip."

"Hey, listen," Herbie said, just as Shali stopped and raised one pointer-finger in the air.

They were almost at the snowfield on the ridge. Except that it was clear to Herb the snow in front of them had not just gently fallen there, direct from up above, the heavens. Instead, it looked as if it had come avalanching down from higher up the mountain, possibly the day before, bringing tons of rock along with quite a weight of ice with it, white and wet and grainy-looking — cold. Basically it was a mass of snow and ice and rocks, all jumbled up together, a heap of stuff that anyone would rather walk around, if possible, than climb up on. But it was also where the whistling was coming from.

"It's . . . sure it is, a signal — an SOS," said Shali. "Coming from up there, somewhere." She gestured at the mess in front of them. "Come on."

"*Weird*," said Herb, and followed her. They started climbing up the jumbled snow and rock and ice. Shali, leading, scrambled up on hands and knees, going very carefully, and trying not to make a sound. At last she peered down on the other side of one big heap of frozen rubble, and when she had, she turned and looked at Herb, her blue eyes big as willowware.

"It's not a *person*," she informed him in a whisper. "It's a *yeti*! It's trapped under a monstro pile of junk."

Herb stared right back at her. Of course he knew

about the yeti — the "Abominable Snowman" to the English-speaking world. Pookie Woodchuck and his men all claimed they'd seen a lot of them; they talked as if the things were just as common on the routes they traveled as are groundhogs by a parkway in Connecticut. They said (as Herb had heard before) the yeti was a hairy biped, built like a power forward in the NBA, but taller, shy and basically benign, good folks if sometimes just a little mischievous and scary. But Herbie also knew that people with his color eyes were meant to call the yeti stories "folklore," with a little, condescending laugh. He went quickly up the slope and lay there on his belly next to Shali.

Yup, no doubt about it (Herbie thought); it was a yeti, sure enough, hairy, huge and lying on its stomach and its side, with one leg and one arm pinned underneath a ton or two of rocks and ice and snow.

"Now what?" breathed the girl, in her companion's ear. "There may be others in the area. You think *we* ought to try to help this one?"

"Of course," said Herb. He didn't have to think. What this trip was all about was Health Care, after all. To him, the figure lying in the snow was no abomination. It was a living thing, pinned beneath some rocks and stuff; its Health was very much in need of Care.

"EXCUSE me," Herbie said, or rather called, down toward the captive yeti.

The thing stopped blowing on its whistle.

"EXCUSE me," Herbie called again. "I don't suppose that you, by any chance, speak English?"

"*Horace?*" said the yeti. His voice was slightly

muffled, but the word came loud and clear. The yeti couldn't turn his head toward the boy and girl.

"Horace, you damn Lapsang-lapper, you." The yeti parodied Herb's voice and style of speaking. "I don't suppose that *you*, *by any chance*, would like to kiss my foot." And he chuckled and continued in his normal voice. "Or failing that, to get your ass down here and cut me loose? Tell you one thing: I *am* getting cold. And I b'lieve I've got a little fracture of the astrogalus, maybe."

Herb and Shali looked at one another. The yeti didn't just speak English; he spoke it like a black American who'd gone to Cornell Med.

"Hor-*ass*!" came the yeti's voice again, but now with just a little sharpness in it. "I've been like this for four-five hours, buddy, and I'm getting to the edge of sick of it!"

"Uh — we're not Horace," Herbie called. "Sorry about that. We're just two people on their way to Baba Malomar's. But you — you really are a yeti?"

"Well — yes," the yeti said. "Although, of course, the very nature of reality ought to be defined, before we talk about who's really who, or what — or almost anything else, I guess."

Herb looked at Shali, eyebrows up. She nodded. And so they swung their feet around and slid down to the place where the yeti was.

Up close, the yeti was a pretty scary sight. From head to toe, he had a coat of thick and silky-looking hair, about as long as, say, a collie dog's. His, however, was a mix of black and gray and pure white hairs, which made him, overall, look gray. His deep-set eyes were black and fierce; facially, he looked to be a cross between Benito Mussolini and a mandrill, or some other large baboon. He had a powerful and well-proportioned body, with enormous calloused hands and feet.

"Hi," said Herb, when they'd hunkered down beside the yeti. "I'm Herb and this is Shali. I've got about a million questions that I'd like to ask you. But I guess we ought to try to get those boulders off you, first."

The yeti heaved a sigh; it sounded like a mix of resignation and regret.

"Yes," he said. His voice had gotten much more formal, talking to this pair of youthful strangers. "I'm Doctor Arthur Bradford Cushing. I hope you'll call me 'Cushy,' though; everybody does. But what I'm thinking is that you two youngsters sure as hell would get two hernias apiece before you got those rocks on me to move. I'm afraid you're going to have to do a little — what did Hawkeye call it? — 'meatball surgery'? Go in some place above my captive elbow here, and cut around a bit. You've got a knife with you, I trust?"

"Sure," said Shali. "But . . . well, I can't believe you want us to perform a — *you* know — *amputation* on you!"

Arthur Bradford "Cushy" Cushing chuckled. He seemed to be relaxing, once again.

"Good gracious gravy, *no*," he said. "I don't want you stickin' *me* with any ol' Swiss army! *I* happen to be five foot nine, when standing on my tippy-toes, and five — or make that *ten* — times better looking than my alter ego, here. I also happen to be mostly African and part American, by heritage, with not a drop of Himalayan blood — not that that's important in the least. No, everything you're looking at right now is *costume*. The real me is underneath. And the master zipper that you have to use to get to me starts out, as luck would have it, on the *yeti's* wrist, the one that's trapped. Which means you'll have to cut into his arm to get to it. Hate to ruin a good suit, but that's the way it goes. Seems as if it's me or it . . . did he say '*Sherry*'?"

"Shali," Shali said. "It's short for Shalimar."

"Of course," said Cushy. "Well, then . . . *shall* you, Shali?"

She looked at Herb. He shrugged why not.

"Why not?" she said.

The total job took pretty near an hour. The yeti's "skin" was more or less the thickness of an asphalt shingle, but a lot more pliable and maybe fifty times as tough. Underneath the skin (in addition to the little doctor) there were lots of lightweight rods and cables, even little motors that the person in the suit could use to help him walk, bound, jump, go "ooga-booga" at a tourist or a yak train, or whatever.

Once they had the zipper working, things went right along. Dr. A. B. Cushing was a short black man with horn-rimmed, tinted glasses, and a light gray sweatsuit on. On the front of it, it said: "I'm a Living Legend." Beside not being tall, he also wasn't fat or young; Herb's guesses were 145 and sixty, but physically in real good shape. Unfortunately, though, a rock had landed not just on the yeti's leg, but on the doctor's ankle, too, and once they had it free, and he had checked it out, he said that he was certain it was broken.

Herb and Shali helped him into extra clothes of

theirs and, following instructions, rigged a sort of chair-sling they could use to semi-carry him between them.

"Luckily for you good young Samaritans — as well as for myself," said Cushy, "we aren't very far from base. When we get close to where we enter it, we'll have to pause so I can blindfold you. And I'm afraid I must insist you spend at least the night."

With that he then produced, from underneath the waistband of his sweatpants a lethal-looking little automatic, not unlike the one that Herb had seen in Hometown, when Felicity had pointed hers at him.

Herb never has remembered clearly much of all that happened in the next . . . oh, eighteen hours. They forced the two of them to take this pill before they left the place, and it made almost everything unclear and him unsure of what was even semi-clear. The stuff he thought he *did* remember was so totally farfetched — impossible — that Herbie knew that telling it to anyone would mean he'd end up on the inside of a cuckoo's nest with walls so high he never could fly over them, they'd see to that. Here are half a dozen items from his sample case of memories:

1. The "yeti" base was carved into a mountainside, and it was a cross between the Xanadu Plaza, Trump Tower and the Hall of the Mountain King.

2. The "yetis" themselves were members of a very secret, very old, society. They were men and women of all different nationalities, most of them with *most* advanced degrees from *very* well-regarded universities. Many of them had made *enormous* sums

of money and/or *major* scientific breakthroughs, before they joined the group; some of them were just great-looking.

3. But all of them had given up on "society" and "civilization" as those words are presently understood.

4. And so, they therefore spent their lives in peace and harmony, playing jokes — or this one joke — on all the rest of humankind.

5. In addition to the "yeti" base, there were some other similarly grand and hidden centers of these people's operations, scattered here and there around the globe. People at those other bases did their stuff as Sasquatch, as the Loch Ness Monster, Champ, and other local legends, and in the drivers' seats of flying saucers.

6. "Visitors," like Herb and Shali, are "treated and released" (if friendly), "absorbed into the group" (if suitable and willing), or "other."

In any case, the next thing Herbie knew for sure, he and Shali were walking *down* a ridge, its snow-capped top behind them, heading for a peaceful-looking valley. This valley, with a small but lovely river flowing through it, was also home to Baba Malomar's palatial ashram, surrounded by lush fields and meadows, orchards and, yes, vineyards, heavy with ripe fruit.

"Can you *believe* that place?" Herb said to her, meaning where they'd spent the night, he thought, meaning all they'd seen and heard including grateful Cushy's parting present to them: "I'm a Living Legend" T-shirts.

"What place?" said Shali.

* * *

For the rest of the way to Malomar's Herb kept turning over in his mind this question: Would he have liked to stay and be a "yeti," if they'd asked him to?

There were a lot of things he liked about the life, the whole idea. For sure. You got to hang around with people who were really smart, in comfortable surroundings, and your every need was taken care of. Also, in your "work" you got to put one over on . . . well, pretty much the world's entire population. That'd sure be something new for him, Herb thought.

The one big trouble Herbie saw with going into yeti-ing was that he wondered whether fooling everyone was quite the sort of high that kept a person happy for a lifetime. Was it enough to give up *Hoping* for, for instance. Or Tyree Toledano? Or Herbie Hertzman, really, for that matter?

30
AT BABA MALOMAR'S

"Shali. Herb. I'm going to tell it like it is, all right?" said Baba Malomar. "Being an American, like both yourselves I guess, I'm not the kind of guy that's comfortable with anything that smacks of caste, or class. I'm not into having servants, even. To me, all people are the same — co-equals. Yah.

"*But*," he added, and he held one finger up, "let's not try to kid each other. What we've got here is an ashram — that's an *eastern* institution — not a spa or a resort. And on an ashram you are going to have a *spiritual* leader, which on this one is myself. And *devotees* — that's everybody else, excluding guests, of course. However, that don't mean there isn't lots of *synthesis* on these fine, fertile acres. In this *eastern* setting I insist on certain *western* principles and styles and attitudes, such as — " He broke off suddenly to say, "Hi, sweetie!"

"Hullo, beloved teacher," said this particular co-equal. Herb had been watching her approach for quite a while. She was wearing steel-toed boots and a light blue silky tank top, skin-tight cutoff denim shorts, a pair of heavy work gloves and a knotted kerchief 'round her slender neck. She was pushing a sturdy wheelbarrow piled high with roofing tiles, and only puffing just a little; her skin was nicely tanned and slick with sweat. Like all the rest of them that Herb had seen since they had started on their guided tour, this devotee was in her twenties, probably, and blonde, and in fantastic shape. Baba was the only guy he'd seen, so far.

They'd been walking three abreast and arm in arm along a wide stone walk, with Baba in the middle. Not being into expectations, Herb had not flipped out when he'd first seen the guy. As far as Herbie was concerned, there wasn't any reason why the guru shouldn't be the shortest of the three of them, and look a little like a beaver, being bucktoothed, chubby and cherubic, in a chocolate-colored robe down to his feet, on which there were a pair of soft Italian leather driving shoes — slip-ons, orange-tan. And it was perfectly all right with Herb that Baba had pink cheeks, no beard at all, and friendly light brown eyes that certainly did not *appear* to see into the deepest secret spots in either his or Shali's soul.

Overall, in fact, he couldn't pass as being physically the same as *any* of the girls they'd seen; physically he looked co-equal to a dish of chocolate pudding, or a couch potato at the age of thirty-five. Herb, who'd never been there, thought he sounded like he came from Philadelphia.

But everywhere the stone walk went — and it

went everywhere around the grounds, Herb thought — it cut through, passed beside, or went around about the lushest, richest vegetation, and the best-kept-up facilities the boy had ever seen.

"The soil throughout this total and entire valley," Baba stated, "is a hundred and ten percent all-natural alluvial, the finest, purest dirt available, I don't care how much you paid an acre. Sink a shaft straight down for fifty feet, and it's the same. I'm talking decomposed organic matter, never under cultivation, containing no impurities, such as your rocks, your sand, your clay. Shali. Herb. This stuff is total *mother*, kid you not. It's so darn fertile . . . Herbie, if you spat your gum out *there*" — he pointed to a garden plot beside the walk — "and stepped on it, in twenty years I bet you'd have a rubber tree to tap."

Herb nodded, smiling, just in case the guy was kidding him. He wouldn't know a rubber tree if one bounced off his head, but he absolutely *did* know lawns and flowers, vegetables and shrubs and bushes, fruit trees, grape vines, and shade trees, tennis courts, a roofed but open-sided gym containing Nautilus equipment, a croquet lawn, an archery range and a riding ring. And he could see, had seen, all of those while on this tour, all of them (just like the girls who worked or played on them) in prime time, class A, number one condition. He was sure he'd never seen so many healthy blades of grass, or such shiny perfect leaves on every tree, or fruit so succulent, blooms so aromatic, tennis courts so straightly lined, or vegetables so ready to be picked they almost cried out "Eat me," as you passed. And speaking of the girls . . .

" . . . devotees all happen to be female at the moment, yah." Baba Malomar was answering a question put to him by Shali. "And, let's see . . . all of them *are* blonde now, aren't they? But that's okay. I test a lot of products from my little lab on them, and so it's better and more scientific, too, to have one kind of subject, only. Hey!" He gave a little laugh. "You can think of them as my white mice, or rabbits, similar in age, sex, body type, IQ, reaction times and friendliness, and sense of humor. You know, I did my first recruiting on a beach near San Bardoo, and there wasn't what you'd call a lot of choice. In fact, when I included 'boredom' as a must-have for admission, the group I ended up with was darn close to self-selected. Of the first eighteen that I approached — pretty much at random — fifteen qualified and later came."

"You mean, a lot of girls like *these*," said Herb, gesturing the way Magellan must have done, a lot, when he got home, "agreed to journey way out here with you, a guy they'd never seen before, before all this was even *here*?" That seemed to Herb to be so borderline miraculous that anyone who brought off such a coup deserved . . . well, sainthood at the very least. But not a billion dollars, necessarily, as well.

"Mmm, yah," said Baba Malomar. "I guess they did. They had your spirit of adventure, I suppose. Hey, sweetie," he broke off to say to someone in a maillot on a racing bike, her long bleached hair straight-streaming out behind. "And don't forget your magic of the Orient, as well as how a lot of them had been discouraged by their deans from taking any further shots at higher education. We also had a few unfortunate misunderstandings (I would call them) over what I said to them about the highs I guaranteed they'd get off of pwolarky."

" 'Pwolarky'?" Shali said. " 'Pwolarky,' did you say? Is that — ahem — the stuff I mentioned wanting to discuss with you, when we first got here? The franchise-type material? The wherewithal to turn a cellar-dwelling Health Care situation into a pennant winner? In other words, *The Product*? If so, I think your name for it could use a little work, still."

Baba shook his head and smiled an enigmatic smile. They were getting close to what looked like a little awninged light refreshment stand, a sort of small gazebo. Herb had seen two others, earlier, spaced around the grounds. Behind the counter of each one, a devotee was apt to be involved with slicing juicy mangoes, which she would then proceed to squeeze (along with tangy citrus fruits) into a frosty glass container. Other, passing devotees would interrupt their work or workouts to flat-belly up and slake their thirsts, thereby (as Baba'd said) avoiding being hit by dehydration. There were also solid snacks available, Herb saw, and all of this completely free of charge, apparently. None of the women Herb had seen so far were carrying wallets; he could be quite sure of that.

"Treats time!" Baba sang out joyfully, when they had reached this latest stand. "Debi, sweetheart, here come three parched throats, I kid you not. And, look, my tongue is even swollen, too. So how about you pour us three nice tall ones, side by side and . . . let me see, I guess I'll have a Ding-Dong, too, all right? Herb? Shali? Say hello to Debikins. And how about a little something sweet? That's other than herself, I mean. The Tastykakes are *very* nice, this year."

The boy and girl both passed on solid food, but they accepted drinks from Debi, an agreeable little devotee in fitted yellow, nearly legless, overalls, who told them that her name was spelled with just one b and e, and that she sure was pleased to meet them.

"Deb," said Baba Malomar, when he had swallowed half a glassful, "Shali, here, just asked about pwolarky. How about you do the honors? Tell her not just what it is, but how it makes you feel — as if they couldn't tell *that* just from seeing you."

"Sure, Baba-shoog," she said. "It'll be my pleasure." She turned and faced the visitors, then squared her shoulders, did a little left-right march in place, and cleared her throat.

"Pwolarky," she said, sounding thoughtful, serious, "is what I like to call a unifying system for a person's life. In it, Play and Work are one, as I shall shortly illustrate."

With that, she half turned to her right, and with a finger traced the letters P L A Y in the condensation on the juice container. Then she put a WO between the P and the L, and an RK between the A and the Y. And there it was for all to see: PWOLARKY.

"Play and Work are one," she said again. "All day and every day, we work at play and play at work. We *are* them, you could say, and they, the two of them, are us. We not only *work* at fixing up, and getting into shape, and making one another happy, but we also *play* at it! You see?" She paused, took one quick glance at Baba and relaxed. Reaching for a rag to wipe the counter with, she tacked on one last thought.

"The whole thing's just a gas," she said. "It really is."

"Isn't she a piece of *work*?" said Baba Malomar, delightedly.

The other two thanked Debi for the cool, delicious drinks *and* the enlightenment, and then the three of them continued on their tour.

"So, all of this," said Shali, with a sweep of her arm that included the ashram's half a dozen gracious wood-and-fieldstone buildings (plus the two under construction), as well as its gardens and its grounds, including the enormous swimming pool, "all this was done by devotees — by Debis past and present?"

"Absolouie," Baba said. "Every bit of it was done by good, old-fashioned girlpower. I can't prove this in a court of law, but — Shali, Herb — I honestly believe that given optimum conditions, blonde young women are the hardest workers in the world. I'd match our good friend Debi there against a Sherpa porter, kid you not. But notice" — finger up, again — "I said 'optimum conditions.' "

"Meaning what?" said Shali, sounding skeptical, to Herb. In his life already he'd observed that lots of girls with darker hair were not great fans of blondes.

"Background first," said Baba Malomar, agreeably. "I'm sure you know the saying 'a hard worker is a happy worker,' right? That line, of course, was doubtless coined by management, some branch of management, at least. Parents, teachers, employ-*ers* — they all repeat it gleefully and often. Hey, why shouldn't they? It sends a message, makes a statement, gives advice — and even happens to be partly true! The both of you know this, yourself: If *you* work really hard at something, you are apt to feel extremely happy — with yourself *and* with the job you've done."

"Ye-es, but," said Herb, remembering how working hard had gone for him, at least up till the time he'd gone to Castles in the Air, "the trouble is, sometimes it's hard to get yourself to work that hard. And so you're not a happy camper."

"Exactly!" said their host. "That's just exactly right. For me, that bromide's incomplete. The way it *ought* to read is this: 'A happy worker is a hard worker is a happy worker.' Follow me? Happy leads to hard, which leads to happy and to hard again, and so on to infinity." He beamed.

"Um," said Shali. "So, I guess the thing you've had to do is figure out some way to make the people here all happy, every day. Seems like quite a challenge, seeing as there's . . . twenty-five or thirty . . .?"

" . . . forty-three, just now," he said.

" . . . and only one of you. How *do* you try to do it?"

"I'd hafta say three ways," said Baba Malomar. "That's in addition to pwolarky." And he chuckled. "First, I don't have any favorites; I treat everyone the same, as best I can. And, believe me, I am happy doing that and I work hard at it."

The boy and girl both nodded. They believed him.

"Secondly," he said, "I do a lot of yakkin', to the congregation as a whole. Each day, every day, we have Transcendent Time, when Baba does his stuff. Face it, I'm the guru here, so it's expected of me. I even changed my name, right off, to help it work right. Sidney Drexel Arthur was okay for board-rooms and the clubs that I belonged to, stateside, but out here . . . ? Could you imagine someone called Sid Arthur being *anybody's* guru? I'm going to tell you something true: After — what? — five years of this, Baba Malomar feels more like me than Sidney Drexel Arthur ever did. Incredible, you say? It's true! Out here, I'm really finally total me. I've returned to my first love, which means that I'm a man of science on the one hand, and, I like to think, I *also* am a man with some attachments to a higher plane."

He nodded to himself and walked a ways in silence, maybe (Herbie thought) engaged in, like, a mini-meditation, knocking back some spiritual tall ones.

"And, finally, there's our weekly practice of — don't laugh — anointment," Baba said.

"*Anointment?*" Herb and Shali asked, almost together. But neither of them laughed. In fact, Herb felt his heart speed up, as if it had some inside dope concerning what was coming next.

"Yah," said Baba Malomar. "Once a week, I lay some unction on my devotees, right on their pretty heads. It's a compound of my own devising. Formally I call the stuff *Easelspirlimine*." He pronounced that "ee-zell-*spir*-li-mean," with the accent on the "spir."

"The girls believe it's hair conditioner," he said. "But my *pet* name for the stuff is 'Bummer Balm.' " He looked at Shali. "And, Shali — yes, of course it's what you've come here for. You and Herb, and Roni and Cecelia."

"And what, exactly, does it *do*?" asked Herb, a little breathlessly.

"Conscientiously applied, one time a week," said Baba Malomar, "it takes away all feelings of unhappiness."

"*Roni and Cecelia?*" Shali asked.

"Yah," said Baba. "They're the reps Amalgamated Pharmaceuticals sent down. They parachuted in last night. It's really quite bizarre, an almost unbelievable coincidence. Physically, they look a lot like devotees. The difference is, they have a cashier's check for more or less a billion dollars, after taxes and all penalties Internal Revenue assessed me for." He grinned and shook his head. "And also they're unhappy."

Neither Roni nor Cecelia *seemed* unhappy — not to Herb, at lunch, at any rate. Roni was the shorter of the two. She had a punky look about her: bleached streak in her short blonde crewcut, with a guess-what-I-got fishnet T above black Spandex running tights. Cecelia's honey-colored hair was cut in bangs and fell in waves well past her shoulders. She had as deep a tan as Herb had ever seen, and he was sure she'd been maintaining it that morning. For lunch, she wore a wraparound short skirt and what the boy assumed must be the top of her bikini. In any case, it left an awful lot of breast exposed. There were just the five of them at Baba's table, the guru and his guests. And, naturally, the conversation centered on this Bummer Balm.

"As far as I've been able to establish, this is tricky stuff," their host was saying to the other four. "It activates the neuropeptides in the brain. Almost at

245

once, within say half an hour of its application, symptoms of unhappiness begin to disappear, or lose their place in Subject's scheme of things. Stupendous? Absolutely. The only thing I can compare it to is what those jokers at Johns Hopkins and at UVA are working on for colds, the common cold. The idea *there* is that you give the person what is called a 'bradykinin antagonist' — weird name, huh? — a drug that keeps your body from producing kinins, which are one of its reactions to the virus of a cold. If kinins aren't there to dilate blood vessels and send out icky messages of pain, discomfort and the like, Subject may still *have* a cold, but she escapes the *symptoms*, what your people" — Baba looked at Roni and Cecelia — "like to call 'colds' miseries.' Likewise, and in this case, a person using Bummer Balm may be unhappy, still — and almost surely is, in my opinion — but with her neuropeptides acting out, she has no noticeable symptoms. She doesn't *feel* unhappy, and (I guarantee) she doesn't *act* unhappy."

Herb could scarcely believe his ears. He felt a sense of awe. This unimposing little man, this Sidney Drexel Arthur, seemed to him to be a new Pasteur, or Curie, the 1990s Jonas Salk.

"Far-freakin'-*out*!" said punky little Roni. She was definitely excited; you could tell. "What you're describing is like *heaven*. Can you imagine *anyone* not wanting it?"

"When you say a subject doesn't *act* unhappy," asked the ever-careful Shali, "what exactly do you mean by that? You mean she doesn't mope around, or cry a lot? Or is there other evidence?"

Baba Malomar refilled his large wooden eating

bowl with Rice-a-Roni (East meets West again, thought Herb), and smiled.

"A ton," he said. "You've seen the girls yourself. They have no neurotic symptoms of unhappiness, none whatever, zip-o. The longer time you hung around the more you'd be convinced of that. None of them is overweight — that's obvious — or listless, take my word for it. They never nag (about my eating habits, say); they never are unfaithful. None of them is into drugs or alcohol or cigarettes. And on top of all of that, I'm satisfied there aren't any harmful side effects — and it also seems to work on everyone."

"Everyone who's female, white and under thirty," Shalimar reminded him.

"Well, yah," he said. "But given all we know about the human brain, I'm confident the stuff'd work the same on Herb, here, or myself. Or Greta Scacchi, were she willing and available. Or Tina Turner, Chairman Mao, or Mr. Rafsanjani." And the guru laughed and winked across the table at Cecelia.

She thrust both fists up in the air and yawned and stretched. Baba didn't seem to mind.

"Jet lag," she explained. "This girl needs her nap. But Sidney" — she put elbows on the table and leaned out in Malomar's direction — "let's not beat around the bush. What you've said is good enough for us. We are very ready, Roni and myself; we have a proposition that, we're very, very sure, you'll totally get off on. With all due respect, we're confident that these kids here" — she flicked a glance toward Herb and Shali — "can't come up with anything that even *touches* all that we'll be putting on the table."

"Well, gollybucks, who knows?" said Baba, almost bouncing in his chair with cheerfulness. "Everybody gets an equal chance on this man's ashram! What I was thinking was: Maybe I could get together with the Shali-Herb proposal later on this afternoon — assuming that they're ready — after naps. And then the three of us" — his finger pointed to himself, and Cecelia and Roni — "might just have *our* huddle sometime after dinner. How's that sound?"

"Delicious!" said Cecelia.

"Para-freakin'-*dise*-ical!" groaned Roni.

"Sure. Okay," said Herb and Shali.

31
PROPOSITIONS

Nap time, Herb and Shali soon found out, was a regular and much beloved component of the ashram's daily schedule. *Everybody* napped, and not just sitting on a chair, reclining on a chaise, or lying in a hammock, say, with clothes on. No, at this man's ashram you took off your clothes and got in *bed*, and lolled around on nice cool sheets. And either slept or not, depending on the usual alternatives.

Herb and Shali didn't. There was too much to discuss.

"I don't know," said Shali. She'd propped her pillow on its end against the wall, and she was sitting up in bed and leaning back against it, one knee up, the other leg extended.

"I don't know," she said, again. "I'm very dual about this stuff, aren't you? Face it, Easelspirlimine is not what you could call a *cure* for anything; it's more along the lines of Tylenol, or Advil, one of those. It doesn't touch the *causes* of unhappiness at all. In fact, it lets you go on being miserable and never feel you ought to lift a finger. To *do* something, you know?"

"Well, yeah," said Herb, "but it would help a person function better, though, like Baba said." He was lying on his stomach with his head on one extended arm, toward the foot of their big bed.

"Oh, sure," she said. "No doubt about it. I don't doubt that all the devotees *do* function great." She made a face, not all that sweet a one, Herb thought.

"Well, that's something, anyway," he said. "I mean, supposing someone's really bummed, had, like, a clinical depression, never mind what from. Wouldn't it be great if Bummer Balm could let that person lead a normal life? Not have to hit their head against the wall, or be strapped down, or something?" He touched her foot, wrapped his hand around it, rubbed his thumb along the underside of it, from underneath the instep to the heel. Herb couldn't yet believe how much he liked . . . her feet, for instance. Just because they were a part of *her*.

"Oh, sure," she said. "Oh, absolutely — mmm." Herb thought she might be speaking to his hand as much as answering the questions that he'd raised. "That'd be *fantastic* — and you're right. It ought to be available to them, the real bad cases. The part that worries me is other ways it could get used, like, 1984-ishly. 'Cause Roni's also right, I bet; almost everyone'd *think* they wanted it. Let some Big Brother start to give it out, and he could keep the people in his country in some kind of docile, mellow state . . . forever. They'd even work like demons, just the way the women here do. Perfect little Nazis."

"*Nazis?*" Herbie said, and he began to laugh. "You say that just because they're blonde — real blondes." He ran a fingernail straight down her sole. She pulled the foot away. "Which makes you envi — "

"Shut up, you," she said, in phony fury. She'd switched her body on the bed and got a palm across his mouth. "You keep on bringing up those blondes, and you'll need Bummer Balm yourself, a double shot of it. All I meant was — "

"Sure, I know," said Herbie, pushing off his gag. "And I agree with you. But still, if we don't get the rights to it, and other people do, that's much more apt to happen. I mean, their *business* is to do a lot of business."

"That's right," she said. "And I'm not saying that we ought to change our plans. All I was saying was that . . . well, this stuff is like an atom bomb. You want to be the only one to have it. But going up against a billion bucks *and* Roni and Cecelia . . ." She paused and pondered that a moment. "Maybe we can tie him down and tickle him until . . ."

"We thought perhaps we'd tie you down and tickle you until you gave us what we're after," Shali said. "But that seemed pretty crude, in light of all your hospitality."

They'd been there for a good three hours, chatting back and forth about . . . oh, everything, it seemed. The ashram and the devotees, Baba's past and present life, all that he'd accomplished there, how great it was. The conversation couldn't have gone any better, Herbie didn't think.

Baba chuckled, liking Shali's thought. Maybe liking the idea of being tied and tickled, Herbie thought. Baba certainly was liking Shali, liking looking at her, absolutely, even though her hair was quite a few shades darker than acceptable.

Herb liked looking at her, too, of course — the more so given what she'd put on for this meeting, an outfit that he'd been amazed to see her pull from near the bottom of her backpack. Not only was it not like anything he'd seen her wear before, it also didn't even look as if it should have had to spend time in a *pack* at all, not ever. A Vuitton overnight bag, maybe, but a backpack, never.

What it was was a completely simple, plain, white tunic of a dress, short, made out of silky, sexy, *almost* see-through, wrinkle-free, synthetic stuff, and worn with just a bright green sash, and sandals. Herb could guarantee the "just"; he'd seen her slip it on, on top of only underpants.

"Don't worry," she had said to him, "this isn't going to be the free-peeks-for-the-fat-boys hour. I'm doing this for me — for how it makes me feel to dress this way; it's called 'creating atmosphere.' "

Oh, right. For sure (thought Herb). And he was thinking: hazy, hot and humid.

That really hadn't been the way it was, however. What happened was that Shali — feeling as she did — more or less became the one who ran their little meeting, smoothly steering them from topic A to topic B, and so on, finding out a ton of stuff about the way the ashram worked, establishing rapport with Baba Malomar. She and Herb found out, for instance, that the present group of devotees, and many of their families, were paying large amounts of money for the privilege of coming there, and that a slew of other girls had applications in, to come the moment Baba had an opening. The guru also told them much about the booming health food business they were doing there, shipping supplements and tonics (*Baba Bits* and *Baba Blend*, both made from products grown or found right in that lovely valley) to stores around the world.

It was pretty obvious to Herb that Baba Malomar was proud of all that he'd accomplished in this setting, and that he very much enjoyed the chance to tell the story to four fresh, enthusiastic ears. He also seemed to like to banter with the two of them about the future fate of Easelspirlimine. Like, whether they could get the secret out of him, as Shali'd said, by tickling.

"Oh, it's not so crude, that method," he maintained. "From what I've heard, some cultures do it, like, an *art* form, even. Seems that what they do — the girls — is fold up paper different ways, so as to look like birds and submachine guns, and tickle guys with *that*. All up and down their *spines*, I think it is. I don't know, of course, from personal experience. It's just a thing I heard."

The guru chuckled and reached down to grab the piece of crystal stemware he'd been hitting on. His guests had both declined his offer of martinis, so Baba drank alone.

"We'd rather stroke you with the facts," said Shali, touching Baba lightly on a brown-robed knee. Herb sensed that this was it, that she'd decided that the time was ripe to hit him with their most compelling arguments, the heavy stuff.

"The truth," she said. "Reality, as it exists, right underneath our noses. It's pretty clear to me that, thanks to your initiative and acumen, you've got a life right here that's much more nearly perfect than the one you had before you came — and one that couldn't be improved by ten or *twenty* billion in the bank. You've got a waiting list of . . . what? How many did you say?"

"About two hundred," Baba said. And, yes, he licked his lips; his eyes glazed over, slightly. "That's counting just the ones who sent in a deposit, though. Inquiries and applications, I'd say . . . oh, another thousand."

"Two hundred comely but presently unhappy girls you know will give you almost every cent they have if they could come and work and play with you," said Shali. "Plus, your net from *Baba Bits* and *Baba Blend*, which, by your own admission, are in such demand that you've had record profits every year you've been in business."

"They *have* gone over great, I must admit," the guru mused. He nodded. The salesman in the guy kicked in real fast when he heard words like "net," "demand," and "profits." "But, hey, why shouldn't they? The stuff that we produce is now not merely natural/organic, but — thanks to Bummer Balm — it's also never touched or tainted by unhappy human hands at any stage of its production. Just *think* about that, Shali, Herb. No one else can match that guarantee. You can almost *taste* the happiness in Baba's products, guys."

"I'll bet you can," said Herb. "But, Baba, just

suppose some madman, like the guy they had down in Uganda, started using Bummer Balm — on everyone. Or even someone well intentioned but not extra bright, a politician with some bad advisors, say, who got to be the President, back home. Wait, let me put it this way. . . . How'd you like it if you *had to* use the stuff?"

Baba didn't have to think that over long.

"I'd totally despise it," he said, quickly. "Governmental interference with my *moods*? Forget it. Hmmm." He nodded his round head a time or two; the guy was clearly thinking that one over.

"I'm going to tell you honestly: You got a point there," he agreed, at last. "And it's a biggie. I'd *like* to take that check from Roni and Cecelia; a billion bucks would represent security. And I would have mobility, again — the right to go back to the ol' U.S. of A. and maybe run for public office, if I wanted to. Who knows how high a billion bucks might take a guy? I might like to see. But the thought that Bummer Balm might be imposed on some guy like myself . . . that's basically obnoxious and I kid you not. The thought does give me pause, Herb, Shali. Like you said, that 'some guy like myself' might even be, like, *me*. Conceivably."

"But, if you kept production *and the secret* in your hands," said Shali, jumping at his hesitation, improvising just like crazy, "you could continue with the life-style you enjoy so much right now, *forever* — and at no risk to yourself. And if, for reasons of your own, you sent the people that we represent a small supply each year, why, you'd be doing more for suffering humanity than any other Nobel laureate in history."

255

"Any *other* Nobelist?" said Baba. "You really think I'd be a . . . well, *contender* for the prize?"

Shali made a face, a gesture. Both of them said this: "*Of course* you would be, silly."

"Step aside, there, Schweitzer, Martin Luther King, Mahatma Gandhi, Florence Nightingale," Herb chimed in. "Say hello to Baba Malomar, *Time*'s Man of the Year, and probably the Decade. You doubtless saw his handsome face on *People* magazine, as well."

"Whereas if you *sell* the thing," said Shali, "you would lose control of it, and of your place in history. A box in *Fortune* or in *Business Week* would be about the best thing you could hope for."

She crossed her long, bare legs a final time, giving Baba still another chance to think their proposition over. After a count of ten, however, she stood up; the dress fell gently into place, perfectly unwrinkled, still.

"Well," the guru said, "you've scored some interesting thoughts, ideas, no doubt about it. You kids are sharp, and more than sharp; you're, like, *good people*. But, in fairness, I should listen to the other side, as well. Roni and Cecelia think that they can beat you; possibly they can. We know they've got a billion arguments to offer, but what else?" And Baba smiled. "I've got to give those girls a chance to show me everything they've got, just like I said I would. You know?"

"For sure," said Herb.

"I do believe I do," said Shali.

Herb and Shali took another walk around the grounds that night, instead of going to dinner. And it wasn't that they didn't like the ashram's food.

"I'm not sure that I could stand the sight of Roni and Cecilia warming Baba up," she said. "He'll have so many bosoms in his face, he'll think he's back in diapers, on the pediatrics floor."

"But how about our chances when they're through with him?" asked Herb. "I felt pretty good back there, when we were done. It seemed to me he took the stuff you said to heart. I mean it."

"Well, I think he did," she said. "The trouble is that Roni and Cecelia are — let's face it — specialists. Amalgamated Pharmaceuticals would get the best. The best of the *best* of the best. I'm sure the two of them are trained negotiators, Harvard MBAs, most likely. And that'd be on top of all their other skills. Chances are they'd be in line for two-three million dollars each, if they bring back a contract. Baba's heart could be outvoted *Shali*, *Herb*" — she said that just the way the guru would have — "by some other organ. Frankly, Herb, I fear the worst."

Herb spent some moments trying to guess — imagine — what-all Roni and Cecilia could/would do to Baba. He found he really couldn't. Maybe it was just as well, he thought. Herb wondered if, with sex, everybody thought that lots of other people knew and did a lot more stuff than they did, better. But he honestly could not imagine how there could be any *feelings* better than the best ones he was having now, with Shali. Did that make him unusual, or stupid, lucky, self-deluding, limited, or shy? (he asked himself). "We were in Big School when the Head came in," he thought. That was the way that Flaubert started *Madame Bovary*.

"If only," Herbie said, "if only we had something Roni and Cecelia wanted even more than that much money. Some fabulously rare and gorgeous jewelry, for instance. Or Eddie Murphy, maybe. Sly Stallone."

"Right," said Shali, drily. "Sure. Fat chance of our . . . hey, wait!"

She'd stopped dead in the middle of the fieldstone path. Her eyes were rolling, *sparkling*.

"Of course," she said. "Of course, of course, of course." And she was hopping up and down, both feet together, with her hands clasped tight in front of her, chest high.

"You got it!" she exclaimed, and grabbed Herb by both shoulders, hopping still.

"But what?" said Herbie. "Settle down, all right? What 'what' I got? Sly Stallone, you mean?"

The girl stopped jumping, anyway. "No, no, of course not, dope. It's something else we *know* that Roni and Cecelia want," she said. "*Must* want. Roni *said*, herself, remember? They're both — what? — *unhappy*! Baba, too."

"And so?" said Herb. "So what? I don't see how their being . . . normal helps us."

"Idiot," said Shali, "think. Suppose that we could find a way to get in Baba's bedroom. Late, late, late tonight. When Baba and the girls are totally exhausted. So fast asleep they wouldn't notice if the earth moved under them. *Again*, presumably."

"That wouldn't be too hard," said Herb. "The getting in his bedroom part. There aren't any locks on any doors in the entire ashram. That's something that I've noticed. You can walk straight into Baba's suite; anybody can. You're probably *encouraged* to —

your kind, that is. So what, though? What would we do then? Take pictures?"

"Hardly," Shali said. "*Then*, we'd . . ."

Though hardly what you'd call a rake, roué, or libertine, Herb had viewed X-rated movies in his life, two of them, in fact. There was a kid who went to school with him whose parents were collectors of the things. They didn't think their son knew that they had them, though, stacked right there behind his mother's sweaters, on a bedroom closet shelf. Their kid knew lots of things they didn't think he knew, including Herbie.

So, anyway, our Herbie, having seen those films, was somewhat prepped for what he saw in person when he entered Baba's bedroom, namely this erotic sprawl of naked flesh, both stretched and curled on Baba's super-king-sized mattress, overlapping lots of different ways.

He had to give the two girls credit — or their exercise instructors, anyway. Roni and Cecelia both looked great, from any angle. Each looked as if she was (or could be) hard *and* soft, round and flat, rough and smooth, wild and woolly, Hammacher and Schlemmer. Herb didn't choose to look at Baba all that much. Just enough to know he had no future in the porno movie industry.

All three of them were totally conked out. On the floor, beside the bed, there was a tall glass pitcher with a little near-clear liquid left in it. There were also empty, black-stemmed glasses, three, two of them tipped over. On the bedside table there was evidence that other ways had also been employed to alter local consciousness.

259

Herb and Shali tiptoed in, and kept on going, quickly, to the dresser; it had four drawers and it was made of blonde mahogany, of course. The graceful, widemouthed urn that both of them had noticed there before was still in place. This vessel had a silver chain, with nameplate, hung around its neck, the way decanters do, sometimes. But instead of saying "Scotch," or "Gin," this nameplate had another sort of mouthful on it: "Easelspirlimine."

Herb stared at it. And suddenly he felt like Henry Morton Stanley must have felt, when he laid eyes on Dr. Livingstone. Or Moses when the Red Sea parted. Or (getting closer to reality) as he had felt the moment that he understood the Big Red Chicken's scratchings. "Easelspirlimine" made *sense* to him; he bet he knew *exactly* what it was. He snuck a glance at Shali; she looked no different than before. He guessed her mind was altogether on their plan.

"I'll hold the urn," she whispered. "And you can be the one to slop it on." She picked up the container and approached the bed, looking at its bareskin cover.

"How much should I use?" asked Herb.

"He said it didn't take a lot," she said. "I'd recommend a good-sized dab, though; we wouldn't want to under-do. And try to rub it in, okay? It sounded like he really rubs it in, on devotees."

Herb put a dollop, first, on Roni's punky 'do, then another on Cecelia's part, behind her bangs. When he rubbed the ointment in, Roni seemed to half wake up. "You bad boy, you," she muttered, touching Malomar and changing her position, slightly. And she giggled. Super-tan Cecilia just accepted her anointment with a kind of queenly nonchalance. When Herb was done with her, his hand was still all covered with a thick layer of the gunk, and he wiped his greasy fingers dry on Baba's head. As he and Shali had it figured, Baba didn't matter, either way.

The first thing Herbie saw, when he and Shali hustled in the dining room at breakfast time, next day (with eyes and fingers crossed), was that the three were there already, fully clothed. That was good, for openers. The next thing that he saw — and this was truly excellent — was quite a little pile of torn-up pinkish paper, right beside Cecelia's plate. When he got close, he read *The Chase Manha*-inscribed upon the topmost scrap.

"Hey, 'morning, guys," said Roni to the two of them. She had a T-shirt on that day, all black except for one word "Masterpiece," in silver, on the front of it. "Guess what? It looks as if we *all* win, this time. Cece tore up the check, just now" — she gestured at the pile of pink — "so you can have the goo, for all we care. We're staying on with our new, all-time, favorite cookie. This Malomar, right here, feels like a million bucks to us." And she reached out to pinch the guru's cheek, and smile into his dark brown eyes.

Which Baba then proceeded to let drop, like Mr. Modesty, personified.

"What can I say?" he said to her, and to the other girl. "Welcome to the loving presence, Roni and Cecelia. And, hey, you weren't any slouches, either." The holy man then shook his head.

"I shoulda realized this might happen," he concluded.

When the meal was over, Baba asked the boy and girl to come with him. They went back to his suite, again. Someone had cleaned up, already — changed the sheets and made the bed and put the toys away. The place looked very nearly . . . monkish, Herbie thought, except for having such a huge expanse of bed in it.

"I got some things to tell you two," the guru said, when they had all sat down. "Amazing and surprising things, perhaps. Don't flip. For instance and get this: I do believe I'm going to give up booze and drugs and Ding-Dongs. When I first woke up this morning, I didn't have the slightest urge to reach for any one of them."

Herb looked at Shali; Shali looked at Herb. A single thought zoomed out of both their minds, collided in the empty space between them: Baba'd been affected by the Bummer Balm, and maybe it *did* matter. They would soon find out.

"But that's not all, there's more," he now was saying. "Shali. Herb. Guess what?" He gestured toward the dresser top, the place the urn of Easel-spirlimine had stood the night before. "There is no 'product' anymore. It's been taken off the shelf; it's unavailable. To you, to anyone. At any price, or no price."

"What?" said Shali, barely croaking out the words. "Unavailable? But why?"

"When I woke up this morning," Baba said, "I saw my situation in a truly different light. It was like a revelation, in a way. But also not. You see?"

He focused on the blankness of their looks. "I will try to make you understand."

"Please do," said Shali, staring at him in amazement, still.

"Revelations sometimes come from seemingly thin air," he said. "Like inspirations, genius-level thoughts, ideas, inventions, or creations. But they also sometimes come from people's mouths, but only if another person's ears can truly hear them."

Baba smiled at each of them in turn.

"Herb. Shali," he went on. "I'm speaking of *your* mouths, *my* ears. Yesterday, you laid a lot of wisdom on me — yes, the two of you. Some of it was mixed with nonsense, to be sure, but that's okay — nonsense has a way of getting into everything. Yesterday, however, I was not . . . in tune with wisdom, all that much. My ears were partly closed, my understanding limited. I heard, but did not see. You understand?"

Herb thought he might, and so he nodded. Shali sat there motionless.

"This morning, though, I understood, I saw," the guru said. "You had it right. I've got it made right here, the way things are right now. Fame and fortune?" Baba snapped his fingers. "Hey, who needs 'em?"

"The Nobel prize?" said Shali, hoarsely. "The *Time* and *People* covers?"

Baba smiled. "Yes, they're the nonsense part — you got it. Who needs that kind of crap? Not me. Those things are superficial trivialities, devoid of any lasting satisfaction. And you want to know the truth? I don't *deserve* them, even."

"Don't deserve them?" Herbie had to ask. "How

come?" Baba'd made a scientific breakthrough, after all; there was no denying that. Herb was pretty sure he'd seen some people on the *People* cover who'd done much, much less than that.

"My great discovery," the guru said, "my amazing scientific breakthrough — you want that I should tell you how I made it? Just by luck, my friends, pure luck."

Baba shifted in his seat, but not from nervousness; he was only getting comfy. He looked to be at peace with . . . well, the universe.

"Here's how it happened," he went on. "I was sitting in the lab one day with nothing whatsoever on my mind — a total blank, you know how it is, I'm sure." And Herbie nodded once again. "And then I started doodling, but not with pen and pencil on a sheet of paper, but with stuff I had around, just sitting on my workbench — chemicals et cetera. I'd grind up some of this and add a pinch of that or drops of something else. And then I'd maybe heat the glop I had until it changed consistency or color, or let off some interesting fumes. Well, one of these *experiments* (ha-ha) produced an end result that was both thick and rich, as well as quite good-looking." He beamed. "Like certain applicants we've had — hey, kidding!" And he shook his head and chuckled at his own good-naturedness.

"So," he then continued, "I just had it in a jar right on that counter top when a devotee named Brandi happened by and saw it. She must have thought it was a styling gel, because, before I knew it, she had put some on herself. And pretty soon she started acting strange — like, different — cheerful, happy, friendly, *eager*, even. I wondered if it was the gunk that caused the change, so naturally I ran some tests on other girls. You know the rest; in two weeks' time, this place was just transformed — into a little slice of heaven, attitudinally. *I* soon figured out the scientific explanation — that whole neuropeptide bit — but that was all I did *on purpose*. The gunk itself was not the consequence of human genius. It was just a gift, like from the gods." And Baba smiled benignly, once again.

"That's an amazing story," Herbie said. "But there's one thing that I don't get. How come you're telling us all this?"

Baba shook his head. "I'm not exactly sure myself. It might be out of gratitude for how you've helped me, how you've made me see what's what. Or maybe it's because I feel a little sorry that you came so far for nothing. Or maybe it's because I'm hoping *one* of you will stay."

He stood up and offered Herb his hand.

"Herbie, thanks for coming," he said, pumping it. "You remember how to go, all right?"

Shali started talking right away, trying to talk the guru into giving her at least a little sample of the stuff and swearing that she'd never mention where she got it from. But Baba Malomar was adamant. The secret would stay where it was, he said. But wouldn't Shali — "hey, no fooling" — want to join it?

"Thanks but no thanks, Baba," she informed him with a smile. "Tempting as your offer is, I'm still with Herbie, here."

She took Herb's hand and squeezed it. Two hours later, they were on the trail.

32
PRESENTS OF MIND

After that, for umpteen days — which was how long it took to go from Baba Malomar's back to the monastery courtyard where the van was parked — Herb's mood swung back and forth as wantonly and wildly as a good aerobics class. Although he'd spent a lot of time in adolescence, he had never felt so certain *and* confused, so man *and* baby, so conforming *and* rebellious, so Siskel and so Ebert. Sometimes it even seemed he felt both miserable and great at once.

One trouble was that Herbie's mind kept leaping out of present time and landing in the future. It seemed as if he couldn't help that. And where, a week or so before, he'd pretty much accepted that his life with Shali, their relationship, was transitory, limited by circumstances he could not control, now he had a very different attitude. Within an hour of the time they left the ashram, he had told the girl he *wasn't* going to leave; he was going to stay "behind" and stick around with her. The Upwardli-mobile could do the same, or go back empty. That was all there was to that, so there.

Except she said at once he *had* to go, he didn't *have* that choice to make ". . . and please, let's not discuss it."

Her answer came so fast, her tone was so abrupt and so convincing that he blinked and didn't — that's "discuss it" — for a bunch of days. Then, casually, he mentioned that there wasn't any reason that he *should* go back to Castles in the Air. He was sure his *parents* wouldn't mind; lots of times they acted very much as if he wasn't there at all, he said. He was also pretty sure that Ses deBarque would be *delighted* if he stayed. Wasn't that what Castles in the Air was all about? To help someone like him find something meaningful to do? Well, what could be more meaningful, Herb asked the girl, than this? Working cheek by jowl with her on . . . *projects*, such as this one.

The two of them were in her sleeping bag when Herbie whispered that, and their clothes were scattered on the ground beside them, but his mind was so much on convincing her, he wasn't even touching her.

"The trouble is," she said, "you just can't understand. That isn't *your* fault, either. It isn't anybody's fault. It's part of life. No one knows what's best for them. They *think* they do, but they don't ever really know. And you know why? Because they're people."

"Well, you're a person, aren't you?" said Herb.

"I guess I am," said Shali. "What do you think?"

"I think if you're a person, too," said Herb, "then you don't know what's best, yourself. For you *or* me. So, how about: Whatever *you* do next, I'll do it with you, and we'll see what happens? *That* seems like a great idea, to me." And when she shook her head, "Why not? Just give me one good reason."

"*Because*," she said.

He said that wasn't any reason, and she knew it. And he gave her just a little pinch. He didn't want to get too serious. As long as things stayed light, he thought he had a chance. When he was trying to talk his mother into something, he would always try to keep it light. Any time she changed her tone of voice and got real serious, he knew that he was sunk.

"It may not be a reason," Shali said, "but that's the way it is. You *can't*. And no one's sorrier than me." She started crying, just a little. *That* was serious, for sure.

"When the time comes, please just *go*," she said, and wiped her eyes. "And if you love me, please don't talk about it anymore."

That was clear enough. Herb sat up straight, now half outside the sleeping bag. He had a strange sensation in his head.

"All right," he said. "I do, and so I won't. I *do* love you that much."

That was the only thing that he could think to say. His mind was out of arguments. "Alice was beginning to get very tired . . ." floated through his brain, the words that Lewis Carroll used to start those great adventures. *He* was going to go, not stay, and she would not, *could* not, go with him. And he'd never understand it.

"Love" had made him "Happy," just as he had thought it would, but he could not hold onto it, or her, the person who had made him love. What would happen to him now?

Well, at least (he thought) he had the secret of the balm, of Easelspirlimine. He hadn't even told her — Shali — what it was; only he and Baba knew. It could be the Golden Fleece that he'd bring back to Ses deBarque. It would be *something*, anyway. And she would be real proud of him, so proud that maybe she would fix it up so he could rendezvous with Shali on his next adventure! Maybe he would spin Space Exploration, and the two of them could take a trip to Neptune or Uranus — or, better, to a distant galaxy, somewhere. A trip like that *could* take forever, Herbie thought.

"I am a pawn of fate," he said out loud, dramatically. "I'm nothing but a minor piece on the big board game of life."

Shali looked at him, but didn't speak.

Or maybe I've *been* pawned, Herb thought, and am an item in a hockshop window, hanging next to a guitar. Whoever'd owned me formerly — my parents? Ses deBarque? — had gotten cash for me. Passersby along the sidewalks would glance up and see the items in the hockshop window. "Nice guitar," they'd say.

Herb couldn't tell what he was feeling. "Numb" seemed like a real good possibility. He remembered seeing baseball batters hit by pitches — on the arm, let's say — and seeing trainers run right out and spray some stuff directly on the spot the ball had hit. The announcer on TV would always say the spray would "freeze" the arm and kill the pain. The

269

guy could keep on playing, even with the injury he had. Herb thought his thoughts were like that spray, all aimed directly at his heart.

A few days after that, Herb had a different kind of thought. Maybe it was triggered by that pawn-shop window fantasy, the thought of someone getting cash for him.

He realized he now had access to the other key to Happiness. Not just the Golden Fleece but (too) the goose that laid the golden egg. Even if he had no Love, back home, he still could have a ton of Money!

After he had showed the thing to Ses, he could *sell* the secret of the guru's Bummer Balm; he knew the way that Easelspirlimine was made! All he'd have to do was get in touch with . . . oh, Amalgamated Pharmaceuticals, let's say. They'd give him millions for the formula. And they were good Americans; they'd never sell the stuff to crazy zealots or ideologues. This (also) wasn't 1984. He'd be set up for life — and whoever *really* needed Easelspirlimine would get some, somehow, whether they could pay for it, or not. *Congress* would make sure of that. Or HEW, or HUD, or *someone* (other than himself).

When Herbie thought of that idea, he once again had something to look forward to. He'd never have to sweat that deal of "doing something with himself," and T.K. could have juicy "sTeaKs," for offerings. And he — he could get himself some *stuff*, the way that Pookie Woodchuck had, and Pema, too, and Sendup.

* * *

That was the first thing he and Shali noticed when the two of them rejoined the yak train for its journey home. The boys had made a *killing*. The evidence was right before their eyes.

The yaksmen all had Rolex watches now, three or four of them per wrist. Around their necks they wore what looked like double loops of tire chains, except that these glowed wickedly and wealthily as only eighteen-karat gold is apt to do. Sendup had swapped his tattered parka for a down-filled Chesterfield (the first that Herb had ever seen), and Pema'd had an artificial plastic ear-top (lined with Gore-tex) made. All the yaksmen sported brand-new expedition boots, $250 models from Asolo AFS, and in their inside pockets there were little black address books, stuffed with names and numbers. In those same pockets, Herbie spotted gilded edges, too — the kind that go on bonds, and stock certificates, and deeds of ownership, CDs.

The yaks, for their part, had acquired bright new horn guards that Herb thought — was pretty sure — were made of platinum; their shaggy hair appeared to have been trimmed and washed and styled, since he'd last seen them. No longer did they carry great, enormous loads; in fact, their only burden (which they took turns with) was a good-sized, well-made steamer trunk — of *Japanese* design, Herb thought. A cargo plane, with a PWA logo on its sides and tail, came overhead each afternoon and dropped, by parachute, hot dinners for the yaksmen and their honored guests, and bags of a nutritious Vitamalya Twenty-eight Grain Mix for every yak. Also, the next day's breakfast, and a VCR, a big-screen Sony, and a microwave, along with half a dozen current films and batteries to run the whole caboodle on. They'd leave all those electrical conveniences beside the trail, next morning. At lunchtime, everybody dieted.

But, after three or four days with the yak train, Herb became aware that something bad was happening. In spite of all the movies and the *haute cuisine*, Shali wasn't looking happy. He asked her why; she told him it was nothing — and she seemed to pull herself together for a while. But then, next morning, he woke up to find her dressed and sitting on a rock, just staring into distant space.

Herb *hated* seeing that; he couldn't stand it. It hurt him much much more to see her sad than to be sad, himself. He knew he had to *do* something, to find a way to cheer her up before the closing credits started rolling on the screen: "Costumes by Abida," and "A Ses deBarque Production."

Because he was, if anything, American, his first idea was: Get her some great present. Something that would take her mind off . . . what he didn't want to think about himself. So, to that end he went and talked to Pookie, hoping that the guy might have the perfect gift in stock, left over.

"Gee, too bad I'm out of sterling silver nose rings," Pookie said, and scratched his head and thought some more. He finally had to say he really didn't think he had the kind of thing Herb wanted — unless he thought a "What Batman Doesn't, Katmandu" wall plaque fit the bill.

Herb said it didn't, quite, and thanked the guy and walked away to grind his teeth in desperation. He doubted that they'd (even) chance upon a dragon he could slay for her. Time was running out and there he was, his head as empty as his hands.

And both of them stayed empty, right up until the time they reached the monastery courtyard, and he and she, the two of them, were standing by the van.

Why he thought of it, and why he hadn't thought of it before, he never knew, but suddenly it came to him. *Of course.* He could give her something that he *knew* she really wanted.

So what if that meant giving up the second key to Happiness? He didn't hesitate. There'd be other ways, perhaps, for him to get some Money. Money comes and goes; Love never ends, not even at "Goodbye."

"Shali," Herbie said, "I've got a little something I've been saving for you. Look."

And on the van's big, dusty sliding door, he wrote two things, and neither one of them was "Wash" or "Me."

First, he wrote the words "eel slime," but oddly, just like this:

E ELS LIM E

And after that came "aspirin," this way:

AS PIR IN

dropping it into the spaces in the eel slime, so's to make the single word:

EASELSPIRLIMINE

"You see?" he said. "Isn't that pure Baba Malomar? A synthesis of East and West, a mixture of his old world and his new one? *And* a Baba-word, to boot — just like 'pwolarky'! He got the formula by luck; now you can have it, too. You can give it to

273

your 'people.' They can use it right — for *everyone*."

Herb couldn't say another word. All that was left in him was sadness. Bawling like a baby, he reached out and gave her one last hug, and turned and dove into the van. She closed the sliding door for him.

But (he thought) at least his present worked. Before the door slammed shut, he saw that she was smiling.

33
STILL MORE FAREWELLS

As usual, the trip did not take long. In fact, it lasted barely long enough for Herb to dry his eyes, subdue his sobs, and start to both appreciate and not appreciate at all, the fact that he had found and given up both Love and Money in this same adventure, back wherever he had been. He wondered what that meant, in terms of what significance it had — *would have* — in . . . well, his other life, his real one. Assuming that he had another life, of course; assuming anything at all was real.

Ses deBarque, as usual, was right there on the runway when he landed — the "runway" being, as before, the tower room at Castles in the Air.

"Well," she said, "that was a long-tailed Louie, eh?" She checked out that opinion on the pendant watch that hung around her neck. "Five minutes *plus*." She whistled. "I was getting worried that you weren't coming back."

Herb gasped. "You mean that's possible?" he said.

She grinned, but she was serious. "Oh, sure. Sometimes, in certain cases," she replied. "But not for you, my dear. I'm much too sweet on you to leave you way out there" — she waved, a trifle vaguely — "somewhere. Let's go sit down — all right? — and have a nice cold drink. You look a little droopy."

Herb was glad to follow her back up to her apartment, to that same peculiar but delightful living room he'd visited before, the one that made you think that you were sitting on a mountaintop. He supposed his eyes were still a little red, but he was not that sad. What he mostly felt, by then, was numb. Again.

"There are some things I ought to tell you," Ses began, when they were seated, holding goblets of that most delicious drink she'd given him before. Its faint, sweet flavor was like nothing Herb had had in any other place. Although it didn't taste like them, it made Herb think of nectarines.

He nodded, thinking he could just accept whatever she would say. He wasn't worried. He seemed to have no expectations whatsoever. No yearnings, either, come to think of it.

"Aspirin mixed with eel slime, rubbed on people's heads, will not help anyone's unhappiness," she said. "Not here. Something worked up at the ashram, sure, but that was there and then, and this is here and now."

Herb took that in. His gift to Shali had been

worthless. He could have given her a set of woven placemats, or a backscratcher.

"Secondly, there is no Shali Sloan. Such a person does not now exist, was never born, and will not die, if you were wondering," said Ses deBarque.

"And neither was there any Zippy or Felicity, I bet," said Herb. "Nor will there be *whoever* on the next trip that I take. But that's all right."

"Two out of three ain't bad," said Ses. "Concerning Zippy and Felicity, you're quite correct. And absolutely, like you said, that *is* all right. But you're not taking any other trips. This was your last one, buddy-ro. In point of fact, I'm closing Castles in the Air and getting out of here. These shoes were made for walking, and I'm goin' home again."

She held her feet up off the ground. Herb saw that she had on a brand-new pair of walking shoes, a pair of Nikes, some design he'd never seen before.

"Air Olympuses," she said. "You know who Nike is?"

"Is that the way you say it?" Herbie asked. "I thought that you pronounced it 'Nee-kay.' I think she was a goddess, back in ancient Greece. Of victory, I'm pretty sure."

"Right on," said Ses, "but no, it's *Nie-key*, rhymes with Tie-key, take my word for it. And that reminds me, just in case you're wondering: I won the Cadillac, all right."

"I guess I'm not surprised," said Herb. And it was funny, but he wasn't. "Congratulations."

"Thanks," she said, "it wasn't hard; you never had a chance. I'm going to give the thing to Sandy Rex; you're more the compact type. I gave the van to my young daughter there, E.T." She gestured at the picture on the table. "The one you said you'd like to meet sometime, remember?"

"Sure," said Herb. He was looking at the picture. Although the girl looked quite a bit like Ses, she also looked (he now could see) a lot like Shali — and Felicity. And Zippy, too, in one or two respects.

"But Ses . . . ," he started, with his mind a momentary jumble of confusing facts, and anti-facts, and arty facts and speculations. "You're going to close this place and leave me on my own?" He stopped. "No, wait. That came out wrong. I *meant* to say: You're going to close this place and go on home? I really did."

"Yup." She nodded. "Yup. It's time."

"But what about *me*?" Herb asked. But he was smiling as he said it, teasing her.

"What *about* you?" she demanded.

"Well, I'm going to *miss* you," Herbie said. "A *lot*."

She grinned. "That's good," she said. "That means you'll think of me, from time to time, and we'll stay friends that way. And probably — who knows? — I'll pop on back and visit you — oh, now and then."

"I hope so," Herbie said. "If I'm not here, I might be up at Hampshire." And he winked.

The boy got to his feet, and so did she. They hugged and kissed each other on both cheeks, the European way.

"Good luck," she said, and looked into his eyes. "Good luck."

34
AND SO

The next thing Herbie knew, he found himself on Sunset Strip, meandering along. He *was* quite tired, but he felt he had a lot of time — and not to kill, to use. He decided that he'd try to hitch a ride, so he might get wherever he was going sooner. He turned around to see a van approaching, and he stretched his arm out to the side, his fingers in a fist, his thumb extended.

It stopped. The sliding door was shiny; he could see his own reflection in the thing. Ignoring it, he opened the *front* door and hopped right in, sat his butt in high-backed, bucket-seated comfort. That made him shotgun-wielder, navigator, maybe — and a step above the passenger he used to be, he thought.

The driver was a girl, the most attractive girl that Herb had ever seen. He smiled at her and she smiled back, right straight into his eyes, as if to send a message into them. "It was love at first sight" was how the writer Joseph Heller started off *Catch-22*, Herb knew. She wore a scent that seemed almost familiar, made him shake his head and sniff again. He thought this was a case of *déjà phew*.

They reached the end of Sunset Strip. Another road went left and right in front of them, a road that Herb had never seen before.

"Which way are you going?" she inquired.

"Well, I'm not exactly sure," he said.

"I think I've got a map in there." She pointed to the glove compartment.

Herb's hand went out, then stopped. Probably, he thought, next to the map in there, he'd find a small insurance ID card, and it would have her name on it. "Ekaterina Toledano" he might read. E.T. And he would have to face the fact he'd had it wrong for all those years, that it was not "Tyree" but "Teri" Toledano.

He looked at her, the driver; she was facing him and grinning. It didn't matter what her name was. He knew he didn't need the map. Chapter I of Vatsayana's *Kama Sutra* had this title, he had suddenly recalled: "Observations on the three Necessities for Happiness on Earth: Virtue, Riches and Pleasure . . ." Begin at the beginning, Herbie told himself.

"Take a right," he said.